A breeze stirred behind Megan

It fluttered the bottom edges of the newspaper articles: GRIM REAPER KILLS AGAIN... POLICE SEARCH FOR MADMAN....

Why did Jack Gallagher have these gruesome articles on his bulletin board? This morning's edition, with a headline on the next victim, had a note scrawled beneath it. In Jack's handwriting was one word...

MEGAN

With a shaking hand, Megan reached out to touch her name, but was distracted by a sound.

Footsteps... and they were behind her.

ABOUT THE AUTHOR

A lover of romantic-suspense reading, native Californian M.L. Gamble followed the "itch to write it herself" and began her fiction-writing career about four years ago in Mobile, Alabama. The author continues to write in her favorite genre, now from her new home in Bayville, New York, where she resides with her husband and two children. Having worked as a field supervisor for a television survey company, M.L. Gamble is able to put this firsthand knowledge to chilling use in her third Intrigue novel, *When Murder Calls.*

Books by M.L. Gamble

HARLEQUIN INTRIGUE
146—Diamond of Deceit

When Murder Calls

M. L. Gamble

Harlequin Books

TORONTO • NEW YORK • LONDON
AMSTERDAM • PARIS • SYDNEY • HAMBURG
STOCKHOLM • ATHENS • TOKYO • MILAN

For Melbourne residents
Richard and Lorraine Gamble.
With love and thanks for bringing three kids up
and never letting them down.

Harlequin Intrigue edition published January 1991

ISBN 0-373-22153-3

WHEN MURDER CALLS

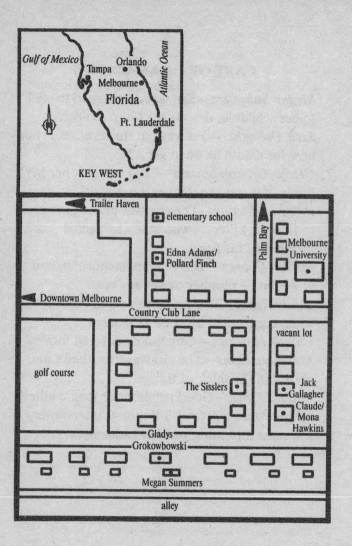

CAST OF CHARACTERS

Megan Summers—She was determined to stick to her schedule, despite the Grim Reaper.

Jack Gallagher—He was out for revenge . . . but how far would he go to get it?

Gladys Grokowbowski—Cold feet cost her her life . . . but was the Reaper the culprit?

Pete McMurphy—The cop was under pressure to find the killer . . . who many suspected was a member of his force.

Darren George—The veteran anchorman had vowed to be number one at any cost. . . .

Sandy Royal—The young newsman chafed when confronted by another's talent.

Claude Hawkins—Gun nut or devoted father?

Mona Hawkins—The girl was "touched" and always in the thick of things.

Pollard Finch—Good neighbor or manic killer?

Elaine Jones—A fired TV-ratings interviewer, she came into money rather suddenly.

Chapter One

"Come on, Thomas. Please, baby, Momma doesn't want you to be late for school."

"Not going." Five-year-old Thomas Summers threw his brush into the wet sink. His face reddening in anger, he crossed his arms and stuck out his lip, a pose his mother knew meant either a tantrum or tears.

Feeling up to neither at this early morning hour, Megan Summers kept a grip on her temper. "I'll get your hair after you finish brushing your teeth. Use your new toothpaste."

"Mom! I can't find my tennies! Mom!" Six-year-old Roxie's yells interrupted the discussion.

Megan fished the sopping brush out of the sink and turned off the tap. She yelled over her shoulder at her daughter. "Look on the porch, Roxie. I think we left them there last night. And bring in the paper if it's there, please."

Quickly she brushed through Thomas's thick blond curls, then squeezed the striped toothpaste out in a neat line. "Here we go."

Thomas turned and ran out of the bathroom. "Not going, Mom. I hate school!"

She followed, toothbrush in hand. "Take this. Now. Go brush."

He scowled, but heard the note of finality in her voice. "I'm not going to give you my sticker today."

"That's your choice, Thomas. But you still have to brush your teeth."

Thomas hung his head, a tear rolling down his chubby cheek. The shrill ring of the phone let Megan stifle the impulse to pick him up and hug him, an action guaranteed to bring more tears.

"Hello?"

"Megan, stop by my house after you walk the kids to school. I need you to do some things for me today."

The gravelly insistence in Gladys Grokowbowski's voice irked Megan. She answered her landlady, who was also the supervisor for her sole part-time job, sharply. "Can this wait until later, Gladys? I've got to run to the post office and—"

"Norma Schultz died. We need to hire a new interviewer to take her place immediately. I'll see you at 8:00 A.M."

Megan sucked a mouthful of air into her suddenly empty lungs. "Gladys! My gosh, what happened?" The phone's dial tone was the response to her question. In typical fashion, Gladys had hung up without any recognition of the laws of common courtesy.

"I brushed. See?" Thomas sidled up to her and bared his teeth to show his mother that they gleamed.

"Good boy," she said quietly, her mind reeling with the shocking news as she put the receiver back in the cradle. "Now let's get that hair."

They returned to the bathroom, and as she helped Thomas dress, or as Thomas allowed her to dress him, his thumb in his mouth, Megan's mind felt as if it were buzzing. With each second she was more horrified at the news Norma Schultz was dead. They'd started work for Tele-Surv on the same day. The national company employed hundreds of people to work in their homes as interviewers compiling TV ratings statistics.

Thomas nuzzled close to Megan as she closed his top shirt button. He jerked his thumb away when Roxie rushed in holding the damp newspaper in her dainty hands.

"Another murder, Mom!"

Megan spun around and picked up the lunch boxes, checking they were both latched. The morning was taking on surreal aspects, and she fought again to keep her voice calm. "Are you reading the headlines by yourself? What a big girl."

"I don't understand this word," Roxie answered. "Grime ripper . . . what is that, Mommy?"

"Let Momma have the paper, sugar." She took the soggy newspaper from Roxie's hands and casually laid it on the floor. "Now go wash the black off your hands. We've got to go."

The little girl's eyes studied her mother's face for a long moment. "What's wrong, Mommy?"

"Nothing. Hurry so we can comb your hair, Roxie."

Roxie frowned, wondering why her usually direct mother had not answered her question. The child put aside the mystery and scampered into the bathroom. "Mom, can Carrie come over and play today?" she called over the noise of the water.

Megan pulled her house key out of her shorts pocket and handed Thomas his lunch box. He slowly relinquished his beloved stuffed bunny to take it. "Teenage Mutant Ninja Turtles catch murderers. Maybe they could come here."

Before Megan could answer, Roxie raced back in, a smear of white foam on her chin. "Can Carrie come?"

"Yes. Carrie can come." Megan felt the knot in her stomach uncurl a little, glad her children were distracted by a new train of thought. She wiped the toothpaste off Roxie. "I'll call her mom when we get home. Now, come on you two, we've got five minutes to walk to school before the bell."

The Florida breeze was brisk and cool, blowing west off the Atlantic. A typical Melbourne morning, Megan thought as she locked the door of their tiny garage apartment and watched her children scamper down the stairs. The blazing blue expanse of sky was unmarred by clouds, and the heavy dew on the scraggly grass ricocheted against her bare legs as she followed behind her children.

But in the midst of the friendly, cozy town she'd known as home for eight years, a madman was on the loose, and he'd killed again according to the headline Roxie had struggled with.

Megan shuddered despite the sunshine, her eyes studying her children. As a single parent, she knew full well the enormous responsibility of caring for these two little creatures. Megan was their only support, their security and protection against the emotional ups and downs of childhood. She certainly didn't need the added worry of physical harm from kooks like the media-christened Grim Reaper.

"Come on, Mom. We're beating you!"

Breaking into a run, Megan smiled and chased after her brood. This was no time to be glum, she told herself. Her life, like most, had its cracks, but moments like these with her kids made it bearable. She caught them at the corner and gave them both hugs.

"Good morning, Mr. Finch," Thomas yelled across the street.

"Morning, Mr. Finch. Morning, Miss Adams," Roxie chimed in after him.

Megan waved at her neighbor, Pollard Finch, a short, muscular little man with tiny feet and a shiny bald head. He was pushing his roommate's wheelchair. This was the way he and Edna Adams took their morning walk around the neighborhood. They waved and nodded, and Megan turned back to her kids. Roxie was talking a mile a minute, her usual bouncy, cheery self.

"Now, don't forget, Mom. You can't do your TeleSurv calling or study or anything. You've got to play with me and Carrie and Thomas."

"I've got a few calls to make, Roxie. But I'll leave time to play," Megan answered gently, registering the begrudging tone in her little girl's voice. Her mind jumped ahead to Norma's death. With her best interviewer gone, her own workload was sure to increase. Unless she and Gladys could cull someone's name from the mound of old resumes they had on hand, Megan's workload would double.

"I hate TeleSurv," Thomas grumbled, his frown returning.

Megan forced her concentration back to her kids. "Don't say that, Thomas. You know those TeleSurv checks bought you that red bicycle you wanted." They all began to cross the street as the light turned green.

"Hurray for stupid old TeleSurv!" Thomas yelled back.

"Can we make cookies, Mommy?" Roxie asked.

"Sure—"

"Not cookies, popsicles!" Thomas interjected.

"We'll make something fun, kids. Now give me a kiss." Roxie did, with a big smile, then turned and ran off. Thomas held on a little longer, and Megan swallowed hard. "Paint me a picture if you get a chance, buddy. The one on the frig is kind of old. Okay?"

"We don't paint today, Mom."

"Oh? Well then, draw me something."

"Ninja Turtles?"

Megan hated the pizza-eating little reptiles, but she smiled. "Sure. Which one?"

"Donatello, no Michaelangelo. He's the biggest."

"Great. He's my favorite." She gave him another kiss. "Bye, Thomas."

"Bye, Mom."

Megan turned away, knowing Thomas's eyes were on her. She didn't allow herself to turn around until she was at the corner. By then Thomas was a shadow walking up the hallway. She could see his blond head bowed.

A sigh escaped Megan, but then the day's approaching events pushed her attention to her own schooling. In her last quarter of study, she had only ten weeks of classes and two finals to get through before she had her master's degree in Communications.

Rounding the corner to her house, Megan muttered, "Think positive, the end is near." She grinned as she realized how much she talked to herself. Her kids had a mother who loved them. They would continue to grow and thrive despite a disinterested father who'd missed his last scheduled visit and who discharged his parental affection by writing a $400 support check once a month.

Though it was hard on them, she would will them through their childhood. Just like she had willed herself to stop wanting anything but the most basic food and shelter.

Her slim fingers touched her face as she jogged down the crushed shell driveway past her landlady's shuttered house. Her budget was a devil to live with. She hadn't bought a new dress for five years. But the thing she'd missed most was buying a decent brand of cosmetics.

She raced up the stairs and let herself in. The woman downstairs could just wait a few minutes to talk about TeleSurv, she told herself. Maybe then she'd stop being so rude on the phone.

Megan closed the door firmly behind her and surveyed the combination bedroom and living area. The children's room was a nook off to the right, the "kitchen" along one wall and the bathroom off to the left of it. Six hundred square feet that never seemed to be in order.

Megan threw the covers on her sofa bed together and folded it up, then checked the clock on the ancient stove. The miraculous appliance cooked only at 300 degrees but never lost a second's time. It was six minutes after eight. Her appointment with her master's adviser, Dr. Darren George, was at ten.

She sloshed a cup of coffee over to the dinette table and retrieved the paper from the foot of Thomas's bed. Curiosity made her focus on the Grim Reaper story.

Taking a gulp of coffee, Megan nearly choked as she scanned the lead story. Though prepared by Roxie to read about murder, she had no inkling the tragedy would strike so close to home.

The Grim Reaper, operating in their east coast beach community for the past year, had committed murder number five.

"It can't be," Megan said aloud, but the pounding of blood through her veins responded to what her mind fought against. "Norma Schultz, 59, a retired beauty operator was found late last night at 319 Palm Court strangled to death," the first paragraph began. Megan's stomach clenched as the acidic aftertaste of bile burned in her mouth. She inhaled deeply, crossing her arms across her chest to steady herself.

Norma Schultz hadn't just "died" yesterday, like Gladys had announced. She was murdered.

In horror, Megan read the rest of the article. Norma had been found by her sister, who'd arrived for a dinner date. There was no sign of forced entry, and the police gave out no other information except to say that "physical evidence pointed toward it being the work of the Reaper."

The address was about three miles away from where Megan sat now. Chilled by the proximity and the fact she actually knew the dead woman, Megan put the paper down. The jangle of the phone made her jump, and she rushed across the room to silence it as if it were a cry in the night.

"Hello," she said, her throat raw.

"Megan? I told you to stop in. Come down here right away."

"Why didn't—" The phone went dead in her hand. Slowly she returned the receiver to its cradle. Gladys Grokowbowski had struck again. She usually communicated with Megan by yelling her name through the rusty screen in her kitchen window when she spotted Megan and the kids coming up the drive.

Megan knew it would be useless to call her back and explain about her ten o'clock appointment, because Gladys never answered her phone. She used it solely as an outgoing line of communication.

Megan splashed water on the breakfast dishes and hurried down the stairs and across the bumpy lawn. She rapped too hard on Gladys's sagging back door and heard the immediate rattle of chains and bolts being adjusted inside.

"It's open, Megan."

Megan reached for the knob and turned it, then walked into the gloomy interior of Gladys Grokowbowski's home. It smelled of old coffee and burnt pans. Gladys was installed at her usual location in the cane-back chair that took up the entire corner of her kitchen. Mail was piled up on the table her elbows rested on, along with clipped coupons, magazines, playing cards and three towering stacks of Louis L'Amour westerns.

"Do you know what happened to Norma?" Gladys demanded.

Megan walked over to the table and looked around for another chair. There wasn't one, so she rested against a metal folding step stool piled high with newspapers. "Yes. It's horrible."

Gladys blinked her watery blue eyes and nodded. She took a long pull off her filterless Camel, then dropped it crackling into the dregs of her coffee. The Limoges cup left yet another ring on the antique table Gladys insisted on eating from.

"It's not that bad. I have several more interviewers we can give her work to. You did fire Elaine Jones, right?"

Megan counted to five before answering. "Yes. I told you that last week."

Gladys nodded curtly. "How'd she take it?"

"She wasn't very happy about it." Something was odd about this conversation, but Megan didn't have time to find out what. "She said she was going to call you about back pay."

"Huh. Let her try it." Gladys dismissed the subject by searching through the pile of mail in front of her. She pulled out two envelopes that had been ripped opened. "Hell of a time for Norma to die." She handed the mail to Megan.

Megan took the jaggedly torn correspondence and stared at Gladys. She was used to the woman's lack of manners, her bizarre, almost hermitlike existence, and the savage disregard for the worth of her obviously expensive possessions. But never in her life had Megan seen another person react in such a callous manner to a fellow human being's death!

"Read those two applications," Gladys ordered. "I've set up interviews so you can hire one of them. Maybe you better hire them both, since Norma can't work anymore."

"Norma can't do anything anymore, Gladys."

The elderly woman stared at Megan, her cheeks caked with what looked like yesterday's makeup. "I think we should hire a man. That kid we used last spring had a great response rate. I think people are too afraid to say no to a man on the phone.''

Megan looked at the envelopes in her hand and bit on the inside of her mouth to keep from yelling. She studied the first application letter, her eyes taking in the strong, clean script. A man by the name of Jack Gallagher stated he was ''interested in obtaining immediate employment'' and gave impressive credentials qualifying him for the position of phone interviewer.

''What do you think?''

Megan looked at Gladys. ''He looks great. When did you get this?''

''Last week.''

''Did you run a new ad?''

''No. It arrived out of the blue. He must have kept the address from a past ad.''

''Hmm.'' Megan felt a chill across her shoulder blades. ''Did you call him?''

''Yes. I made an appointment for you to see him at one-thirty today. He's going to meet you at McDonald's, across from Melbourne University. That's convenient for you, right?''

As if Gladys cared, Megan fumed to herself. Swallowing a sarcastic response, Megan reminded herself how much she needed the few hundred dollars she'd earn from the eight-week calling survey. ''Yes. What about—'' she searched the next application letter ''—Michelle Jackson? Did you set an appointment for her, too?''

''Yes. I had her resume left over from last fall. She says she's still interested and will see you at two. But I want you to hire the man.'' Gladys took a gulp from the liter bottle of cola sitting at her elbow, then wiped her mouth on the back of her hand. As usual, she wore five rings, the enormous diamonds glittering in the dim light. She seemed surprised to find Megan still with her when she reached for the cola bottle a second time.

''Well? You can go now.''

"Are you okay?" she inquired, then instantly regretted her question.

"I've not been okay since I lost my boy, Megan. But if you are asking after my health, the answer is no. My heart's acting up." Gladys focused on Megan's face. "Don't pay to worry about people who aren't blood relations, Megan. You can't trust anyone who isn't a blood relation. It would pay you to remember that."

Feeling a flush of embarrassment, Megan nodded. Gladys often referred to a long-ago tragedy that had claimed her only child, but she never provided the details. Today she seemed more emotional than usual. Megan's good manners had formed a goodbye on her lips, but she turned quickly and let herself back out into the hot sunshine.

She hurried up the splintering stairs, vowing she'd tell Gladys Grokowbowski just what she thought of her when she and the kids moved from this rat trap. Let Gladys think for a moment about how impossible she was to get along with, Megan fumed. She will have a heck of a time finding someone who will do yard work, run errands and work as TeleSurv's assistant field coordinator just to get a break on the rent!

Inside the house, she flew at the breakfast dishes with a vengeance, then showered, dressed and applied her makeup. She took ten minutes to make popsicles, shoving the plastic tray gingerly into the freezer. Making a mental note to get brown sugar, Megan set off on her fifteen-minute walk to the university.

She was going to get her internship assignment today from her adviser, and it was an important meeting. If things went as planned, the internship would be her entrée into the Miller Advertising Company. The firm had just landed a big account, and she had heard from the job placement counselor that two staff positions were going to be added in September.

Megan intended to fill one of those jobs. She could get through a last, unemployed summer with the kids, then when they went back to school, she could go to work full-time. Hurrying her steps along, she climbed the stairs to the humanities building, unable to keep a huge smile from her face. *Only a few more months of Gladys, TeleSurv and poverty!* The last vestiges of anger and hostility toward her boss dissipated with the thought.

Maybe you're right, Gladys, Megan found herself thinking. I need to worry about my family. Not you.

THE MAN'S HAND was steady as he snipped the front-page article from the *Melbourne Press*. He laid the heavy metal scissors down gently, then walked over to the cork bulletin board and neatly pinned the news clipping to it. His dark eyes roamed the crammed surface of newsprint, but he didn't pause to read the stories.

He knew the details of each story on the first four Grim Reaper murders by heart. The fifth would only contain the same careful manipulation of withheld information and unmentioned clues. America may be a nation with a free press, he thought, but the needs of a police investigation still kept the most interesting facts of a crime secret until after a conviction.

Crossing the Florida room, a covered porch with floor-to-ceiling louvered windows, the man kneeled beside the bookcase and withdrew one of six black leather notebooks. He jotted down several facts, pushed it back into line, then withdrew a second binder.

He opened it to a page near the middle. The letter from Eva Merritt was neatly folded in half. He took it out and read it, then refolded it and put it back inside the page marked "TeleSurv Standings for Melbourne-Palm Bay." The previous fall's network ratings were listed beneath, with the net increases and decreases in households watching a particular channel highlighted in red.

Next to station WABR was a +3.4.; beside station WMMB, a -2.9. The man shut his eyes, deep lines of humiliation and anger marring his lean face. For two years he'd been news director at WMMB, and during that time he'd given the job his all.

The sixty-hour weeks and lack of any other life had paid off, for the affiliate station had moved to number one in the ratings. He'd been a hero to the owner and the advertising manager, and several consumer groups in Melbourne had honored him for his programming of relevant local shows.

Then last fall's TeleSurv results had come in and stunned everyone. He'd left before he'd been asked to. The pain and humiliation his ego had wrestled with returned, but he threw them off.

Now was not the time for self-pity. Now was the time to prove that he had been wronged. And exact the necessary punishment for the crime.

The man stood and replaced the second notebook, shoving it with more force than warranted. The twin statuettes on top of the bookcase rattled, and he grimaced at the sight of them. He wrapped a hand around the neck of the identical women each portrayed and carried them to the hall closet. With a clank he deposited them on the top shelf.

Shutting the door with a bang, he concentrated on his meeting later today. With any luck he'd be able to sniff out a lead and find out from the inside who at TeleSurv surveys was working with the man who'd masterminded the scam.

His eyes rested on the Grim Reaper articles as he walked back onto the porch. When the truth came out and his old station called to beg him to take his job back, he would. And he'd be right on top of current events, having kept up with the Grim Reaper story with an angle no one would ever guess.

MEGAN WAS TOO STUNNED to cry. She was almost too stunned to breathe. For a woman who prided herself on careful planning, she had never dreamed the present situation was likely to happen. But it had, and she'd better come up with a plan to salvage her life, she thought in panic.

"Megan, are you okay?" Darren George's smiling face loomed close to her. His hand pressed her shoulder. "I don't want you to worry about this. It means waiting until next fall to intern at Miller Advertising, but that's no big thing. I'll get you an internship at WABR for now. Two internships will look better on your resume, anyway."

"I can't wait for Miller. I'm graduating at the end of this quarter."

"I know. But you can take eight class hours above your master's for credit—"

"—You don't understand," Megan interrupted quietly, "I've spent every penny of my loan and grant money going to school for three straight years. I don't have enough to register for more classes. I need to get a job by September 1, not go back to school."

He blinked, then smiled his 1,000-watt grin. "No problem. So you take the internship at my station and be done with it. I know you're interested in working in advertising, so I'll let you work with the network sales and marketing people instead of the news folks. Okay?"

Megan smiled weakly. She knew she was fortunate having Darren George, WABR's senior anchorman, as her adviser, but her disappointment was intense. "Thank you."

"Megan, you're divorced aren't you?"

"Yes." Her ex-husband's face flashed into her mind. Dean Summers had once been a student of George's. She wondered if that was the reason for his question.

"It must be tough. School and motherhood, I mean."

Megan nodded, unsure of what he was trying to say.

"Well, okay then. Can you start tomorrow?"

"Yes. Can I put my time in during the day? My kids are in school, and I'd like to work during those hours."

"Sure. We don't care how our interns clock their hours. As long as they get twenty in."

Megan rose as Dr. George grabbed his jacket and prepared to leave for his eleven o'clock seminar. She held out her hand. "Thanks for everything, Dr. George."

He pressed her hand between both of his. "I'd do whatever I could to help you, Megan." A good-looking, if theatrical, man in his early forties, Dr. George fancied himself an object of lust to his students. He was tall, blond and deeply tanned. He had pale green eyes and reddish eyelashes, and a small mole near his top lip.

She withdrew her hand and smiled, her muscles complaining of his overly ambitious handshake. "Thank you.

When can I pick up my appointment letter for the internship?"

"Be at the station tomorrow at nine. I'm doing a special investigative report on the Grim Reaper murders. It'll be a good time to introduce you around."

It crossed her mind to tell him she knew the latest victim, but she swallowed the impulse. One of the cardinal rules of working for TeleSurv was that no one know what you did. Confidentiality was a major factor in their surveys, particularly in smaller markets like Melbourne where bribery could affect the outcome of the random sample.

"I'll see you, then." She turned and left as a fresh wave of sorrow and shock washed over her at the news of Norma's death.

With a heavier heart than when she started out, Megan headed to her last scheduled honors class, "Ethics in Journalism."

Her sadness seemed an ironic rebuke for her own response of thinking of poor Norma's death in terms of protecting her job. I sound like Gladys Grokowbowski, she thought with a wince. For the second time this morning she felt a chill cross her back.

Chapter Two

Megan watched the man approach her across the busy fast-food restaurant. He was firmly muscled and had thick, sun-streaked hair and dark eyes. In need of a haircut, he was freshly shaven and had a clean, just-showered smell.

Silently she concluded he took vitamins and jogged—his grip was the self-confident one of a man who took care of himself. "Hi. Are you Jack?" she greeted him, half rising from the booth.

"Jack Gallagher. Megan Summers, right?"

"Right. How'd you know me?" she quelled the tingle she felt at his touch and sat down.

Jack smiled briefly and followed suit. "Mrs. Grokowbowski said to look for a girl with dark circles under her eyes and red hair. You're the only one who fit the bill."

Megan's smile stiffened at his less-than-complimentary description. Leave it to Gladys to make such a lovely introduction. Involuntarily she touched the area under her right eye. "Dark circles, huh? Are they that bad?"

Jack studied the woman across from him. She looked too young to be the mother of two, which was another detail Gladys Grokowbowski had thrown in. The faint dark traces were clear beneath the delicate layers of skin. Atypical of redheads, her coloring was pale and golden, untouched by a single freckle. Her eyes were dark blue, set under darker brows, and above full, shining lips.

Jack usually objected to lipstick, but on Megan Summers it seemed the right touch. "No, they aren't. Kids keep you up at night?"

"Take your pick. Kids one night, thunderstorms and a leaky roof the next. Then there's studying, working and reading when I get into one of my binges. Sleep is something I do little of."

She began to redden at this stream of information she'd unleashed. The look in his eyes—that indicated attraction—heightened her color further. "But enough about me. Can you tell me a little about your work experience, Jack, and why you're interested in being a TeleSurv interviewer?"

Pleased she'd steered the conversation so deftly toward him Megan listened as he gave perfect answers to her questions about the TeleSurv information manual.

After twenty minutes of chatting, Megan sipped at the still-steaming coffee from the foam cup. "Well, that's about the whole story with TeleSurv. They sell their quarterly reports to the television, radio and advertising companies that subscribe to their service for big bucks, but they pay us the salary I've outlined. My good interviewers usually make $500 a survey."

"Five hundred dollars for calling seventy-five households each of the first four weeks? To tell them they've been randomly selected by TeleSurv to take part in the survey, right?"

"Right. Then the second four weeks you call your people who agreed to keep the viewing diaries and answer questions, and urge them to mail the surveys back to TeleSurv on the correct dates."

Jack Gallagher nodded, his expression serious. "And you never use your real name?"

"That's right. For TeleSurv, you're John Martin. And my female callers are Ann Davis." Megan smiled, noting the concentration this man was giving their conversation. It was a good sign. If he was this interested in TeleSurv, he'd be less likely to hand in incomplete assignments. "Do you have any more questions?"

He was studying the application form she'd handed him, his brow furrowed. "Why do they ask on this application if I've worked for a radio or television station in the past twelve months?"

"They're nervous about any sabotage of the survey."

He looked directly into her eyes. "You're kidding."

"It's been known to happen in the past. An interviewer who supports the interests of one station or another can influence viewers. Offer them money to put down they watched a certain TV program, or whatever." Megan watched as he reread the form. "You've not worked for a TV station before, have you?"

His glance met hers. Now was the time to test his ability to play the dangerous game he'd begun. Now was the time to lie through his teeth.

"No. As I put down on my resume, I'm a magazine writer. I've been self-employed for the past five years. Right now I'm between assignments, and I thought this might be an interesting job."

"It is. People are really friendly and surprisingly willing in this part of the country to take part in the survey. I understand they have a much harder time in places like Chicago and New York where, even when people have agreed to take part, they throw the survey booklets away like junk mail."

"Floridians are pretty laid-back," Jack replied, lacing his long fingers together and leaning toward Megan, his concentration fully on her. "Are you from here?"

Her face began to warm again. Why, she wasn't sure. "Yes, born in Orlando, years before Disney made it famous. My folks are still there, but my sister and I moved here to go to school a few years ago. She finished, I married and dropped out. Now I'm back at it." Megan silently cursed her second barrage of personal information.

It was awkward, to be sitting here with an attractive, attentive man. She realized at that moment how long it'd been since she'd gone out socially. *Four years. I've not had a date for four years!*

"It must be tough working and going to school with kids."

"Are you married?" she blurted, surprised at her boldness.

"No. Not anymore," Jack answered. "But isn't that an illegal question to ask of a prospective employee?" His teasing tone took the sting from his words.

"Yes, it is. But since you asked about my kids, I thought you might have—" her voice died away and she flushed. "—I'm sorry, Jack, I didn't mean to pry."

He surprised her by reaching across and squeezing her hand. As soon as she noticed his touch, he moved away. "You're not prying. I have a thirteen-year-old son. He's lived with my ex-wife for the past eight years. She's done a great job under incredibly tough circumstances."

Megan nodded, relieved no animosity colored his tone. "They're not here in Melbourne?"

"No. They're in Kansas City. A world away." He looked directly into her eyes. "Being separated from my son is the worst thing I've ever had to face."

"I bet," Megan replied. They sat in silence for a moment.

"Your husband must be supportive."

"I'm divorced," she answered, too quickly. "Now, unless you have other questions, I'm going to say 'Welcome Aboard.' I've got an extra assignment because..." Megan stopped, wanting to be tactful about Norma, but then found herself announcing the dramatic truth. "Because one of my interviewers was killed."

"Killed?" Jack's head snapped up from the form he was signing.

"Yes. She was the latest victim of the Grim Reaper. It's horrible. I only heard about it this morning."

"Norma Schultz worked for TeleSurv?" he asked in surprise, realizing his mistake too late.

"Did you know Norma?" Megan shot back, her look perplexed.

"No," Jack said, shaking his head. "I just remember the name. I was reading the paper a few minutes ago. Bad habit

I have of retaining trivia. Was Ms. Schultz a good friend of yours?'' His heart pounded erratically as he tried to prolong the discussion.

"Not really. But it's such a shock when you actually know someone who's met with violence."

"I'll bet. Too bad the police have such a poor chance of catching this guy."

"What do you mean, Jack?"

Slowly he unclenched his right hand, willing himself to sound casual. "Serial killers are the worst kind to find. There's seldom any rhyme or reason to their patterns."

"It seems to be a symptom of our times. Too many people with grave problems fall through the cracks, never get the psychiatric help they need. Did you see the editorial in last Sunday's paper?"

He nodded. "Yeah. I'm sure the editor of the paper is not real popular with the cops this week."

Megan shrugged. "The writer made a good point. I just hope the inference about a cop being involved in the crime is wrong."

"That's true. If the Reaper has a gun and badge, he could easily catch his victims unaware." Jack looked directly into Megan's worried gaze. "But no one has proved that he's doing that, so you can still trust the cops. For now, anyway."

Something in his voice warned her. He wasn't deliberately scaring her, but the truth of his words was impossible to dispute. "Well, enough bad news. I'll get the scan-ads to you tomorrow and you can go through the material and see if you have any other questions."

"Scan-ads?"

"TeleSurv address scan forms. Sorry, we call them that. Let Gladys or me know if you don't receive them in the mail. The post office loses the envelopes all the time." Tears burned behind her eyes at a new thought. "A couple of weeks ago Norma's assignment was damaged, and we had to get her forms rerun." Megan's voice cracked at the mention of the dead woman, but she went on, "Norma was a great worker. She was so worried TeleSurv was going to be mad at her. But . . . well, let me know if you don't get your work."

"Thanks for your concern." Jack smiled, inclining his head to the left, a habit he had when he was nervous. "So I'm hired?"

She smiled and held out her hand, anticipating his touch with more interest than she knew she should. "Yes. You're hired. Calling starts a week from today."

"Thanks, Megan." Jack shook hands and eased out of the booth. "Can I call you if I have questions? Or should I get back to Mrs. Grokowbowski?"

"Call me. She pretty much stays out of the picture."

"Okay." He turned to walk away, but then faced her again. "How long have you been doing this?"

Megan craned her neck back to meet his eyes, wondering at the strained note in his voice. "For a little more than a year. Why do you ask, Jack?"

He shrugged and looked away. Megan had the feeling he wanted to say more, but about what she couldn't imagine. He was a quick man, and the intricacies of TeleSurv weren't lost on him.

He turned his dark eyes back to her. "I was just wondering if you got burned-out after a certain amount of time. Mrs. Grokowbowski mentioned she'd been the coordinator for four years and seldom kept interviewers more than a couple of surveys."

That was a bizarre comment for Gladys to have made, Megan thought. Most of the interviewers stayed on much longer than that. Was Jack Gallagher worried about job stability? she wondered. He must really need the money. A wave of camaraderie surged through her. "Don't worry about burnout, Jack. Or about getting assignments. Good interviewers always have work."

Out of the corner of her eye Megan spotted a girl she bet was her two o'clock appointment. "Call me if you think of anything else."

"Thanks, Megan." He forced himself not to reach for her slim fingers a second time. A desire to touch her overwhelmed him for a second, but he overcame it. For some reason he felt he could trust her. "I'll be talking to you."

Hopefully he'd get the chance to do that, he thought. Jack pushed the door and felt the burst of heat from the midday sun wash over him. But time was running out. He had to get the information from Megan Summers as soon as possible. Before the Grim Reaper struck again.

MEGAN PRESSED HER HAND to her forehead, feeling the dampness with despair. Her hair needed a perm, which she couldn't afford. Despite the time she'd taken with it this morning, it was now completely limp. When she got to the bus it would be a frizzy mess. Her first day as an intern at WABR, and she would arrive looking like a straggly dog.

Oh well, Megan thought. Dressing for success was just one more thing that would have to wait for a steady paycheck. The first thing she was going to buy was a tube of frosted Scarlet Kiss lipstick she had nearly drooled over at the cosmetic counter in Maas Brothers. Megan had pressed the button on the light pole and was waiting for it to change when an ancient white plymouth pulled up alongside of the curb.

"Good morning, Megan. Can we give you a lift?" Pollard Finch asked through the open window, his thick glasses glinting in the sunlight.

Megan waved to Edna Adams, who was installed with pillows and supports in the back seat beside her folded-up wheelchair. She was holding a huge white Persian cat. "Are you sure it's not out of your way? I'm heading to the bus to catch the 93 downtown."

"You're going our way, Megan. We'll drive you."

Megan crossed in front of the gleaming chrome grill and opened the passenger door. Inside, the car was frosty, the air conditioner blowing full blast. It felt good, but would do little for her hair, she realized with a grin.

"Thanks very much, Mr. Finch."

"It's my pleasure, my dear. I've been meaning to do something nice to thank you for being so good about the recycling crates."

It took Megan a moment to figure out what he meant, then she remembered. Early in January he'd commented to her on the sidewalk in front of Gladys's house, how much it distressed him that Gladys never took in her crates. The City of Melbourne was at the forefront of waste recycling, requiring its citizens to separate paper, metal and glass into color-coded crates. Gladys never moved them to her backyard after the refuse was picked up.

Megan knew it was because Gladys rarely went outside at all, but instead of explaining that to her neighbor, she'd simply taken in Glady's crates along with her own since then.

"You don't have to thank me for that, Mr. Finch. You were right, it was an eyesore."

"People just don't think of the pollution they cause," Pollard Finch replied. "Noise pollution with those abominable radios; eye pollution with trash and litter everywhere you turn. It's a crime against all of us, Megan. One each person needs to combat. America is choking on trash!"

She nodded, unsure of what to say to this surprising barrage from her neighbor. Her feet rested next to a laundry bag full of shirts, light blue garments with patches on the sleeves. "Are you with the post office department, Mr. Finch?"

"Yes. Twenty-nine years and eight months' service, as of Monday. Twenty-nine years of perfect attendance, the highest in the southeast region." His hand grasped the smooth black steering wheel so hard his knuckles showed white.

"Those are records to be proud of," Edna Adams added from the backseat.

"They certainly are," Megan agreed. "Do you work here in Melbourne?"

"Not anymore. I've recently been transferred to Palm Bay station. They're trying to get me to retire and think that bit of harassment will do the trick. It won't, though," Pollard added with a dry laugh.

"Are you coming to the homeowner's meeting tomorrow night, Megan?" Edna asked. "We're going to vote on purchasing Neighborhood Watch signs, you know."

"I plan to, Miss Adams," Megan said. "With this Grim Reaper character roaming through Melbourne, I'd say we need to do something."

"I agree, my dear," Edna replied.

"Where can I drop you, Megan?" Pollard asked as they approached downtown.

Megan pointed to the WABR building at the next corner. "Thanks so much for the lift. I'll see you both tomorrow at the meeting."

Waving goodbye, Megan hid her mirth as her neighbors drove off. They were a strange pair. Gladys had said it was scandalous, two people old enough to know better, living together so openly, but Megan found it charming. Edna Adams and Pollard Finch seemed to be devoted friends and probably saved a ton of money by setting up house together. They lived in Edna's huge white house across the street from her kids' grade school. Pollard kept the yard and grounds as immaculate as he did his car.

I'd rather have those two as neighbors than Gladys, Megan thought as she walked into the lobby of WABR. They minded their own business and seemed to really care about their neighbors.

She gave her name to the receptionist and was immediately ushered down a thickly carpeted hallway to the newsroom. Things were quiet. The morning news show had wrapped, and the weather forecaster, a pretty girl with amazingly long nails, was chatting with the tall young man Megan recognized as broadcaster Sandy Royal.

Blonde and handsome in an almost aggressive way, Royal looked about twenty-five. He was the son of the station owner and the co-anchor of the five o'clock news. Darren George had used him in one of Megan's classes as a prime example of what some called the "Twinkie element" in broadcast journalism. Good-looking model types who were hired to read the news, instead of journalists who were trained to report it.

They both ignored Megan, who self-consciously took a chair and tried not to look as if she was listening to their conversation.

"I'm going to take my buddy's boat out tonight. Why don't you come with us?"

"How big's the boat?"

"Forty-two feet. Bring your roommate if you want."

"Why? Think you can handle two dates, Sandy?"

He grinned wolfishly. "I'll share. And if she's as good-looking as you are, my buddy will flip."

Before Megan could offer a sarcastic rejoinder, anchorman Darren George's voice boomed across the room as he came through the door. "Hey kids!"

Megan smiled, relieved. "Hi, Dr. George."

"Megan! Did they load you up with work already? Why are you others just sitting here?" He turned a sardonic smile on Sandy. "Come on, big boy. I know daddy owns the station, but the Grim Reaper's out there, waiting for you to find him. Megan here is going to help you."

"I thought you had that little gig wrapped up, Darren," Sandy shot back.

"I'm doing my own series on the guy, but Mitchell okayed you sidebarring me." He turned to Megan. "Mitchell Kostos is our assignment editor. Come on with me and meet him. He thought it would be great if Sandy had some assistance on the research side."

"I can handle my own research, Darren."

"Of course you can, dear boy. But think how nice it will be to have the lovely Megan here to help."

Sandy turned his eyes to her, clearly dismissing her six-year-old cotton dress with a blink. "Help? What kind of help can a *student* furnish me, Dr. George?"

"Megan here can do some interviews, take notes, even think, dear boy. Since you've got your sights on a network gig, don't you think it would be nice to have someone to help you do all that?"

"Look, Darren—"

"Mr. Royal," Megan interrupted softly, "I've watched your feature reports for the past few months and I'd be really grateful if you'd let me do some background work for you."

Both men turned their glances to Megan. Sandy's eyes glinted. "Thanks . . . Megan, is it? Okay, sure. I can always use an extra pair of legs. Be at the Melbourne Police Department tomorrow at ten and I'll introduce you to the detective heading up the case."

"Great, Sandy," Darren George said with a smile. "I'm sure having someone to check the facts will help you. Meet us in my office in about ten minutes. We'll discuss the whole thing then."

Megan felt the tangible animosity between the two men. As she let Darren lead her out of the waiting room, she noted the embarrassment on young Royal's face. The weather girl seemed to be enjoying herself, which probably meant she wouldn't get her boat trip, after all, Megan thought to herself.

"So, Mrs. Summers. How do you like big-time TV news?"

"It's very—"

"—Very boring, back-stabbing and disappointing," Darren finished for her. "But don't worry about that. You'll get great experience. Maybe even a job out of this, if you're interested."

Megan's spine stiffened at the steadily increasing pressure Darren George was applying to her arm. She knew better than to put the skids on any job offer, but she felt panicked over George's apparent memory loss over what her primary assignment at the station was going to be. If she was going to have any kind of shot at all at Miller Advertising, she needed to put time in the marketing department. Not babysit Sandy Royal. "I appreciate what you're offering, Dr. George. But I thought I was going to be working with the marketing people."

Darren George stopped abruptly and let go of her arm. "Megan, this isn't the time to turn down an opportunity of a lifetime. The Grim Reaper murders have gone national! This could make your career!"

"But I'm not interested in being a journalist. My thesis had a strong public relations—"

"Trust me on this, Megan." Darren returned his hand to her arm. "Help me keep tabs on this story, and I assure you you'll end up with a job in whatever field you want."

They resumed walking. Despite his words, Megan was sure that it wasn't the story, but Sandy Royal, that Darren wanted her to keep tabs on.

AT EIGHT-THIRTY MEGAN closed the door to her children's bedroom, delighted that both had gone to sleep without the usual fight. Roxie had read the bedtime story, and Thomas had refrained from whining.

Such victories were the measure of a mother's day, Megan thought to herself as she settled down at the dinette table. She glanced at the stack of mail. It was time to write out the checks for the monthly utility bills, but she didn't feel like putting herself through such a deflating experience just yet. She had $408 in the checking account, a small fortune to her, and it would be great to let it sit there for a day or two before she paid out $300 of it to the power, water, gas and telephone companies.

Stuffing the bills away in the kitchen drawer, she tossed out the junk mail, two pizza ads and a sweepstakes mailing. Then she remembered Thomas loved playing with the magazine stickers inside so she retrieved the buff-colored envelope and left it for her son and his collection. The kid was mad for stickers. Once she had to reprimand him for going through people's trash to claim the treasures they had tossed out as rubbish.

Megan unzipped her briefcase and pulled out the material Darren George and the assignment editor had given her to go over on the Grim Reaper case. There were photocopies of all the Melbourne Press clips, as well as the AP wire stories that had gone out nationally.

There were also computer printouts on all five victims, Norma Schutlz included. Vital statistics, next of kin and the like, plus copies of the police reports on the first two victims. Megan wondered where the others were.

She pulled out a pad and jotted down the names of each of the Reaper's prey. Darren George had told Sandy to plan his sidebar on the backgrounds of the victims to reveal any common denominators in their lives. The police were certainly doing the same thing, Megan had realized, but George had insisted they do their own investigation. He seemed convinced the dead were linked in some important way to their killer.

As Megan wrote down their names, ages and occupations, she wondered about the theory that the Reaper was posing as a cop. He'd evidently gained access to his victims' homes without breaking in, which led some to think he masqueraded as a public official.

Megan sighed, then added the addresses to her list.

Leslie Fielder, 37, pizza parlor manager, 618 Palmetto.

Joy Motherhood, 29, housepainter, 124 1/2 Century Blvd.

Monique Patrick, 51, owner of Monique's Gifts, 333 Brevard Blvd., Palm Bay.

David Dunton, 44, Automobile Tire dealer, 9 Bayside Dr.

Norma Schultz, 53, TeleSurv Surveys, 319 Palm Court.

The occupation section on Norma's vital statistic sheet listed "telephone solicitor" as her occupation, but Megan noted the more specific information. She wondered if she should call the police and give them this detail but discounted that thought. Surely TeleSurv had no bearing on the woman's death. The jangling of the telephone interrupted her thoughts.

"Hello?" Megan answered.

"Megan. Come down here and pick up the staff assignment sheets. They need to be mailed to TeleSurv first thing in the morning."

"Hi, Gladys. Yes. I'll come in a few minutes." It surprised Megan to hear the labored breathing of the older woman. She sounded as if she was having trouble catching her breath. "Are you feeling okay, Gladys?"

"I'm having some damn reaction to my heart pills. Doctors don't know what the hell they're doing these days."

Megan bit her tongue. She knew Gladys was told to cut down on her caffeine consumption, advice she ignored. "Can I do anything for you?"

"Just get this damn stuff in the mail."

The line went dead and Megan grimaced. The woman was impossible; she reacted to kindness like a snake would to a boot heel.

"Mommy!"

Megan crossed the room and peeked through the door. Thomas was sitting up in bed, rubbing his eyes. "What's the matter, honey?"

"Can't find bunny."

She spotted the well-mauled stuffed rabbit beside Thomas's bed and picked it up. Her boy cuddled against it, then stuck his thumb back into his mouth and went back to sleep instantly. She straightened the sheet around Roxie and tiptoed out.

Ten minutes later Megan pulled her tennies out from under the couch and put them on. She then took a couple of minutes to unfold the bed inside. When she got back from running down to Gladys's, she'd shower and think about the Reaper in bed. Great company, she thought, allowing a moment's self-pity. *I wonder if Jack Gallagher sleeps alone?*

Annoyed at her randy thought, Megan hurried down the stairs and across the lawn. All the outside lights were off at Gladys's house, not an unusual occurrence. Gladys often remarked how the power companies were the most corrupt of all government-controlled agencies, and she went out of her way not to give them her money. Megan reached for the screen door, surprised to see it cracked open.

Gladys usually unlocked the doors when she was expecting her, but she never left them open. Megan checked on the ground for the envelope Gladys wanted her to pick up. It was nowhere in sight. Megan felt the skin on the back of her neck prickle as she pushed the door wider and peered into the dark kitchen.

"Gladys?"

There was no answer.

Chapter Three

Megan stepped a foot inside the door. The screen creaked in complaint as she held it open behind her. "Gladys? I'm here to pick up the staff list."

A faint "cuckoo, cuckoo" from a clock deep in the house echoed off the kitchen walls, but no voice responded to her.

She let the screen door close slowly behind her and took another step into the cluttered room. The tobacco scent was thicker than usual, and fresh. Megan crinkled her nose as her foot touched something liquid, her shoe slipping as she moved backward. A broken crystal glass was smashed on the linoleum and a dark substance pooled around it. Megan leaned down and picked up the goblet and examined the floor. It was splashed everywhere with cola.

Megan stood erect. "Gladys? Are you decent? I'm coming in." The image of Gladys, dead from a heart attack, sprang to mind, but she dismissed it. The old bat was probably in bed with the TV on and just forgot to leave the list, Megan thought.

She took a step across the pool of soda. Behind her she heard the sound of soft footsteps. Clutching her hands into fists Megan jerked around as the screen doorknob creaked behind her.

Roxie stood there staring at her, her blue eyes wide with fright. "Mommy. I couldn't find you!"

"Oh, baby. I'm sorry." Megan splashed through the mess on the floor and was out in the thick night air in a flash. She scooped up her daughter, who now began to sob, and hugged her. "What's wrong, Roxie? Did Thomas wake you up?"

"No. The phone did. It was ringing and ringing. I got scared when you didn't answer it. So I looked outside for you."

Megan carried her daughter back up the stairs. "Who was on the phone, honey?"

"I don't know. No one was there when I picked it up."

Roxie was nearly asleep in her arms when Megan made it back into the house. Her daughter was getting big, but her forty-five-pound weight seemed light and incredibly dear at this instant. She was surprised Roxie had ventured out of the house in the dark. It was more her style to call her from the steps. "Go back to sleep, honey."

"Are you going to stay here with us, Mom?"

"Yes, baby. I'm going to stay right here. Now go to sleep."

Damn, she thought as she looked out her front screen. She'd left the door at Gladys's wide open. Megan picked up the phone and dialed her boss's number. After twenty rings she hung up in disgust. When was Gladys going to learn to answer the phone!

Megan started for the door. She'd given Roxie her word that she'd stay in, but she couldn't just leave the door open down at her landlady's. Before Megan got far, she was startled by vigorous knocking on her front door.

She stood frozen. No one ever just dropped in on her like this, especially after nine. Maybe Gladys had heard her and had actually ventured out...? "Who is it?"

"Megan?"

The deep male voice was familiar. Jack Gallagher? she thought. What on earth? Megan pulled open her front door. "Jack! Hi!" Through the screen the light from the house shined into his eyes, darkening the color to black embers.

"Hi, Megan. I'm sorry to drop in on you like this, but I wanted to return this application." He waved an envelope at her. "I know you needed the industry disclaimer, and like a fool I left the restaurant with it."

"Thanks. You didn't have to make a special trip, though." She opened the door and reached for the document, aware of how tall he was suddenly, a fact that hadn't sunk in when she'd met him earlier. His hair was dry now, and she noted how it curled around the bottom of his ears and neck. He had a very strong neck, thick and tan. She could see his muscles flex at his collarbones, because the top buttons of his shirt were undone. Her earlier thought of him brought a spot of heat to her face. Megan stepped back and beckoned him in. "Come in and have a glass of lemonade or something?"

Jack didn't move. He glanced into the tiny apartment, registering the fold-out bed with the dainty white nightshirt tossed across the pillow. "I don't want to mess up your routine. If you were getting ready to go to bed..."

Embarrassed at the sight of her pink-flowered sheets, Megan laughed nervously. "No, I've got a lot of work to do. Please come on in for a moment."

Jack crossed the entry and stood awkwardly near the door. "Where are your kids?"

"They're in the room over there. Sound asleep, I hope. But we need to keep our voices down or they'll be out here to investigate. They're nuts about company."

Jack smiled. It was the first genuine show of emotion she'd seen from him in their two brief meetings, and Megan was struck by how handsome it made his features. His teeth were even and white.

"My son was the same way when he was little. Never wanted to go to sleep until the company left."

Several questions that were none of her business passed through her mind, but Megan didn't ask any of them.

"The divorce was my fault."

"I'm sorry," she responded. "But I know from experience there are always two people at fault to some degree."

"Sometimes. Sometimes I think it is just one person's choice. What happened with your marriage, Megan?"

"The malady of the eighties. My husband wanted to do 'his thing,' and it didn't include his college dropout wife and two runny-nosed babies." She flushed, hearing the hurt in her voice.

"I bet he regrets it."

"I doubt it," she answered sharply.

For a moment they both stayed silent while fighting back emotions too raw to reveal to a stranger. Jack continued, "I was driven by my job and didn't let much else get my attention. Guess you could say I was a twenty-four karat fool."

She smiled and stiffed the impulse to reach out and squeeze his arm, wishing her children's father felt some of the regret reflected in Jack Gallagher's face. She motioned to what she hoped was the cleanest of the three aluminum dinette chairs at the table, unnerved that this man had shared such a personal insight with her. "Please sit down. Would you prefer coffee?"

He settled his lanky frame onto one of the chairs. "Lemonade will be fine, thanks."

She poured out two glasses and brought them to the table, piling her books and tablet with the Reaper murder victims on it on the third chair. Jack had seemed to stare at it for a moment, but when she had formed a question for him, his expression was blank. She searched her fatigued mind for a neutral topic. "Do you live near here, Jack?"

"Yes. Just two streets over. Off Country Club Drive. I figured I'd just drop the stuff off. I didn't think you were home."

"Oh?" Megan sat and took a gulp of lemonade, trying to quell the butterflies in her stomach. With Jack Gallagher sitting here with her she seemed to be seeing her apartment for the first time. The shabby clutter dismayed her.

"I called and let it ring for quite a while. Just a few minutes ago."

She put her glass down and mopped up the ring of condensation left behind on the Formica table. "I was downstairs at Mrs. Grokowbowski's. My six-year-old, Roxie, got to the phone finally, but you must have hung up already."

Jack's expression changed. "Gladys Grokowbowski lives downstairs? In the front house?"

"Yes. What's wrong, Jack?"

He blinked, the muscles on either side of his jaw twitching. "She have a boyfriend?"

The absurdity of the question nearly made Megan laugh aloud, but Jack's tense demeanor cut the giggle off before it formed in her throat. She swallowed, her nervousness returning. "Why do you ask?"

Jack stood and walked to the front door, opening it to look at the dark house below. "When I turned into your driveway I saw someone on the front porch. A man, I think. He stood there in the dark. I said good evening, but he didn't reply. When I was climbing the stairs to your place I looked back and saw someone, it may have been the same guy, crossing the street."

He didn't add that something about the guy had unsettled him. From the taut lines around Megan Summer's appealing mouth, it was the last thing a young mother alone with two little kids needed to hear.

Jack met her eyes, then glanced to her hands. She was twisting the bottom of her T-shirt with one of her fingers.

"Are you sure of what you saw, Jack? I've never known Gladys to have any male visitors. And she never uses the front door." Suddenly the bizarre incident with the spilled soda and open side screen door rushed through Megan's mind.

"I'm sure someone was on the porch," Jack replied.

"Something must be wrong." Quickly she told him what had happened a few minutes before he arrived. "Can you go down and poke your head in the door and call her?"

In answer to her question, Jack moved through the door and out onto the landing. Before he pulled the knob closed he turned to her and said, "Stay here, Megan. Lock the door and call the police if I don't come right back."

Before she could answer he was gone. She locked the door and paced back and forth. Stopped, cleaned up the lemonade glasses, took her tennis shoes out of the sink, then paced some more. She went in and kissed the kids, then returned to the tiny living area and picked up the books and tablet off the dinette chair and moved them to the table beside the sofa bed. She sat down for a moment, aware she was trembling.

How had such an ordinary night turned out to be so terrifying, she wondered? Dread that something was wrong, horribly wrong down at Gladys's house, coursed through her. Gladys would never open the door for someone she didn't know. Unless it looked absolutely safe. *Like it would if it were a policeman!*

Megan tried to put the thought aside, but could not. A lump of fear, bitter and hot, burned in the pit of her stomach.

She had been in the house. Her baby had stood crying, unsuspecting on the side porch. What if the stranger lurking on the front had . . .

The sound of Jack's knock nearly made her cry out with nerves.

"It's me, Megan. Let me in."

Megan hurried to the door. She said a short prayer that she would open it and find Jack looking sheepish, so her own fears could evaporate. She flung the door open to admit him, but her eager smile froze on her lips.

Jack was pale under his tan and there were spots and smears of red on his clothes. "Call the police, Megan. Gladys Grokowbowski has been murdered."

THE NIGHTMARE EVENING continued on. At least the kids hadn't wakened but once, Megan thought. When the first batch of detectives had arrived, accompanied by the siren and lights that seemed to chew through the walls of her house, they'd both started to cry.

She'd gotten Roxie and Thomas back to sleep and pulled the door to their bedroom closed, only to be confronted by a Minicam and the harsh lights of WABR's night crew coming through her front door.

They'd monitored the police calls and shown up minutes after the squad car and ambulance had turned into the narrow drive. Mitchell Kostos, the burly newsman she'd met earlier, yelled gruesome questions at her. "Can we have a statement, Miss Summers? Did you find the body? Was it knifed, shot or strangled?"

Before she could answer, the detective who seemed to be in charge, Pete McMurphy, ordered them back down the stairs. Jack took her by the arm and sat her down, then clunked a glass full of whiskey in front of her.

"Drink it, Megan. It'll help."

She picked it up, wondering idiotically how he had found the whiskey at the back of her spice cupboard. But he was so tall, she thought. Of course he could see behind the jars.

Jack sat across from her at the dinette table, staring at the milling cops while the noise downstairs echoed up to them, mixed with cries and excited voices from the neighborhood. In the sky overhead she heard the whacka-whacka-whacka presence of a helicopter as its high-voltage spotlight mingled with the flickering red-and-yellow lights strobing against her front windows.

Finally some of the commotion died down, and she and Jack were left with Sergeant McMurphy and Officer Judy Barnes, a middle-aged bleached blond in a too-snug uniform.

Megan put the glass of liquor to her mouth, tasting the burning strength of it with her lips, but feeling nothing as it traveled down her throat.

"Now, Mr. Gallagher, I need to ask you just a few more questions and I'll let you and Miss Summers get back to what you were doing."

Megan cut her eyes to the detective, uneasy with the implication behind his statement. Jack seemed not to notice and shook his head in cooperation.

"What time was it that you found Mrs. Grokowbowski?"

"I'd say about nine," Jack answered.

"Miss Summers called in at 9:13," Officer Barnes interjected, her voice full of questions it wasn't her place to ask.

McMurphy frowned, then looked at Megan. "How long did you and Mr. Gallagher wait after he found the body before you called 911?"

Her throat felt incapable of speech. Megan swallowed and inhaled deeply. "I called as soon as Jack came in."

"Right away? You didn't fix him a drink or talk?" The chair legs of the detective's seat scraped against the linoleum as he moved a few inches closer to the table. Officer Barnes scooted up nearer behind him, and Megan felt three pairs of eyes on her.

"No. I opened the door. Jack said Gladys had been killed. I turned and picked up the phone and called."

"I see." McMurphy made a note on his small lined pad. "And what time did Mr. Gallagher get here tonight?"

The phone rang and Officer Barnes grabbed it. "Who's calling please?" she asked. She put her hand over the mouthpiece. "A Darren George wants to speak to Miss Summers."

The two police officers exchanged glances, then McMurphy nodded curtly. "Tell him she'll call back."

"He's a personal friend. I'll take it now. If you don't mind," Megan shot back. She caught a look of surprise from Jack, but she wasn't sure if it was due to the fact she knew the anchorman or that she was being tough with the cops.

"Fine," McMurphy responded. Megan rose and took the phone. "Hello?"

"Megan! Are you okay? Sandy just called me and told me you found the Reaper's latest victim. I couldn't believe our luck!"

She sensed Detective McMurphy's disapproval and didn't feel like discussing the night's events with so many onlookers. Her glance returned to Jack, whose attention was focused somewhere faraway. "A friend of mine did. I'm sorry, but I can't talk now, Dr. George. I'll see you tomorrow at the station."

"Okay. Sure thing. Get in as soon as you can. This is a real break for us, Megan."

"I'll see you tomorrow." She hung up the phone, wondering how much explanation she should give. "I'm doing an internship at Dr. George's station. Coincidentally he's working on a feature story on the—" her tongue stuck to her teeth "—Melbourne murders."

McMurphy nodded. "Lucky coincidence for you both." He watched Megan closely as she returned to her chair. "Now, where were we? Okay. When did you say Mr. Gallagher got here tonight?"

"About ten minutes or so before he found—" she inhaled again "—Gladys."

"And right before he arrived you were downstairs in the Grokowbowski house." The detective stopped for three heartbeats. "Did you see Mr. Gallagher out on the street when you brought your daughter back upstairs?"

"No. But then I wouldn't have, since my back was to the street."

"You might have turned around. Mr. Gallagher said he did exactly that when he was at your front door—looked down and saw the man from the front porch across the street."

A knot of fear and impatience grew in Megan's stomach over the questions. She felt guilty for not noticing more. And guilty for being irritated at the policeman. "I didn't see anyone on the street."

McMurphy made another note. "Okay." He smiled at Jack. "So you found the body about nine, checked around for the murderer, then came back upstairs to Miss Summers's house—"

"—It's Mrs. Summers. Mrs. Megan Summers. I told the 911 operator that," Megan interrupted, overwhelmed suddenly at the redundant questioning. She stood and crossed to the sink, rinsed out her glass and turned. Officer Barnes's hand was resting casually on her holster, which infuriated Megan further. Good grief, she thought, did these people think she and Jack had killed Gladys?

"Did you know Mrs. Grokowbowski well enough to enter her home without permission?" Officer Judy demanded.

She whirled around. "Yes, I thought she might be ill so I went in. It was the decent thing to do."

"Mrs. Summers thinks it's very odd that Gladys Grokowbowski would have admitted any man to her home," Jack added. He flinched as all three onlookers turned to him. "That may be a clue as the Reaper's actions. I read recently some people think he may be a cop."

"He's not a cop." Officer Barnes sputtered, walking up to and standing within inches of Jack. Her chubby knuckles clenched on to her holster. "Some irresponsible people in the media have speculated he's posing as a cop. But there's—"

"—That's enough, Judy," McMurphy cut in. He gave her a withering look, then turned to Jack, who was leaning back in the chair, two legs off the ground. "So you follow the Grim Reaper story, Mr. Gallagher? Got any private theories on our man?"

Jack sat the chair legs down easily, pushing his heavy hair back off his forehead. "None. How about you?"

Megan saw the deep flush crawling up McMurphy's neck. Suddenly she wanted them all out. The game of cat and mouse and innuendo was too much to cope with. "I'm sorry. Can we do this tomorrow? I really need to check on my kids and get some rest."

McMurphy nodded, made a final note and snapped his pad closed. "Certainly. Mr. Gallagher, I'll be in around 9:00 A.M. Could you and Miss—excuse me—Mrs. Summers come in and give a complete statement at that time?"

"I'll be there." Jack met Megan's glance. "Can I come by and get you?"

She nodded, then watched without a word as he led the two policemen to the door. It was a relief to her that he assumed the role of host. Jack closed the door gently, then crossed over to the dinette table to lean on the back of the chair. He had washed the blood off his hands and arm sometime when she wasn't watching, she noted numbly.

"Are you going to be okay, Megan? Can I call someone to come stay with you? Or do anything?"

"No. I'm fine, thanks." She swallowed again and crossed her arms across her chest, feeling the trembling return. "Do the police think it was the Grim Reaper?"

A look of anxiety and shock mingled in Jack's eyes, radiating tension out across the planes of his high cheekbones. "I don't know."

"McMurphy didn't say, but I heard the ambulance man and the the coroner discussing the method with which Mrs. Grokowbowski was killed. One of them said it looked like the Reaper." She felt the tears falling, as the trembling got worse. "Dear God, Roxie was right there! I was in the house!"

"Hey, Megan. It's going to be okay." Jack crossed in a single step and took her in his arms. His own numbness was replaced for a moment by his revulsion over the night's events, and the reverberations the killing was having through Megan Summers's life. The image of Gladys Grokowbowski's open eyes, reflecting the terror of her last vision, had scorched itself into his brain. The trickle of blood was still warm when he'd touched her, and his skin burned at the memory.

Jack moved his tingling fingers to the nape of Megan's neck and hugged her to him, liking the way her head tucked into the hollow of his throat. She was slight, but strong, and made no move to relax against him.

"You're bound to be in shock, Megan. Take it easy, though. You're safe. The kids are safe."

She felt safe in his arms. For an instant she reveled in his muscular embrace, but then she stiffened and pulled away. "I know. It's just all so horrible...."

"It is horrible." Releasing her, he reached for a tissue and wiped her face. "Here. Blow your nose. When I leave, lock the door and try to get some sleep. Tomorrow things will look brighter."

She took the tissue and blew her nose. It had felt warm and wonderful in Jack Gallagher's arms, but she couldn't allow herself to lean on him. He was a stranger, a man she didn't really know at all.

She was all the kids had in life to depend on, and it was time to buck up. Her trembling stopped, and Megan took another deep, shuddering breath. "Thanks, Jack. I'll see you about, when eight-thirty?"

"Eight-thirty will be great." He wanted to reach out and brush the strand of silky red hair stuck against her damp cheek, but he refrained. She made it clear she neither wanted nor took any comfort from his touch.

"Thanks. Good night, Jack."

He walked to the door and moved the lock into the engaged position, then turned back to her. He wanted to tell her what was on his mind, but he could not afford the luxury of the truth now. Besides, discovering the fact she knew Darren George personally changed everything. "The murderer has no history of striking twice in the same place, Megan. The kids will be okay."

She nodded her appreciation for what he was trying to do. "I'll see you tomorrow."

When the door clicked shut she prayed he was right, but had a premonition that she was not okay. And wouldn't be until the killer was caught.

Chapter Four

"Why'd Mrs. Gladys die, Momma?" Roxie asked in an anxious voice. "When am I going to die?"

Megan leaned down and hugged her daughter. "You're not going to die until you are a hundred and twenty-five because you always eat your Cheerios. Now hurry up, sweetie, the bell has already rung."

"Didn't Mrs. Gladys eat her Cheerios?" Thomas asked with a solemn look.

She only told her children Gladys had died in order to explain the commotion last night. Megan knew they would assume she'd died of natural causes, and for now she was going to let them continue thinking so. It might be a bad way to handle such a tough topic, but she was anxious for the kids to get into their classrooms and immerse themselves in the distractions of normal routine.

At any rate, Megan told herself, now was not the time to explain the facts about how vicious life could be. A few minutes ago she'd made an appointment with Milton Butz, the principal, to tell him about last night.

"She probably didn't honey. And she smoked and drank soda all day. All unhealthy stuff. Now scoot. Momma will be here to walk you home."

Both children hugged her tighter than usual and walked through the doors into the hallway quietly. She watched them for a moment, wondering if she should call their father. But what would he do? she asked herself silently.

Nothing, which is what he did best, her mind replied as she entered the administration building.

Mr. Butz was speaking to someone on the phone, but he motioned Megan to sit down and he'd be right with her. She sat in the child-sized chair on the opposite side of the counter from him, swallowing a fleeting feeling of guilt. Ever since the fight she'd had in the fifth grade with Pam and Barbara, two rotten kids who had delighted in double-teaming her, sitting in a school principal's office was cause for anxiety.

She let her eyes drift around the room. A few feet from Butz the school secretary sat typing, about twenty-two words a minute, Megan noted. *Our tax dollars at work.* To the left of the woman sat a heaveyset, big-boned girl in her late teens.

Megan recognized her as Mona Hawkins, a mentally handicapped teenager the school district employed in a work skills program. Mona stared at her for a moment as Megan waved, then turned back to the three-by-five-inch cards she was alphabetizing. She studied a chart of the alphabet in front of her for several seconds, then filed a card. Mona glanced again at Megan.

Megan smiled widely, hoping her encouragement showed. Mona looked away without changing her expression and stared again at the letters.

"Mrs. Summers?"

Megan blinked and stood quickly. "Good morning, Mr. Butz."

"Good morning. Won't you come into my office?" Milton Butz held back the short gate that granted entry to the administrative area.

To the tap, tap, tap of his secretary's typing, Megan walked by the principal, her lungs inhaling the clean scent of Old Spice after-shave. The smell reminded her of her father, and she found herself relaxing the first time since last evening.

Behind the closed door of his office, Mr. Butz listened to her story of the events of the previous night, at one point jotting down a note to himself in a black notebook he had opened on the credenza beside him. His expression was sympathetic. Megan appreciated the fact he did not over-react to her mention of the Grim Reaper.

"So what I'm most concerned about, Mr. Butz," Megan said as she leaned closer to his desk, "is that if Thomas or Roxie show any unusual behavior, that I be notified immediately. At this point I don't think they're too scared, but once the other kids at school start talking about what's sure to be in the papers, it may get very hard for them."

"Rest assured I'll discuss this with their teachers, Mrs. Summers. Both of your children are well-adjusted, so we'll operate on the assumption they'll weather this just fine. Children have remarkable resiliency." His eyes were kind as he stroked his salt-and-pepper mustache.

Megan extended her hand. "Thanks very much for your time, Mr. Butz."

He shook it and both of them stood. "If I'm not being too personal, Mrs. Summers, may I ask how you're holding up under this strain? It must have been quite a shock for you to know someone who was murdered?"

Two someones. Squelching that line of thinking, Megan smiled. "I'm doing fine, really. It's nerve-racking for everyone in town, with a madman running around loose, but I'm going to be careful."

The principal's voice dropped to a confidential level. "The police are quite sure last night's crime is the work of the Grim Reaper?"

"That's how they're all acting, but I've heard nothing officially. I'm sure it takes them awhile to compare all the evidence and everything."

"Of course." Mr. Butz walked around his desk and opened the door for Megan. He laid his hand on her arm and gave her a small, comforting squeeze. "Do be careful, Mrs. Summers."

"I will," she replied as they walked out into the blast of heat from the morning sun. "But I'll feel a lot better when the police apprehend this character."

Mr. Butz's expression turned serious. "We all will, Mrs. Summers. Let's hope the police find him before he murders again."

With the principal's words echoing in her mind, Megan said her goodbyes and walked to the front of the school. She didn't relish walking by Gladys's house, or talking to the two policemen manning the barricade while the forensics people worked inside.

Earlier, Thomas had wanted to stop and play in the police car, but Megan had hustled both children by the scene and hoped the police would be through by the time the children returned from school.

Walking briskly out of the school parking lot, Megan spotted Edna Adams and Pollard Finch on the sidewalk in front of Edna's home. She waved back their greeting, then jaywalked over to the opposite side. "Good morning, folks."

"Good morning, Megan. Are you okay? Is there anything we can do for you?" Edna replied. She sounded out of breath.

"Thank you, but I'm fine, really, Miss Adams."

"This is an outrage. Murderers running around on the loose. The police in this town are a bunch of incompetent imbeciles," Pollard Finch sputtered, gripping the handles on Edna's wheelchair. "Decent citizens are at the mercy of the criminals."

"It really is a mess, isn't it?" Megan replied. She wanted to reassure her neighbors, but in the glare of the morning light the facts were hard to deny. "But I'm sure the police are doing their best. They'll catch this guy soon."

"Don't feel a false sense of security, Megan," Edna replied.

"Edna's right, Megan," Pollard cut in. "A madman killed Gladys. Despite locks and alarms and a well-trained police force, none of us are safe from a madman."

"How did you both hear about it?"

"It's in the newspaper, dear. Page one," Edna answered.

"I haven't seen the paper yet."

"Pollard nearly had an attack when he opened it a few minutes ago. I made him sit down and drink his juice, he was so pale." Edna reached up and patted Pollard's left hand.

"We're going to have to band together, Megan. Are you coming to the Neighborhood Watch meeting tonight?" Pollard demanded.

"Yes, I am."

The balding man jerked his head toward the sound of an approaching car. The sun reflected off Pollard's glasses, nearly blinding Megan. She turned her head in time to see the beige Volkswagen turn the corner. It made a racket as it approached, and Pollard Finch's words were drowned out. The car stopped beside them, and Megan saw Jack Gallagher behind the wheel.

His hair was damp from a shower, and his face was nicked and scabbed in two places from a hastily done shave. Megan felt a jolt of relief at seeing him. "Good morning, Jack. Is it eight-thirty already?"

"I'm early," he said. He opened the door and unwound his long legs from the car, joining the trio on the sidewalk. He saw the suspicion on the two older people's faces and understood it immediately. The Grim Reaper's victims were not only those he killed, but all of the citizens who lived with the fear that they could be next.

He turned his smile to Megan. "How are you doing this morning? The kids okay?"

"I'm fine. They were full of questions, but generally they're in good shape." She turned to Edna and Pollard. "This is Jack Gallagher. He and I were visiting last night when—" her voice faltered "—Gladys was found. Jack was very helpful with the police." She introduced her neighbors to him.

"Well, thank goodness you were there to help Megan," Edna replied. "Do you live close by, Mr. Gallagher?"

"Yes, ma'am. I've rented a house over on Amherst. Off Country Club."

"You live alone?" Pollard asked, a sharp edge to his question.

"Yes."

Pollard nodded. "Welcome to the neighborhood, son. We were just reminding Megan of the Neighborhood Watch meeting tonight. It's over at the Roberts's there." He pointed a plump finger at a house a block away. "Why don't you come with Megan? Get to know the folks around here."

Megan felt herself flush slightly. Nothing like putting Jack Gallagher on the spot, she thought. Not that she minded in the least spending another part of an evening with him, but the man was her employee. He'd been very nice to come take her to the police station today, but she knew he was probably doing that because she was his boss. She glanced at him and saw that his smile had faded.

"I would like to get to know the neighbors better. So far Claude Hawkins is the only person I've met, besides Megan." His voice had a soft edge to it when he said her name, surprising them both.

Edna snorted, ignoring the edge. "That gun nut? Don't judge us all by him, Mr. Gallagher. Most of us are much nicer than Claude the Crank."

Megan and Jack laughed with Edna. Pollard nodded curtly and pushed the wheelchair forward. "See you both tonight," he said.

"Bye now," Megan said. She shook her head at Jack's inquiring look. "Please don't feel obligated by those two. They're great people, but they tend to be a little pushy. I've met Mr. Hawkins and he seems very nice."

"I don't feel obligated. Would you like to come to the meeting with me?" His dark eyes were unreadable, but his words were spoken in the same warm tone.

She would, Megan realized, but she couldn't bear taking advantage of him. "I have to walk my kids to the sitter's, but I'll see you there."

"Okay."

There was no doubt about it, Megan thought with an irrational pang of disappointment. Suddenly he seemed relieved.

"So tell me about Claude Hawkins," Jack asked as Megan stepped off the curb into the street. "He collects guns?"

"Yes. But only antiques. His main interest is in swords and ceremonial Japanese daggers. He lost his leg in World War II and says he traded his limb for a hobby."

Jack walked around his car behind Megan and opened the VW's door for her. He had to shut it twice to get it closed. Megan struck him as a woman who always looked for the good in people. He wondered how blind she was to the darker side, and how forgiving. Last night he'd struggled with the information she knew Darren George. In the light of day, any criminal action on her part seemed improbable. He had decided that at their first meeting. Still he had to stay open to the possibility that his gut instincts were wrong. He had to get more facts.

Jack got in and they drove the short distance to her house, chatting about Edna and Pollard and Claude.

Megan tensed visibly as they pulled up in front of her home. Jack noticed that she took care not to make eye contact with the cops leaning against the patrol car talking.

"I'll just slip into something more presentable and be right with you," she murmured to Jack once they were inside her apartment.

He sat at her flimsy kitchen table and listened to the sound of water tinkling in the basin, then hangers brushing against a doorknob in the back. Now is the perfect time to look around, Jack realized.

Clearing the table of cereal bowls and juice glasses allowed him to cross into the kitchen. He opened two drawers by the sink, finding only silverware in one and coupons and a checkbook in the other.

He listened and heard the unmistakable sound of an electric toothbrush. Quickly he flipped the checkbook open. The entries were neat and carefully subtracted, showing a balance of $408. A list was folded inside, tallying utility bills due of nearly three hundred dollars.

Also in the drawer sat a dish of quarters labeled Milk Money. It held about four dollars, he estimated. He slid out a sheet underneath the change and found it to be an invoice from Pediatric Associates of Melbourne. He opened the bill. It was for an annual checkup for Roxanne R. And Thomas

D. Summers, and a booster shot for Roxanne. The total was $113.

On the bottom of the notice, in the same careful hand, Megan had written in pencil, "Pay when TeleSurv check comes April 1."

Feeling like the worst kind of cad, Jack closed the drawer and walked back to the table. If Megan Summers was in on the scam he had suspected her of, she sure as hell was not hiding payola in her checking account. Just as he sat back down she came out of the bathroom.

Her red hair was pulled up into a cloth band at the top of her head and pinned neatly into a chignon. She was wearing a crisply starched pink oxford blouse and a short black cotton skirt. The skirt showed fade marks along the seams fitting snugly against her hips, probably from years of ironing, Jack thought.

She had on nylons and heels, black leather and well-polished. Tiny gold hoops twinkled in her ears, the only touch of decoration besides the battered watch she wore on her right wrist.

Her lipstick was bright and her smile nervous. With a jolt Jack again realized how lovely Megan was. And how sexy.

The best, or worst, depending on the situation, kind of sexy, Jack thought. The open, needful kind of sexy that promised to give as well as take. It surprised him to feel such a strong attraction. Involuntarily he shook his head and straightened his shoulders. "You look very nice, Megan. Are you going to school after we see Sergeant McMurphy?"

She crossed to the counter and noticed the cereal bowls in the sink. "Thanks, Jack. And thanks for clearing the table." She turned her back and quickly rinsed out the bowls. "No, I'm doing an internship at WABR for the next twelve weeks. Then I'll finally be done with school."

"I forgot. You said you were working with Darren George, right?"

"Right."

"How's he to work with?"

Megan detected a guarded tone in Jack's voice. "Nice. Competent. He has a bit of a temper, I hear." Then, feeling a touch guilty, she added, "But he's very good at what he does. Which is why he's successful, don't you think?"

Her question seemed to fluster him. "I guess so. Yes."

Megan wiped her hands dry on the towel and retrieved her bag and notebook from the end table beside the sofa bed. She was glad suddenly she had closed the sofa up before she walked the kids to school. Being in the same room with a bed with tousled sheets and Jack Gallagher would be altogether too distracting.

Why that thought made her feel giddy she didn't stop to examine. "Are you ready?"

He stood up. Even when she wore heels he was much taller than her. Her mind recalled how strong and firm his hands had been when he'd held her against him last night.

"Yes."

He took the key from her and locked the front door, pulling on it to check the lock. Silently they walked downstairs. The yellow plastic tape reading "Melbourne Police No Admittance" was wound around the sawhorses, flapping in the breeze. Megan caught her reflection in the cops' sunglasses but turned away quickly.

The police made her nervous. They were constant reminders that the unimaginable had happened right outside her door. There'd been no time to glance at the paper, but suddenly she pictured the blood splattered on Jack's shirt. As she slid onto the leather seat in Jack's car, she imagined how gruesome the "evidence" was that the men were collecting inside.

When he backed out of the driveway, she asked the question that had been on her mind. "How did Mrs. Grokowbowski die, Jack?"

His jaw clenched and his hand tightened on the gear shift knob as they crossed I-91 and headed for the precinct office. "It looked like a knife, Megan."

Swallowing hard, she slipped on her sunglasses and hugged her arms across her chest. "I can't remember if the papers have ever said how the others were killed. Do you know?''

He didn't reply immediately. They stopped for a light at Airport Blvd., then made a right with a grinding of gears. Megan glanced at Jack and then out his window. They were passing Trailer Haven, the Airstream trailer park her kids always begged her to visit. The smooth, silver vehicles glowed brightly in the sunlight, and Megan began to feel clammy. The Volkswagen had no air conditioning, and beads of perspiration had collected on her forehead. She wiped her brow, wishing Jack would hurry up and answer.

''I do know. Yes. They were all killed by some kind of blade. The victim's throats were cut.''

Her moist hand moved to her throat. Pollard Finch was right. No one was safe from a madman who chose a method of killing that was up-close and personal. He had to enjoy it, Megan realized in horror, and for a moment she was unable to think of anything but a knife biting into Gladys Grokowbowski's skin while her children slept a few hundred yards away.

MEGAN MOVED UNEASILY in the hard-backed chair. She and Jack had been talking with Sergeant McMurphy for forty minutes, but little progress had been made.

One thing was very clear to Megan, however. Despite the arctic air conditioning in the office, her hands were sweaty. McMurphy was implying, both in tone and content, he thought of Jack as more than a spectator in Gladys Grokowbowski's murder.

He thought of Jack as a suspect.

''. . . Now let me ask you again, Mr. Gallagher. Did you ever meet Mrs. Grokowbowski in person?''

''No. I spoke with her on the phone twice. The second time for less than a minute.''

McMurphy turned to Megan. ''You never saw Mr. Gallagher at Mrs. Grokowbowski's home?''

Megan narrowed her eyes. ''The first four times you asked me this question I didn't mind answering it. But now I think it's rather rude, don't you, sergeant?'' She knew it was a ridiculous tact to take with a cop, but she was getting angrier by the second. Repeatedly asking her to contradict Jack while he was sitting in front of her was embarrassing to them both.

"I'm not trying to be rude, Mrs. Summers." He looked down at the report in his hands. "Okay. You two can go. We'll get back to you."

Megan rose swiftly, but Jack remained seated. He crossed his arms across his chest and stared at the cop. "About that story in the *Melbourne Press* that the Reaper must be a public officer of some kind, I was wondering what you made of that."

"The bastard's no cop." McMurphy shot back, snapping the folder onto his desktop.

"Do you have any leads as to who he is?" Jack asked quietly.

"No. Do you, Mr. Gallagher?"

Jack smiled, but tension radiated from his body. He uncrossed his arms. "Like any citizen, I only know what I read in the papers."

McMurphy leaned forward, pointing a finger at Jack. "Well, Mr. Good Citizen, let me tell you this. One of my detectives pointed out to me this morning that the man who found Gladys Grokowbowski's body lives within three miles of the other five victims."

Megan gasped, her eyes widening at the combative tone in the police sergeant's voice. She glanced at Jack and was amazed at the calm expression he wore as he registered the implication of the cop's words.

"Sounds like an interesting lead. For what it's worth, I'd agree the Reaper is probably a local boy."

"Do you now?"

Megan could keep silent no longer. "Speaking of leads, don't you think it's of interest that both Gladys and Norma Schultz worked for TeleSurv Surveys?"

Both men's eyes slanted toward her. "What are you talking about?" McMurphy snarled. He grabbed a folder from the left-hand basket on his desk and thumbed through it. "Norma Schultz was working for..." He looked up at Megan. "My report doesn't list a name of her employer. How do you know who she worked for?"

"Because she worked for me. Rather, we were both employed by the same firm. TeleSurv Television Surveys in Maryland."

"And Gladys Grokowbowski worked for them, too?" McMurphy's voice had lost its venom.

"Yes. She was our supervisor."

Jack moved restlessly in his chair and cleared his throat. Megan looked at him, wondering if she should add that Jack had been recently employed the same firm. She decided against that. He would surely lose his job if he was identified as an employee in the press.

Which was something she herself was now in danger of, she suddenly realized. "I need to ask you to keep the fact that I work for TeleSurv confidential, Sergeant McMurphy. It's one of the terms of my employment."

In answer to his question, she explained TeleSurv's policy. He agreed to keep the fact out of his next press release, but wariness had now replaced anger in his tone. "I appreciate your information, Mrs. Summers. I may need some further information from you about this 'lead.'"

"I'll do whatever I can, sergeant."

"Me, too," Jack said. He stood and offered his hand to McMurphy. "Let me know if the man who found the body can be of further help."

McMurphy shook his head with the distracted look of a man who has too much to think about. With a nod to Megan, he picked up his phone. "Get me the captain."

Dismissed, Megan and Jack walked silently through the din of the precinct office and out to Jack's car.

"Are you okay, Jack?" Megan asked as he held the door for her.

"Okay? What do you mean?"

Megan stared at his face, noting how thin his mouth was when he clenched his jaw. "McMurphy was pretty off the wall with his questioning. About you knowing Gladys, I mean."

"The man's just doing his job, Megan. Don't over-react."

His comment irritated her. "Sorry."

"Why didn't you tell him I work for TeleSurv?"

"I don't want you to lose your job. And, and..." she floundered.

"And you're afraid that would give McMurphy another reason to suspect me?"

"No," she answered quickly. "Why didn't you tell him?"

"For the same reason." Jack leaned into the car and gave her arm a squeeze. "Thanks for your concern, Megan."

She returned his smile, but could feel his distraction. She felt very uncomfortable and realized she was in Jack's car without an invitation. Quickly she stepped out and brushed her hands down her skirt. "I need to get over to the television station now. And it's just down the street. Thanks for the ride over here."

"Going to see Darren George?" He made no move to convince her to get back in the car.

"Yes." There was something in his voice that made her pause again. Did he know Dr. George, she wondered? "He's been my adviser in school for the past two years. And he was nice enough to offer me an internship at his station when the one I was suppose to have fell through."

"I thought no employee of TeleSurv could work at a radio or television station."

Megan's smile faded. So that was what was behind his questions! He thought she was breaking her own rules. "I'm not *working* at a station. You don't get paid for internships."

"So TeleSurv said it was okay."

She shifted her weight from one foot to the other. Suddenly she felt clammy and tired. It had never occurred to her to check with the advisory staff in Maryland about her internship, but maybe she should have, Megan realized. With a flash of panic, she realized that it would cost her the job if they said no. But if she didn't do the internship, she wouldn't graduate.

Angry that he was acting more like an interrogator than an employee, she clenched her teeth. "I don't really think that is any of your concern."

"You're right." Jack shut the door with a bang and then struck his hands into his shorts' pockets. "So I'll see you at the meeting tonight."

She was tempted to say no, but knew she had no alternative. "Right. I'll bring your TeleSurv materials with me instead of sticking them in the mail, okay?"

"Yeah. Whatever's easiest for you." Jack sensed Megan's embarrassment and confusion over his behavior, and he was surprised at how badly it made him feel. But he had no other recourse, he told himself. For her own good he needed to distance himself from her and break the emotional ties that were beginning to bind them together. The fact that he didn't want to distance himself—in any manner—suddenly hit him. What he wanted right now was to put his arm around her; fill his lungs with her scent, which had been tickling his senses for the last hour.

But that was out of the question. He had business to attend to. So far Megan had remained silent about his employment with TeleSurv, even though she surely knew how interested McMurphy would have been with that information. Which meant Megan Summers trusted him, or, as his conscience pointed out, she was planning on using that information for another purpose.

He had to find out which. His reasons for seeking out Gladys and applying for the TeleSurv job along with the lies he had told Megan burned in his mind. His thoughts were interrupted by Megan's voice. All the warmth and friendliness had vanished.

"Goodbye, Jack. Thanks for the ride."

"No problem. See you tonight."

Megan walked away, her stomach in knots. She told herself it was because she was hungry, but the flush of heat on her cheeks contradicted that. Jack Gallagher was distancing himself from her because he thought she'd come on to him. And he also seemed to think she was unprofessional, or worse.

Her eyelids stung, and Megan realized she was close to crying. Stiffening her back, she blinked away the tears of self-pity and walked quickly down Central Avenue. Who the hell cared what he thought? she told herself.

Jack's VW roared off in the other direction, and the sound made her hurry faster.

It was time to concentrate on the matters at hand, she decided. Taking care of Roxie and Thomas. Finishing school. She glanced down at the folder of research she had been given.

The Grim Reaper had inadvertently involved her and her family by striking close to home. She'd use whatever energy she had left at the end of every day to strike back.

That, surely, would leave her no time to think of Jack Gallagher.

Chapter Five

Darren George's office was teeming with activity when Megan arrived. The anchorman was sitting on his desk in his shirtsleeves, his tie askew, yelling into the phone. The assignment editor was pinning sheets of paper to a bulletin board on one wall while George's secretary and the girl Megan recognized as a feature reporter were sitting on the floor shuffling through folders of papers.

Sandy Royal was nowhere to be seen.

Megan hovered by the office door, unsure if she should enter or wait.

"Megan! Come in! Come in!" Darren George caught her eye and gestured for her to shut the door, then stood and snapped his fingers at the women on the floor. "One of you get Megan to makeup. I want Studio C set up for an interview in ten minutes."

"Makeup?" Megan asked. The woman who took her arm smiled and led her back out the door and down the hall. Megan finally stopped her at the door to the makeup room. "Now wait a minute. What's going on here?"

"Darren is going to interview you about the Grim Reaper for the eleven o'clock bulletin."

"What?" Megan shook her head in disagreement. "Look, there must be some mistake. No one has said anything about interviewing—"

"—Lynn, for heaven's sake," Darren George yelled behind them. "Let's move our feet, girls!" He grasped Megan's arm and gave her a beaming smile. "Now, sweetheart, don't worry about a thing. Take all the time you need with your answers."

The girl named Lynn opened the makeup room door and Darren pushed Megan through it. "And don't worry if you cry," he added. "Tears are a nice touch. Everyone understands how much you went through last night."

Two young men walked toward Megan, one holding a makeup sponge and the other a brush. Lynn was just shutting the door behind her when Megan's temper gave way. "Don't come any closer," she warned the two men. She whirled around and flung the door back open. "Lynn! Wait a minute. I'm not doing any interview."

The girl turned, shock and nervousness on her face. Before the reporter could reply, the door next to Megan's makeup room banged open. Darren George strode out, his shirt covered with a white cloth that was pinned to either side of his collar. His face was coated with pancake makeup, which also covered his eyebrows, lashes and lips, giving him a ghoulish appearance.

"What's going on Megan? What's wrong?" Darren demanded.

She folded her arms, refusing to act intimidated though she was shaking with nerves. "Dr. George, I never agreed to be interviewed about the unfortunate happenings last night. And I don't want to be on TV. I have no wish to be part of the publicity. I have two small children who are going to be under enough pressure without their mother appearing on a news show, giving out all the gory details."

She glanced toward Lynn for moral support, but the girl had disappeared. Her eyes met Darren George's, and her trembling got worse. The man was livid.

"You have a duty as a citizen to cooperate in the police investigation, Megan."

"I have cooperated, Dr. George. Fully. But I don't see how appearing on a news interview helps the police."

"I see." Darren's skin was growing red under the makeup. "You're right, of course. All you would be doing is helping the station where you are interning. All you would be helping is your career!"

His unspoken threat hit her like a ten-pound weight. "I'm sorry. I'm not going to do the interview."

Darren nodded curtly and turned on his heel, slamming the door behind him. Megan's knees began to feel weak. She turned and walked back toward the news offices, unsure of what do do next. As she turned the corner to Dr. George's office, she came face-to-face with Sandy Royal.

"Hi."

"Hi?" Sandy shot back. He stopped and put his big hands on his hips. "Where the hell were you? I've been cooling my heels at the police station, wasting valuable time. You've been here?"

She had missed her appointment with him at the police station, Megan realized numbly. "Oh, Sandy, I'm sorry. I was down there, but I forgot—"

"—You forgot?" He leaned one palm on the wall, his eyes slits of rage. "Well let me tell you something you better not forget. When I tell you to do something, you do it. I've got important work to do, and I don't need some airhead pet of Darren George's screwing me up!"

Megan swallowed, too humiliated to respond. She shook her head that she understood, and turned and went into Dr. George's office. Lynn and the secretary were there, staring at a television. Neither commented, though Megan was sure they heard every word Sandy Royal had spoken.

She sat down and stared at the television with them. The words Special Report flashed on the screen, then Darren George's face.

"Good morning. Melbourne police confirmed this morning that last night's murder of Mrs. Gladys Grokowbowski was being regarded as the sixth crime of the Grim Reaper."

Megan's eyes burned. She clasped her hands together and stared at the pictures of the coroner's car, the dark windows of Gladys's house, the stretcher bearing a blanket-covered corpse that yesterday had been a woman. Megan blinked her eyes several times to clear them and tried to concentrate on what Darren George was saying.

"...And police still have no leads on this serial killer's motives. Sergeant Peter McMurphy is holding a press conference at 4:00 P.M. tomorrow and Action News will be there." Darren beamed his best smile at the audience, then "Wheel of Fortune" flicked back into view.

Less than a minute passed before Darren George returned. Megan was still sitting, but she jumped to her feet at his entrance. He glared at her, then snapped orders at the other women. They scurried out and left her with the angry anchorman, who was doing little to disguise his unhappiness.

"Did you see the bulletin?" he asked coldly.

"Yes."

"It would have been a hell of lot more exciting if you'd done an interview." He sifted through some paperwork on his desk, then snapped down his intercom when it rang "Yes?"

"Your attorney is on line six," his secretary's voice announced from the speaker on his desk. "He wants to talk to you about your aunt's will. Can you talk to him now?"

Darren George shot his eyes toward Megan then quickly looked away. "No. Tell him I'll be at his office at 2:00 P.M." He hung up and sat on his desk, reading a folder.

Megan began to get angry. She'd done nothing wrong, she told herself. And yet everyone was treating her like a turncoat or the village idiot. She needed this internship, but eight weeks of being ignored would be impossible to stomach. She wasn't going to let their bad manners intimidate her anymore. "What would you like me to work on, Dr. George? Should I dig into the backgrounds of the victims like we discussed yesterday?"

He glanced up, a bored look on his face. "Why don't you go find Sandy? Let him guide you. It's obvious you're not interested in taking my advice."

Biting back a two-word epitaph she had used only once before in her life, Megan nodded and walked calmly out of his office. This side of Darren George was a shock to her.

The kindly professor who was concerned about his students had been replaced by an egotist with a one-track mind, and that track was focused on getting Darren George ahead, other people be damned. "Nice" was how she'd described him when Jack Gallagher had asked. Nice was not a word she would use today!

She knocked sharply on Sandy Royal's office door and wondered what else she'd have to contend with when Darren George's Dr. Jekyl and Mr. Hyde personality resurfaced.

AT TEN MINUTES TO SEVEN Megan closed her babysitter's front door and hurried down the steps. Inside, Roxie and Thomas were gleefully spooning out peanut butter cookie dough. Neither seemed to notice that their mother was leaving. Thank goodness for small favors, Megan thought with a sigh as she headed for the Roberts's house.

Megan shifted the heavy parcel of TeleSurv material she'd brought for Jack and sighed. Tonight's meeting would probably be the same kind of situation, curious questions from well-meaning neighbors. But as far as Megan was concerned, any question was unwelcome if it concerned the Grim Reaper.

She rang the Roberts's bell and was greeted by several curious stares, but Pollard Finch was there and took charge of her, hustling her over to a table with Edna.

"We told everyone to leave you alone tonight, dear," Edna whispered as Megan sat down. "You've been through enough."

"Thank you, Miss Adams," Megan replied. She looked around at the twenty assorted people gathered in the Roberts's huge den, seeing Jack Gallagher was not there. His car hadn't been parked in front, and she fought the same sense of disappointment she'd felt earlier.

The meeting was chaired by Vic Roberts, a friendly retired plant manager from Cleveland. "Thank you all for coming tonight. We have a lot of items on the agenda, so let's get to them."

The group quickly passed an agreement to buy Neighborhood Watch signs and post stickers on front-door windows. They also agreed to invite a member of the police department to come to speak to them about ways to safeguard their homes.

Midway through an argument between Rose Sissler and Myra Rosenberg about hiring a private security company to patrol the neighborhood, Megan saw Claude Hawkins and his daughter Mona come in.

Claude had on denim overalls and a plaid shirt. He favored this outfit even in the height of summer during his twelve-hour stints at the local swap meets. Mona kept her head down and sat docilely by her father, but glanced sideways and returned Megan's smile.

The group voted to shelve the security patrol idea until Myra could get all the rate information.

"Now we can get some refreshments," Edna whispered. "Pollard made maple bars."

Megan grinned, but everyone's attention was brought back to the issues at hand by Claude Hawkins's gravelly voice.

"Can I speak for a minute?" he asked.

"Yes, Claude," Mr. Roberts replied. "We're glad you could join us tonight."

Claude nodded and got to his feet, favoring his artificial leg. "I just want to tell you all one thing. If any of you want to get a gun, I've got several I'll go cheap on. Nine millimeters, twenty-twos, though I don't recommend them much 'cause of the little bitty holes they leave in people."

An uneasy murmur crept through the crowd. Megan heard Myra Rosenberg arguing with her husband Ralph.

"And I got machetes, swords, daggers, switchblades and even some acetylene torches for those of you that get nervy around guns," Claude added, then sat down next to his daughter.

Megan shuddered at the thought of having a firearm in the house, but saw from the serious looks on several faces that many were interested in arming themselves.

"Damn fool," Pollard muttered to Edna, squirming in his chair. "Claude Hawkins is out of his mind if he thinks any of these folks could do anything but shoot themselves with guns. I'd never have a gun."

"I agree," Megan said. "You're always reading about people hurting themselves with their own weapons."

"And all the children that have been harmed!" Edna added. "Sometimes I feel like I'm living in the Wild West. Everyday someone's shot dead."

While conversations swirled around her, Megan fought a feeling of light-headedness. Up until now she had always been pragmatic, worrying only about her budget and the day-to-day crises affecting her kids. But the thought of living among neighbors armed to the teeth while a murderer prowled around on the loose was frightening.

She was only one woman. Maybe she should call the kids' dad, she thought. Maybe he'd come for a visit, at least offering temporary support sand protection for Roxie and Thomas against the madness of the world.

She stood, and her foot knocked over the package she'd brought for Jack. While the crowds discussion got animated over the subject of guns, Megan reached down and picked it up. "I'm going to use the phone and call my babysitter, then run this over to Jack Gallagher's house."

She took five singles out of her shorts and handed two to Edna. "Would you please give this to Mr. Roberts for the signs?"

"Surely, dear. Be sure to lock yourselves in tonight."

"I will, Miss Adams."

"Aren't you going to get some refreshments, Megan?" Pollard asked.

"No. Thanks, anyway."

"We'll save some maple bars for the kids, Megan," Edna said.

"The phone is through there in the den." Pollard Finch stood and walked with her to the den, then continued on into the kitchen.

Megan found one of the Roberts's college-age sons in the den, and asked about the phone. He recognized her name from his parents' conversations about Gladys's murder and waylaid her for several minutes with questions about the Reaper.

Finally Megan managed to call and tell the sitter she'd be a few minutes late, then hung up and headed up the street to Jack's. From the Roberts's there were two routes to Amherst Avenue, and Megan chose the one she judged shortest. The sky was darkening and the clouds swollen with rain over the ocean were marked with aggressive swirls of red and pink and gold. Megan loved Florida nights, and for a moment she relaxed.

Heat lightning flashed against the horizon off to the east, and Megan hurried her steps. She turned up Amherst, a pleasant street lined with typical Florida houses built of cinder and stucco. Small homes meant for the retirement years. Spiky palms jutted over every fence, and gaudy azaleas and bougainvillea provided color against the thick green lawns spilling onto the sidewalkless streets.

Jack's house was halfway down, his Volkswagen parked in the driveway under the carport. She knocked at the front door. No lights were on in the living room, and the louvered windows were cranked closed.

Megan rang again. She was nervous over the thought of facing Jack, both because of the strained way they had left each other and the bruising her ego had taken at the television station. She pushed her hair behind her ear and wiped her hand on her shorts, noting that she had a dollop of what looked like spaghetti sauce on her sleeve.

Great, Megan thought. Thomas the Stainmaker strikes again.

Megan turned and looked up and down the street, wondering if Jack had walked up the other way to get to the Roberts's and she'd missed him. After ringing the bell and listening to it squawk hollowly through the house, she was sure he wasn't home.

Well, I'll leave the TeleSurv stuff in his car, she decided. She walked down the cracked sidewalk to the carport. The Volkswagen was locked.

Frustrated, Megan peered around the side of the house. A short chain-link fence stood open. Hoping to find a patio table or screened porch where she could leave his work, Megan went into the backyard. It too was dark, but she was rewarded by finding a small screened-in room. There was a slab near the door, but the rumble of thunder in the distance warned that any package left there was liable to get soaked.

Megan tested the pitted aluminum handle, catching a spicy whiff of scent that seemed familiar as she opened the door. Floridians were careless with locks, she scolded silently.

"Jack?" she yelled, stepping inside. In the gloom she saw a neat, small den. There were several green plants and a large desk. Beside the desk sat a bookcase, full of identical black notebooks standing in a neat row. As her eyes compensated for the darkness, Megan made out three bulletin boards on the opposite wall.

Carefully she laid the TeleSurv package down on a metal folding chair and started to walk out, but words printed on the papers pinned to the bulletin board leaped into her brain, making her body freeze into motionlessness. A breeze stirred behind her, fluttering the bottom edges of the newspaper articles.

The headlines blared: "Grim Reaper Kills Again!", "Victim Number Three Slain by Melbourne Reaper," "Police Search for Madman."

In shock, Megan walked slowly toward them. Why did Jack Gallagher have these gruesome things? she wondered. As she got closer she saw that several paragraphs in each article were underlined. The one from this morning's edition, trumpeting a banner headline about Gladys, "Reaper Takes Sixth Victim," had a note scrawled beneath it. In a firm hand he'd written one word.

"Megan."

Her heart rate sped up, racing jerkily ahead as she had trouble drawing enough air into her lungs. Megan realized she was nearly hyperventilating. With a shaking hand she reached out to touch her name, but her attention was suddenly distracted by a sound.

Footsteps. Stealthy footsteps. She looked toward the thicker darkness and saw a figure posed in the doorway. Of medium height, the person was silent, dressed in a dark blue one-piece jumpsuit with shiny silver zippers. The intruder's face was covered with a black ski mask, the mouth and eyes grotesquely outlined in flourescent purple. It was the most terrifying sight she had ever seen.

Screaming in horror, Megan turned and ran for the door. The man caught her from behind, his leather-gloved hand slapping against her mouth as his other arm locked around her neck.

With a crash they fell to the floor. Megan scratched and yelled, managing to struggle to one knee and reach for the door. The masked man reached for her and pulled her back, but she overturned the chair onto his back, the package of TeleSurv materials spilling to the floor.

He stood and reached toward the desk for some hidden object, but Megan kicked him in the groin and he fell to the floor. She felt a surge of hope that she could escape and scrambled once more toward the door on her knees.

One thought played over and over. She had to get away. With that in mind, Megan stood and flung herself at the screen. The latch caught and she beat her hand against it, steeling herself against another assault.

The door finally gave way and Megan stumbled, screaming, out into the backyard. She tore around the corner and ran down the drive. "Help! Someone help me." A man rushed toward her from the street.

"Megan!"

She stopped as Jack Gallagher grabbed her into his arms. "What's happened? Megan, what's happened to you?"

"Inside," she panted against the viselike grip of fear squeezing the breath from her. "A man is inside your house, Jack." Tears choked in her throat and her trembling legs made it hard to stand.

Jack started to move back toward the house, but realized that was the last place to take Megan. "It's okay, Megan."

He wrapped both arms around her and hugged her, slowly leading her across the street. "It's okay," he murmured as he knocked on his neighbor's door, the brass nameplate identifying it as the Sissler residence. "We'll call the police."

An elderly man answered the door, fright and concern flashing across his face. "What's going on here?" he demanded, looking first at the sobbing Megan, then back at Jack.

"I live across the street, Mr. Sissler. This woman's just been attacked by a burglar in my house. Can you call the police and let her come inside?"

"Of course, young man. Come in." He removed the stubby pipe hanging from his mouth and held open the screen, motioning them in with a tobacco-stained hand.

Jack's arm slid gently from Megan's shoulder. "Go inside, Megan. I'll be back in a moment."

"No—" she dug her nails into his arms "—don't go back in there, Jack. He's a madman, you could—"

"Sh-h-h. It's okay. I'm not going to do anything dumb."

He hugged her quickly and nodded to Mr. Sissler, who took Megan by the arm. "I need to go see if he's still there," Jack said. "Go inside, Megan. Call the police now, Mr. Sissler."

He pulled away from her grasp and ran into the night. Through swollen eyes Megan watched him, terrified it might be the last time she would see Jack Gallagher alive.

JACK RACED UP HIS DRIVEWAY and along the side of his house. He stopped at the corner and peered around. The screen door of the Florida room was standing open.

He looked around quickly for a weapon, choosing a three-pronged gardening spade lying beside the hose. Cautiously he stepped into the den. "Who's in here?" he demanded.

The house was quiet, the hum and click of his answering machine as it rewound made the only sound. He flipped the light switch and flooded the den and living room with light, then continued down the hall. The kitchen and two bedrooms were empty. He turned on all the lights as his pulse returned to normal. Though he searched thoroughly, he knew he was alone. In the closet lay the two Emmy awards he had put away in disgust days before. Fleetingly he wished he had left them out. Megan could have bashed the bastard with one, he thought ruefully.

Jack walked back into the den and looked around, aware now of a siren in the distance. His glance fell on the bulletin boards full of clippings, and his fist clenched into a ball. He dropped the tool to the ground, hurrying as the siren grew louder. Jack removed each newspaper article and hid them in the bottom drawer of his desk.

As he closed the drawer the wail of a second siren swelled in the evening air. It was then he saw the knife lying beside the desk on the floor. It was from his kitchen, an eight-inch blade with a massive wooden handle.

He used it for cutting up chicken. Heaven only knew what the attacker had planned to do with it, Jack thought. A sudden wave of nausea welled up in his throat, and he grabbed the leather chair back. *Megan. Dear God, he could have killed her!*

"Open up, police!"

The command shouted at his front door prompted Jack to regain control of himself. He left the knife lying where it was and let the cops in the front door.

"Are you Jack Gallagher?" the officer in charge demanded.

"Yes. Come in, please." He met the eyes of the three uniformed patrolmen, noting the female cop who was walking across to the Sissler's. He recognized her as Judy Barnes and hoped Megan wouldn't freak out at the sight of her unfriendly face again.

The cops re-searched his house, and he pointed out the knife lying on the floor. One of them lifted it into a plastic bag to be dusted for prints.

Jack followed two of the men out to the backyard while the third began to brief a new group of plainclothes detectives who'd arrived on the scene. The intruder had evidently escaped undetected by scaling the chain-link fence in the backyard. The fence was covered in vines, and on the other side was a heavily overgrown vacant lot.

One of the cops pointed to a strip of navy-blue fabric hanging from the twisted prong at the top of the fence. "Riley, bag that!"

Jack stayed in the yard while Riley and the other cops climbed over the fence and began searching the lot. The powerful beams from their flashlights cut yellow swaths across the blackness, leaving him in the dark.

"Can you come in here please, Mr. Gallagher?" a voice called from the back door. "We have some questions we'd like to ask you."

"I'll be right there," Jack called back. Slowly he walked toward the back door, his mind reeling with a thought that had just occurred to him. He was involved in two separate investigations. One was to try to prove Darren George and the people at his station had fraudulently tampered with a TeleSurv survey that had cost Jack his job.

The second was to stay up with the Grim Reaper story so that he'd be ready to go back to work when he was offered his old job back.

But now two TeleSurv employees had been murdered. And a third, Megan, had been attacked.

Jack stopped at the door and looked in. Officer Judy Barnes was smiling at him with a skeptical look on her pudgy face, while a distraught Megan huddled on the corner of his sofa.

"You seem to be very unlucky, lately, Mr. Gallagher," Judy remarked with a challenge in her tone.

"How's that?"

"Always showing up right after the Grim Reaper."

"We don't know that's who did this, do we, officer?" Jack replied with a snarl.

"No, we don't," she shot back. "But you can bet we'll find out."

His stomach turned as Megan's head jerked up in anxiety. "We all hope you do. Where's Officer McMurphy tonight? I thought he was the number one guy on this case."

Barnes looked surprised, but quickly recovered. "We've called him. His wife will find him and he'll be right over. I'm sure he'll be interested in talking with you."

"Are you okay, Megan?" Jack asked.

As she shook her head yes, a new idea struck Jack. One that filled him with a fear greater than any he had ever imagined before tonight. He turned toward Megan and met her eyes, praying that he was wrong.

Chapter Six

"Drink this, Megan."

She took the steaming mug of coffee from Jack, recognizing the pungent smell of alcohol. Without argument she brought it to her parched mouth and took a gulp.

It scalded her tongue and the inside of her lip. "This is hot. What's in it?"

"Brandy." He sat on the couch a foot away from her, trying not to reach out and touch her. "Drink some more if you can."

Megan took another sip, appreciating the warmth radiating down the passage from her throat to her stomach. It made her feel less disconnected from life, which is how she reacted as soon as the cops had mentioned the Reaper. "This is two nights in a row you've had to pour me a stiff drink."

"It's two nights in a row circumstances called for it."

Tears stung her eyes. She blinked them away, cringing at the scratchy feeling. "Thanks for calling Mrs. Allen."

"No problem. She said both your kids fell asleep a little after eight. I'll drive you over there and help you get them home to bed in a few minutes."

His kindness made her hands tremble again. Megan brought the coffee back to her mouth. She was unwilling to ask the next question, but she had to. "Do you think the man was the Grim Reaper, Jack?"

"I don't know, Megan." He swallowed hard. "No one's ever lived to give the police a description."

"I wasn't much help there, I'm afraid. Medium height. Bigger than me, but not much heavier. Strong. And he didn't kill me. That's all I know." Something from her memory buzzed in the back of her head, some other detail she could not remember.

"He didn't say anything?" Jack hated to ask her this question again, but it amazed him that her assailant had not spoken.

"Zippo. I screamed. He grabbed."

Her comments agitated the generous helping of guilt Jack had served himself. He wondered again with dread if the attacker hadn't spoken because he knew Megan would recognize his voice.

Jack walked over and slammed his back door to be sure it was shut, then locked it. "If I hadn't been such a damn fool and left this door unlocked, it wouldn't have been so easy for the jerk to get in here!"

"It's not your fault, Jack. I'm the one who invited myself in." She sighed. "Trying to save you some time waiting on the post office. Where were you, anyway?"

He sat beside her, lacing his fingers together as she drank deeply. "I was out walking, then I stopped by the meeting. Mrs. Adams told me you'd left to come by here." The fact that he'd been "walking" in Gladys Grokowbowski's backyard, searching for an entrance to her house, gnawed at him. If he had gone to the meeting, the night's events would not have occurred as they did. "Are you sure you're okay?"

"Yes. I feel a little stiff, but I'm okay."

He thought of the knife and a shiver of fear crept across his stomach. "You should have gone to the hospital like the police wanted."

Megan shook her head. "I'm okay. Besides, that would have really freaked my kids out." She turned and met his eyes, touching his knee lightly with the palm of her left hand. "Are *you* sure you're all right? It must be unnerving to know someone broke into your house." She glanced around the room, a dart of remembered fear chilling her. Something was out of place in the surroundings, but she couldn't immediately figure it out.

"I'm fine," he answered brusquely.

"Despite Officer Barnes's insinuating remarks?"

"Despite the woman's acid tongue, yes, I'm really okay." Jack crossed the room and retrieved the bag of TeleSurv materials she had brought for him. He wanted Megan to think of something other than her attack. It was too difficult to bear the pinched lines of worry between her blue eyes, particularly since it was his fault that they were there. "Let me see what you've got here. I may have a couple of questions about the forms."

For a few minutes he pawed through the stuff, having Megan explain the difference between a miscellaneous and a calling cost and pay record. Then he gently questioned her about the "Plan No Viewing" form for people who wouldn't be home during the ratings period.

The last item to discuss was the calendar. He pulled out the hot-pink sheet and studied it, asking her some obvious questions. Out of the corner of his eyes he saw her relaxing, and his own nerves calmed in response. Megan was a delight. If he hadn't had a secret agenda, he'd want to get involved.

"Okay. I'll just pin this up and make sure I pay attention to the mailing dates. Though, since we live so close, I'll probably just drop my work by your place, if that's okay."

"That'll be fine," Megan answered carefully. Despite his caring demeanor, she told herself not to expect anything from Jack. Every time he offered his friendship he immediately pulled back if she responded, almost as if he regretted it. "I'm home most days by two, then I walk up and get the kids," Megan said, smiling.

Despite everything that had happened tonight, she found herself glad to be sitting with Jack, talking to him, chatting about the inane bookkeeping procedures of TeleSurv. Heck, she realized, she might as well admit she liked being around Jack Gallagher. Period.

Jack walked back to the couch and held out his hand for her empty coffee mug. "Want some more?"

"No, thanks. I'll never get to sleep tonight." Megan got off the couch slowly, wincing as she straightened her leg. The tackle the intruder had thrown on her had given her knee a real whack. She tucked her blouse back into her jeans then ran her hand through her hair.

Jack remained where he was, only a few inches from her, and she saw how closely he was watching her. His dark eyes were concerned, and his mouth was stretched taut.

"Hey—" she touched his arm "—don't look so serious. I'm okay, really." A wave of goose bumps ran up her arm as her fingers registered the warmth of his skin and the hardness of his muscle.

"You're sure of that?" He covered her hand with his own and felt her breath on his face.

"Yes." Megan noticed how dark his lashes were against his skin, lining his eyes as if by makeup. She began to tremble again, her knee aching from the fall, but she didn't want to move. She felt expectant, but wouldn't let her mind formulate the exact thing she hoped would happen. The regret if it didn't would be too much to handle right now.

He took a step closer and brought her hand to his chest. His head was tilted toward her. Jack wet the corner of his lip with his tongue, his jaw moving as if he were about to speak.

Megan waited as a dizzy, liquid uneasiness flowed through her body. Before he could say a word, the gong from a clock in another room sounded and she jumped. He squeezed her hand and they both grinned, breaking the mood of intimacy.

"Let me put this in the kitchen, then we'll go get your kids." Jack let her wrist drop and disappeared from her sight.

Megan ran her hands up and down her arms to get her blood circulating again and then paced around the room. She felt upset, keyed up again. And it had nothing to do with her attack, she knew. It had to do with Jack Gallagher, and how her body had just responded to being so close to his.

Okay, she told herself. He's attractive. He's eligible. But it doesn't mean he's interested, he's only being nice. Despite her cautioning, a smile played around the corners of her mouth. Then again . . . she thought.

Her glance drifted back to the bulletin boards, empty save for the TeleSurv calendar. Her heart lurched as her memory flashed a picture of how the cork surface had appeared earlier tonight.

At that moment Jack stepped down into the Florida room. Megan felt fear return with him, utter and urgent.

"You ready to go, Megan?"

She couldn't move. "What happened to the clippings, Jack?"

He glanced quickly at the board, then back to her face. "What clippings?" It was a stupid response. He realized his mistake the instant the words flew from his mouth. The color that had returned to Megan's face drained, and she took a step away from him.

"The news articles about the Grim Reaper, Jack. Did the police take them?"

He heard the hysteria in her voice. He knew her question was really a plea, a plea for him to give her a reasonable explanation of what he was doing with them. And why her name was written on the bottom of one.

"Megan," he began but stopped. It was clear from her stance that she was suddenly terrified of him. Her reaction made Jack search for some kind of white lie, but all his past lies to her clogged his mind.

"Megan, it's not what you think." Jack stopped again. This was not how he wanted to handle her fears. He wanted to hold her. He wanted the look of trust she beamed at him a moment before to return.

But he knew trust was about the last thing Megan was going to feel for him for a while. He planted his feet and crossed his arms. "I took them down before the police came in. I didn't want the cops to see them."

"Why?" Her voice was strangled, and she took another step backward.

"Because that cop woman and Sergeant McMurphy made it pretty clear they think I might be involved in this mess. Finding out that I've been following the news about the Grim Reaper closely wouldn't go far in convincing them they were wrong."

"Are they wrong?" In her confusion, Megan blurted the terrifying question out like a schoolgirl.

He waited two seconds before he answered. "Yes. They're wrong. I've got professional reasons for following this story. I'm a writer, remember?"

For a full minute they stood and faced each other. The westerly breeze kicked up off the Atlantic and blew through the patio. On the windy current Megan heard trees full of leaves shimmying in the night, and she shivered at the sound.

"I see," she finally said.

"No, you don't. And I don't expect you to." Jack dropped his arms to his side and pulled his keys out of his jeans. "There are some things I can't talk to you about, Megan."

"Why?"

The perfect lie materialized. "Because of personal reasons that have nothing to do with you. Now let's go get your kids."

Stung, Megan raised her chin defensively. "I really can manage on my own. Thanks." She turned away, but he caught her arm.

"I'm taking you over to get your kids and driving you home. Let's not argue, okay?"

Jack's face showed he was weary, nearly as exhausted as she was.

"Okay." Megan followed him out to the car and stood quietly while he unlocked the Volkswagen. She watched him as he walked around the car and got in, starting the car quickly.

They sat in the dark for a moment, then Megan cut a glance at him. He was looking at her.

"I'd never do anything to hurt you, Megan."

Her small remaining doubts about him being connected to something criminal disappeared, but her ego still smarted from his prior remark. "I expect not, Jack. After all, we're just fellow employees, nothing more. No real way to hurt each other, is there?"

He gave her a blank look, then tensed his arm as he moved the gearshift into reverse. Her wounded feelings didn't bother him. Actually, he realized, he was glad she was hurt.

He had discovered a few things tonight. Some, like the fact that TeleSurv workers and the Grim Reaper were related in some way, confused him. Others, like the fact that he must consider that Darren George might be the murderer himself, filled him with dread. But one fact scared him, coming as it did completely and full-blown out of the blue.

He was falling for Megan Summers.

This warm-hearted redheaded woman with the bright lipstick and the worn-out clothes touched him. Something about her pride and courage snagged in his gut like a fishhook, paining him in a way he had felt only once before. Sitting next to her now, he had the same raw sense of connection he had experienced holding his son after he was born.

Megan made him feel needy, Jack realized. She made him aware that he had an appetite for whatever it was that was unique about her.

He shook his head as if to clear it and rolled down the window. Megan appeared to be dozing, her head was back and her eyes were closed. Lacy shadows from willows they drove past raced down her neck, leaping to cover him as well when he turned the corner.

Circumstance brought Megan Summers into his life. Jack turned his eyes back to the road as a new thought settled in. It was up to him to keep her there.

MEGAN STEPPED FORWARD in the line, trying to keep her impatience from showing. The four-station post office counter had only one clerk behind it despite the fact that eight patrons were in line.

The customer at the counter had a bag of third-class mail. She was arguing with the postal worker as he scanned a thick book of regulations, apparently deaf to her questions. A second clerk stepped up and consulted with him, both of them ignoring the customer.

In front of Megan an elderly man held two poorly wrapped packages. She knew he was going to have a devil of a time convincing the clerk to mail them. They were sealed with Scotch tape and looked as if packaged with a soft box. On top of that, it was addressed to a serviceman in West Germany.

At this rate, I'll be here until Christmas. She glanced at her wristwatch, then up at the clock on the wall. It confirmed she had five minutes to get to the television station. Her hand tightened on the envelopes she was holding. The utility bills had to go out today or the phone company would turn off her phone.

The woman at the counter finally walked away, lugging her unmailed letters with her. Two other clerks came on duty. One motioned Megan forward, then ignored her while he cut open a cardboard box full of first-class stickers. She bit her lip as the man methodically sliced through the reinforced tape with a small ripping knife. She cringed as the blade skidded against the glued surface.

A minute later Megan was out in the sunshine. She folded the ten and the five back into her wallet, put the receipt where she could find it and stuck the stamp book in her zipper pouch.

She and the kids would walk over and give Jack his money back after school, Megan decided. She smiled as she remembered the gallant way he had paid Mrs. Allen for her last night, and how tender he was getting her cranky kids into bed.

Inside the television station, Megan exchanged greetings with the receptionist and made her way to Sandy Royal's office. She knocked, then peered through the narrow strip of glass next to his door. His desk was a mess of papers but he wasn't at it.

"Megan? Looking for me?"

She whirled around to face Darren George. "No, sir. I was going to meet Sandy here. Have you seen him?"

"Yes. He's in my office. Come on along, sweetheart. Kostos is in a tizzy, and we're having a meeting. You'll love it." He took her arm and led her up the hallway to a large conference room she had not been in previously.

She was surprised at how calm and friendly Darren George was today, but did not regret his change in mood. He was much easier to deal with when he was flirtatious. George held the door for her and got her coffee while she quietly took her place by Sandy.

He glanced at her and nodded, then turned his attention back to the blackboard where Mitchell Kostos was sketching out the particulars on the special George was doing on the Reaper.

"Okay, now, Sandy. You need to get the tape on the McMurphy interview in by tomorrow. We're patching together the shows of the victims' houses, and Darren thought it would be good to contact the neighbors at all six homes for cutaways."

Sandy turned to Megan. "Has anyone asked Mrs. Summers here if she's willing to go on camera about the Grokowbowski case?"

"We're not using Megan," Darren George announced.

Megan let a breath of relief escape. She didn't know why Darren was coming to her rescue, but she was glad she didn't have to fight the publicity battle again.

Sandy shrugged. "Are we still even considering the Grokowbowski woman a Reaper victim?"

"Unless you've heard otherwise. But like I told you yesterday, I want you to concentrate on the angle that the victims might be related through their occupations," Darren said.

"For your information, Darren, I have caught some rumors that the cops don't think her murder fits the bill of particulars."

"In what way?" Darren asked, instantly alert.

"She was killed much later in the day than any of the others, and the wounds are different. Plus something was fishy about some physical evidence found on the old lady, but I can't get my source to be specific about that."

"Those guys don't want any leaks on that kind of evidence," Kostos remarked. "It ruins their ability to tell if a confession is legit or not."

"Any weirdos confessed yet?" Sandy asked, a hopeful edge to his voice.

"Yeah. The ex-Marine from Satellite Beach who claims to have lived with Charlie Manson before he shot Reagan." The group laughed at Kostos's joke.

"I would bet our boy here is never going to confess," Darren announced.

All the people in the room looked at him. "Why do you say that, Dr. George?" Megan asked. Her heart was racing with excitement at being in on the meeting, but something in her resisted listening too carefully to the details. Sandy had passed her a folder of photocopied police reports whose gory details were making her hair stand on end.

"It's just an opinion," the anchorman continued. "But I think most of these serial sickos are acting for themselves and their mommies and daddies who never loved them. They don't get off on confessing to the camera and seeing their life stories on the tube."

"If you're right, it sure makes it harder for the cops to find him," Kostos replied.

"And for you to tie up your report. Right, Darren?" Sandy added.

"Not really." Darren grinned. "Makes a better story that way, don't you think? It'll let us do a follow-up story every five years or so. You know, 'New evidence proves Reaper is . . .' It'll be good for ratings."

Megan felt herself growing red at this remark. She turned quickly back to Kostos, who was reading from a list of possible interviewees.

"Good idea, Darren." He looked down over his protruding stomach. "I'll mention it to the big guy."

"What about this Jack Gallagher guy who found Gro-kowbowski's body?" Sandy asked, doodling on a yellow lined pad in front of him. "He might know something important."

His question made Megan sit up straighter.

"What about him?" Kostos replied. "You think he can tell us something the cops won't?"

"Maybe. What do you think, Megan?" Sandy asked. "He's a friend of yours, isn't he?"

"Yes, he is. I know he's cooperated with the police."

"Did he tell you anything about the murder scene, Megan?" Darren George had reached his hand across the table and touched her arm. He was smiling, but she felt some of the animosity he'd shown toward her the day before returning.

"No."

"I say we get him on film, Mitch," Sandy said.

They all stared at Kostos now. He was using his fingernail to scrape something from his tie. "Yeah. What the hell." He looked up and pointed his finger at Megan. "This guy Gallagher. He ever work in this business?"

"No, not that I know of." She started to tell them about TeleSurv, but she stopped. Telling these guys she worked for TeleSurv would be the stupidest thing she could ever do. "He's a writer."

"Humph." Kostos looked back down at his tie. "The news director at WMMB was a guy named Gallagher. Big, good-looking guy with a one-track mind focused on work. Bright. Drove a beige vintage VW my boy had his eye on. He was really up and coming until a few months back. I understand he quit when our station knocked him out of the top spot."

"Before he was asked to leave, no doubt," Darren George added, then chuckled. "His programming shot way over the heads of all the little folks. He did all those stories about AIDS and teen pregnancy last year, right?"

"That's the man," Kostos said. "Won himself a couple of Emmys."

Darren George stiffened. "Emmys are nothing but polit-
ical payoffs. Don't sound quite so impressed, Mitch."

"At least not until Darren wins one. Or I do," Sandy cut
in.

The two men exchanged hostile looks. Before they could
pursue what was obviously a hot topic, Kostos continued.
"Well, it's too bad it's not the same guy. That Gallagher
would be a man who'd remember the facts."

"Yeah. But it's never that easy in this business," Sandy
said.

"If something's easy, Sandy boy, it's seldom worth it."
Darren smiled a sharklike grin.

Kostos stood and went back to the blackboard. "Okay,
now, tomorrow I'm sending the Minicam out to..."

Megan fought to keep her concentration focused on the
meeting. But several inconsistencies and a flash of instinct
jumbled together to make her brain ache. She was acting
supervisor now, and it was her job to check on the qualifi-
cations of her employees. If her Jack Gallagher was the
same Gallagher Kostos knew, then Jack had lied to her
about his past.

Which meant, she realized as she pressed her perspiring
hands down on her skirt, that he'd jeopardized his job with
TeleSurv as well as her own. Her mind flashed to the bulletin board covered with Grim Reaper clippings.

And maybe a whole lot more.

MEGAN RAPPED on Jack's front door, then turned to where
her children were waiting on the curb.

"You two stay there and don't set a foot in that street."

"Okay, Mom," Roxie and Thomas chorused back.

Above them the sky rumbled ominously. An afternoon
storm was minutes away, and she still had to get to the market.

The door opened, and Jack's surprised face greeted her.
"Megan! What are you doing here?"

She stuck out her hand with the five dollars she owed him,
trying not to register the fact that he looked handsome and
disheveled in a sexy way. His T-shirt had the arms ripped out

of it, and she could see big sections of his side and chest. He was lean and strong, to say nothing of muscular. His upper arms bulged as he pushed his hair back off his forehead. He smelled clean and male, and his tanned skin gleamed with a fine coating of sweat.

The shock of arousal she felt turned her gray mood to black. "It's what I owe you from last night."

He crossed his arms and looked beyond her out to the street. "Why are your kids sitting out there? Bring them in. I was just working out with the weights, but I can stop and we can all have something to drink."

"We can't." She waved the money at him. "Will you please take this."

His eyes darkened. "No, I'm not taking that. Now why don't you tell me what's wrong, Megan?"

She exhaled, then stuffed the money back into the pocket of her denim jumper. He wanted to be direct, well that was fine with her. "Did you work as news director at a television station in Palm Bay six months ago?"

He blinked, then rocked back on his heels. "Come on in, Megan. We need to talk."

"So it's true!" Her disappointment in him matched her accelerating level of fury. "You rotten, lying... You're fired! You lied on the TeleSurv papers, and you lied to me last night about being a writer! You've jeopardized my whole survey and quite possibly my job. I can't believe someone who passes himself off as a decent person would screw around with other people's lives like this."

He grabbed her hand but she jerked it away. "Don't."

"I can explain if you'll give me a chance."

"I gave you a chance, Jack Gallagher." Before she could go on, the shrieks of her children made her turn toward the street. A flash of lightning lit the sky, followed a moment later by the crash of answering thunder. Silver-dollar-size raindrops were pelting the kids, who were rolling around in the middle of Jack's lawn.

"Roxie, Thomas! Stop it!" She turned and ran toward them as the rain fell harder. They were wearing slickers, but both had wet strands of hair plastered to their faces. She dragged them up the drive and stood under the carport.

Listening to their giggles, her temper cooled a little. She saw the front door of Jack's house was closed. Great, so that's it, she thought. I didn't even get to tell him what a complete and total creep I think he is! Behind them a door creaked open.

She turned as Jack came out of his utility room into the carport. He was carrying two Popsicles. "Hey kids, why don't you eat these while your mom and I decide what to do about the rain?"

"We're going," Megan retorted, pulling Thomas toward her.

"In that?" Jack asked, motioning at the storm.

When she didn't respond, he handed the popsicle to Roxie.

"Thank you," Roxie replied sweetly.

Thomas didn't take the one he was offered until Megan nodded her approval. Silently she led her kids after Jack through the utility room and into his covered patio. They stripped off the kids' rain gear and went to the kitchen where Jack had turned the television on to "Sesame Street."

"Want some coffee?" he asked her.

"No."

"Can we go out on the porch and talk while the kids finish their Popsicles?"

Megan looked at Thomas. "Will you be okay, honey?"

He smiled happily and licked his fingers where the cherry juice was trickling down. She patted Roxie on the head and followed Jack back out to the porch. Stiffly she took the chair he offered.

The rain was falling in torrents now, and the wind was kicking up. The lightning came closer, making the lights dim but not cutting the power off completely. As much as Megan wanted to get away from Jack, she was glad she wasn't out there with the kids.

She looked at him. He was leaning forward in his chair, his hands clasped together, balancing his elbows on his knees.

"You ready to listen for a minute?"

"To what? More lies?"

His gaze stayed on her face. "I'll tell you the truth."

"Sure. But I meant it when I said you're fired. It's a rule." Megan suddenly felt foolish, her prim pronouncement reminded her of something her seventh grade physical education teacher would have said.

"I understand that. Rules like that make TeleSurv a very prosperous and respected company." Slowly he began to take her back through his professional life. Jack detailed the past ten years quickly, stopping when he got to the past year.

"The bottom line is that I was good. In demand. Well-paid. I'd lost my wife and child because I put them firmly in the number two position of my priority list. But I told myself it didn't matter. And strangely enough, it didn't matter, Megan. I worked sixty, seventy hours a week. I didn't have time to miss anyone.

"Anyway, everything was going fine. I was doing lots of public service programming, winning awards for the station and sponsers for issues that had been shunned in the past. The demographic studies I'd done told me people wanted more substance than fluff in their news, and I convinced management to back me to the hilt." He fell silent, his head dropping down while he stared at the floor.

"So why'd you get fired?"

He smiled ruefully. "The September TeleSurv ratings showed our station had lost nine thousand viewers from the previous survey. It was the biggest drop in the station's history."

Despite her resolve to stay angry, Megan felt her sympathy aroused. "They blamed you for all of it?"

"Sure. I had more power than any news director ever had. I was a natural to be blamed."

She watched him closely. He was the picture of honesty, and misery. Her temper cooled even more. "So that's why you were collecting that information on the Grim Reaper? You're trying to get back into the news business?"

"I hope to eventually. The Reaper is a big story. When and if I ever do go back to local news, I didn't want to be short on details."

"So what's this all got to do with me, Jack? Did you decide to come to work for TeleSurv and get your revenge somehow?"

He nodded. "That's a rough way to phrase it, Megan. But it's pretty right. Except that it wasn't TeleSurv I wanted to get revenge on. It was the TeleSurv employees who fixed the survey."

"Fixed the survey? What are you talking about?" Her anger flared. She heard her kids' voices rising and knew she should go see to them, but she felt rooted to the spot. "Are you telling me you think I cheated on the September survey? Is that it?"

"I didn't know who did, Megan," Jack answered flatly. "But I have proof that someone did."

"Proof?" Her tone was of complete disbelief.

He got up and retrieved the letter from Eva Merritt, handing it to her without another word.

Dear Mr. Gallagher:

My name is Eva Merritt. Last month I was contacted by a woman who said she was with TeleSurv Surveys. I agreed to take part in her survey.

The reason I'm writing it to complain. After I got the survey diary, a man called me. He said his name was Mr. Martin, and he urged me to report on my survey that I watched Darren George and the WABR news. He said I would get a bonus for this information from sponsors interested in helping Melbourne grow.

It sounds to me like this Mr. Martin wants to help Melbourne grow like a bull wants to help a cow, if you get my drift. I hope your station can look into this for me.

Megan read slowly, her stomach churning as she got to the end. The letter was dated five months ago. "This is unbelievable. TeleSurv would never condone this kind of pressure.''

Jack stared at her, saying nothing.

''I'll call my staff supervisor in Maryland and pass this information on to him.'' Megan's voice faltered. ''Did you do anything about this?''

''I tried to. I sent a copy of it to the Federal Communications Commission (FCC), and to Sherman Royal at WABR. Then I made an appointment to go see Mrs. Merritt.'' Jack's jaw tightened into a line of anger.

''Well? Did she have any more to say?''

''Eva Merritt was dead when I went to see her, Megan. She'd drowned a few days before.''

''My God! How horrible!'' Megan's hand clenched the letter.

''Horrible? Yes. And suspicious. You see, Mrs. Merritt was confined to a wheelchair, Megan. As far as anyone who lived at her apartment complex knew, she'd never gone near the pool before.''

''Jack, do you know what you're implying!'' Megan jumped to her feet and began to pace. ''I think you're overreacting to this. What did the police say?''

He stared hard at her. ''They said it was an accident. The FCC dropped their investigation, refused to contact other citizens who had taken part in the survey, and Sherman Royal said he had never received my letter. Case closed.''

''Well, then, close it.'' She looked down at the letter. ''I will send a copy to my boss, though. Just in case.''

''I'd appreciate it, Megan. You see, I'm afraid that whoever called Eva Merritt may be resorting to bigger crimes to keep this scandal quiet.''

''Like what?'' Megan shouted, turning on him. She had bright spots of color on her cheeks. Her hair was full of electricity from the storm, and it stood out in a hazy foam of softness around her face. ''Pushing old ladies into swimming pools?'' she whispered.

He said nothing.

''The next thing you'll be telling me is that you suspect Darren George of setting the whole scam up!''

"He had the most to gain."

Megan met Jack's dark eyes and felt a jolt of surprise, followed quickly by terror. "But why, Jack? He'd have to be a monster to do that. Why don't you just accuse him of being the Grim Reaper while you're at it?"

Jack nodded. "Okay. I think Darren George might be the Reaper."

Chapter Seven

Megan listened silently while Jack outlined his reasons for tying Darren George to the TeleSurv scam and the murders.

"Aside from Eva Merritt's 'accident', it's too coincidental that both Gladys and Norma Schultz were both employees of the company," Jack concluded. "And now that you've been attacked..."

"In your home," she retorted.

"Which proves the point even more, Megan. Until a few minutes ago *I* was an employee of TeleSurv, too."

She made a wry face at that and began to pace. "But if your whole point is that whoever 'fixed' the survey, if it was fixed, is suddenly nervous and silencing those who worked with him, why would he attack you? And if the Reaper is involved, why were those other people killed who weren't employees of TeleSurv?"

Jack shook his head and sat down on the couch. Out of the corner of his eye he saw Roxie and Thomas peeking around the corner of the hallway. He pretended not to see them. "I didn't say I had it all figured out."

Suddenly Megan flashed onto a piece of information Sandy Royal had mentioned earlier. "I heard a rumor today at the network that the police think Gladys may have been killed by someone other than the Reaper."

"Hang on." Jack shook his head suddenly, not wanting her kids to hear this discussion. He pointed to the hall, and Megan stopped short.

"Hey, you two," she said with a smile. "All done with the Popsicles?"

"Can we have another?" Thomas asked.

"Thomas—"

"Sure you can, buddy," Jack replied. "If it's okay with your mom."

"Too close to supper. Speaking of which, we'd better go wash your hands and get to the store." The rain had faded to a drizzle, and with any luck they'd get home no wetter than before, she thought. She hustled the kids down the hallway to Jack's bathroom and cleaned them up, then went to retrieve their rain gear.

Jack was waiting for her. She saw he had donned shoes and a less-revealing shirt. He chivalrously held Roxie's coat for her and pulled on her rain boots while she chatted about her friend Carrie.

Thomas watched Jack solemnly, and Megan wondered what her son was thinking. He had asked several questions about who that "man" was who had carried him to bed last night. "Okay, guys. Thank Mr. Gallagher for the treats."

"Thank you, sir."

"Thank you, Mr. Gallagher." Roxie gave him a quick hug and followed her mom to the door.

"Megan," Jack called.

"We can discuss this later, okay?" she said, then turned and faced him, a hand protectively on each of the children's shoulders.

"Can I come, too? I'm out of everything. I could drive us all to the market, then maybe to McDonalds. My treat."

The kids squealed, and she gave Jack a halfhearted dirty look. He was a parent and surely knew you never mentioned plans like that in front of two kids without expecting a yes answer. "We appreciate it, but—"

"—Please, Momma." Thomas pulled on her dress. "I love McDonald's. You never take us!"

"Thanks. You've got yourself three dates for dinner." Following Jack outside, she felt unsettled and still angry with Jack, but she was intrigued by the facts linking Tele-Surv to two dead women.

Though she was sure Jack was mistaken, she knew she had to hear more of his theories, even though the implications raised fear inside her.

Another thing she couldn't help admitting to herself was that she was pleased he'd made the offer. Despite his misrepresentation about his past, Megan liked him. She enjoyed spending time with him.

"Sit down, troops. Let me help you with the seat belts," Jack said.

While he was strapping the kids in, Megan stood by the car and waited. Her attention was caught by an insistent tapping behind her. She turned and saw Mona Hawkins standing at the large picture window in the house next door.

Megan waved, but the girl didn't smile. She stopped tapping and stared at Megan, then motioned to her to come over. Megan walked across the squishy thick matting of grass and the crushed shell driveway. Mona's face was very close to the glass.

"Hi, Mona."

Mona didn't reply, but she pressed a piece of paper against the window for Megan to read.

Megan's smile faded as she recognized what it was. The TeleSurv staff report for spring, listing the names, addresses, phone numbers and assignments for the TeleSurv employees. "Megan" was scrawled across the top in familiar handwriting.

It was the document Gladys Grokowbowski had called her to come and get the night she was murdered.

"Megan?"

She jumped at the sound of Jack's voice. "Come here," she said, then turned to Mona. The window was empty, the heavy curtains swishing back and forth where the child had stood.

"What is it?" Jack asked.

"Mona. She has the staff report Gladys left for me."

"The one the police didn't find the night she was murdered?"

"Yes." Megan glanced again at the window. The drapes were still now.

Jack squeezed her arm. "Go wait with the kids. I'll knock on the door."

"Should we call the police?"

"I don't know. Let me find out where she says she got it."

Megan walked back to the car where her children were beginning to whine with impatience. She watched as Jack knocked loudly a third time, but the front door remained closed.

The sound of an approaching car made her turn toward the street as Claude Hawkins pulled into the drive. He was behind the wheel of an ancient Chevy pickup, the red paint faded to brown and chipping. He nodded at her and stopped the truck.

"Hey there, Miz Summers."

"Hello, Mr. Hawkins." She glanced toward his house and saw Jack walking toward them. Mona had not answered the door.

"Momma. When are we going to McDonald's?" Roxie yelled from the inside of Jack's car.

Thomas began to cry. "Momma. I forgot to bring Bunny!"

"Looks like you got your hands full there," Claude chuckled and limped toward the car. "Hey now, you rascals. Leave your mama be. She's talking to Old Claude." He reached into his overalls and pulled out several wrapped peppermints and two shiny disks Megan couldn't quite see. He handed them through the window to the kids.

"Mr. Hawkins?"

Claude turned from the excited children shouting their thanks and reached out his hand to Jack. "Evening, Mr. Gallagher. How are you?"

"I'm fine, sir," Jack replied. "But I wonder if you could do Mrs. Summers and me a favor?"

"What's that?" Claude asked, patting his clothes as he looked for something in his pocket. He pulled out a nicotine-stained pipe and stuck it in his mouth.

Jack and Megan exchanged looks. "Could you ask Mona to come out here for a minute?" Megan said. "She has a piece of paper she was showing me through the window."

"What kind of paper?" Claude asked, looking over toward his house. His truck blocked the view of the window.

"It was a typed list."

"We need to know where Mona got it, Mr. Hawkins," Jack said. "It may be important."

Claude took the pipe out of his mouth. "It ain't been stole, has it? You know the girl's slow. Sometimes she takes things but don't know it's wrong."

"It's nothing like that, Mr. Hawkins," Megan assured him. "It's a list of names that she may have found on the street or something. We just want to see it and ask her if she can remember where she found it."

"Mona don't go nowhere without me." Claude stuck the pipe back in his mouth. "I ain't remembering her ever finding nothing." His tone had lost its friendliness.

Jack sensed the man's tension. "No one's going to accuse her of anything, Mr. Hawkins."

"You can bet on that, Gallagher," Claude said sharply. He walked toward his house. "I'll go see about this."

Megan touched Jack's arm as they watched Claude. "He's worried about Mona. I remember hearing at the school once that Mona had walked into a neighbor's house unannounced. The police were called because some minor damage was done. Claude's probably worried we're going to make trouble."

"I've seen her out walking at night, but she's never spoken to me when I speak to her."

"She goes out walking by herself?" Megan asked.

Jack nodded. "Yeah. Worried me, too. I wonder now if Claude knows she does that?"

At the mention of his name the front door of Hawkins's house slammed and Claude walked toward them. He stopped beside his truck. "Mona don't know nothing about no list, Miz Summers."

"But I saw it! Just a few minutes ago. She had it in her hand."

"I think you're making a mistake, ma'am," Claude said, a steely tone now wiping all the easiness from before out of his voice. He pointed his pipe at Jack. "I'll thank you to stay off my property when I ain't here."

With that, he turned on his heel and stomped back toward his house.

"Mommie! Are we ever going?" Roxie wailed.

Jack and Megan started at each other briefly, then got into his car. He backed out slowly as the kids began to harmonize on the Ronald McDonald song, and turned the headlights on. It was starting to rain again. "Are you sure of what you saw, Megan?" he finally asked as they turned onto Airport Boulevard, racing past the shimmering silver Airstreams in the Trailer Haven park.

"Completely." She answered in a flat voice.

"What do you make of it?"

She turned, her blue eyes wide with surprise. "I can't imagine how she got hold of it. Unless the murd—" Megan stopped and glanced behind at her kids, who were playing paddycake and giggling. "Unless the m-u-r-d-e-r-e-r dropped it on the street or somewhere the other night."

"Don't overreact now. Maybe one of the ambulance drivers or the cops dropped it."

"I'm not 'overreacting.'" She crossed her arms, then uncrossed them. Jack was right. Since Gladys was killed, she realized she had wondered about every person she saw on the street, worrying it might be the killer. "You know, maybe she found it in your yard."

"My yard?"

"Remember the visitor last night. Maybe he had it. If he was the—" Megan licked her lips and stopped "—the person who was at Gladys's, that would explain how he knew about you being an employee of TeleSurv."

Jack nodded, his expression stormy. "Good guess, Megan. I only wish we had some real proof these crimes are connected to TeleSurv."

"I thought you were sure of that a few minutes ago."

"So did I. But now I'm not sure of anything." With all the fragments of the mysteries wrapping themselves around him like a many-tentacled beast, he was admitting the truth.

"I'm sure of one thing," Megan said softly. "We need to call Sergeant McMurphy about this."

He let out a deep breath he'd been unconsciously holding. "Okay." The golden arches came into view. "But let's feed the Indians first. We'll all feel better after we eat."

Megan agreed, but in her heart she knew he was wrong.

THEY DIDN'T HAVE to call McMurphy. The cop was waiting for them when Jack's VW pulled into Megan's drive.

He was alone, leaning against the side of a banged-up Ford Fairlane that looked like it had chased its share of speeders.

"Evening, folks," McMurphy said as they got out of the car.

"Hello," Megan replied, letting Jack take the bulky grocery sack from her arms. She walked the kids up the stairs and unlocked the door while Jack and the cop followed her. Once inside she asked the men to take a seat, then she ran the bath for the kids and hurried them into it.

"Scrub up, now. Thomas, I mean it when I say use the soap. And remember your ears!" Megan left the door to the bathroom ajar and crossed over to the dinette table. McMurphy was sitting with his hands folded, watching Jack put away her groceries.

She felt a flash of annoyance at Jack for doing that chore, but not because she minded his help. It was how it made her relationship to him look to McMurphy. She could feel the policeman's mind whirring away, judging them on a level of intimacy that they were not.

"Well, sergeant, to what do I owe this visit?" she asked as she sat across from him. Jack joined them at the table, sitting backward on the chair and leaning his chin on his right hand.

"I had a few questions about the matter we discussed in my office." McMurphy looked at Jack, then smiled at Megan. "If I've come at an inconvenient time..."

"No. It's a little hectic right now, but I can take a few minutes."

McMurphy's glance went back to Jack. "I don't mean to be rude, but this conversation is related to a murder investigation—"

"—And you'd rather not have me here?" Jack asked, rising as he spoke. "No problem."

"Wait a minute, Jack," Megan said. "I don't see any reason for Jack to leave, sergeant. As a matter of fact, he and I want to tell you about something that happened tonight." While Jack stood with his arms crossed, Megan filled McMurphy in on the list she'd seen in Mona Hawkins's possession.

"You're sure of what you saw?" McMurphy asked sharply when she'd finished.

"Yes."

"Did you see the list?" he asked Jack.

"No."

McMurphy pulled on a dog-eared notebook. "You evidently know about the fact that two employees of TeleSurv were murdered, possibly by the Reaper, I take it." His pencil scratched quickly on the paper. He didn't meet Jack's eyes.

"Yes. As a matter of fact, I was also an employee of TeleSurv," Jack answered.

"What?" McMurphy looked at Megan. "Mrs. Summers neglected to tell me that little fact."

Megan swallowed hard. "There's something else you should know about, too. Tell him about the letter from Eva Merrit, Jack."

He did, but not before he gave Megan a look that told her he had not planned in divulging that aspect of his private investigation.

"So you're a newsman," McMurphy responded when Jack had finished.

"I was. I may be in the future. Right now, I'm unemployed."

He scribbled a few more lines in his book. "Newsmen sometimes see stories when all that's there is coincidence."

"I understand the same is often true of cops," Jack shot back.

McMurphy chuckled. "'Fraid so. You should have mentioned this little connection to Officer Barnes last night when you had that prowler, though. Might amount to something."

The tension in the small room was making Megan's nerves feel like they were crackling. She read suspicion in McMurphy's voice, and tension in Jack's. Though she understood the reasons for both, the two men were annoying her. They were dancing around each other like a couple of bullfighters looking for the biggest share of applause.

"Excuse me, gentlemen. I need to get my kids out of the tub." She got up and went into the other room. It took ten minutes to wash and dry off her children, and another ten to get pajamas on and drinks of apple juice. Megan allowed them to go tell Jack good-night, but she stayed in their room.

She knew McMurphy would again misunderstand when Jack appeared at the door carrying both kids, but their smiles of delight made her dismiss her worries about what the cop thought.

"You have heavy kids, Megan. They need to go on diets. No more cheeseburgers."

Roxie squealed with delight when Jack dropped her onto her bed, and Thomas giggled when he got the same treatment.

"Good night, kids. Thanks for letting me go with you," Jack said, kissing them both on the forehead. He squeezed Megan's knee. "I'm leaving now. You going to be okay?"

"Of course," she answered with more pique than she felt. "Thanks for dinner."

"Want me to come over later? We can talk about things."

She felt a flush of yearning spread down her chest, surprising her with its intensity. She did want him to come back tonight. "No. I need to start survey calls. And I need to hire someone to do your assignment. That's going to take most of the evening."

He nodded. "So I'm still fired?"

"Yes."

"Okay. But I want to see you tomorrow. If we put our heads together, maybe we can come up with something the cops overlooked."

His request startled her, but she nodded. "I'm doing some research for my internship, maybe something will overlap." Megan stood, uncomfortably aware of the fact her kids were watching her closely. She kissed them both, then reached for the light and snapped it off.

Her arm brushed against Jack's chest as she passed him in the doorway, sending a flash of heat across her body. Quickly she walked back to the dinette. "I haven't offered you anything, sergeant. Can I get you some coffee?"

"No thanks."

Jack held his hand out to McMurphy. "I'm going now, officer. If I can do anything more, let me know."

McMurphy shook his hand. "I will. And I'll check into the Merritt woman's drowning."

"Thanks."

McMurphy cleared his throat. "By the way, I take it you've recovered from last night?"

Jack stopped at Megan's front door, his hand resting on the knob. "Yes. I was surprised you didn't come to the house. One of the patrolmen said you have a standing order to be informed of any kind of attack that might be linked to—" Jack remembered the kids, who were undoubtedly still awake "—anything unusual."

"That's right." McMurphy looked angry for a moment, then his face fell into a mask of blandness. "I wasn't on duty last night though, and when I got home, my wife didn't give me the message about the attack. I only heard about it this morning when I read the report." He paused. "I'm not convinced it has anything to do with our investigation."

"Oh?" Jack said.

"Really?" Megan added. "You think it was just a random break-in? Even though Jack was an employee of TeleSurv, too?"

"Yeah. I do. The MO is too different. He never leaves anyone alive. And that knife. Not the kind our boy uses."

A chill went down Megan's back. "What knife?"

Jack exchanged a look with McMurphy, then hurriedly explained. "One of my kitchen knives was on the floor by the desk, Megan. I thought you knew that."

"No, I didn't." Her hands began to sweat as the memory of the attack came clearly into focus.

McMurphy reached out and patted Megan's arm. "Don't worry about it. Now, let's get on with a few details."

Aware he was dismissed, Jack was irritated. Not a big believer in intuition, he nevertheless felt a sudden distrust of McMurphy. But there was nothing he could do about it now. "Good night. I'll talk to you soon."

"Thanks, Jack." Megan watched him shut the door behind him.

"Seems like a nice guy," McMurphy offered.

"He is." She smiled. "Now, what can I help you with?"

"My captain is interested in pursuing the TeleSurv angle of this case. We'd like your help going through some material we took from Grokowbowski's house the other night."

"Material?" Megan asked.

"It's all TeleSurv stuff. It was scattered around all over her bedroom and more of it was dumped out in her closet. Maybe it connects."

A chill ran up both arms, making Megan tense her shoulders together. "Of course I'll help however I can. You want me to tell you what the documents are. Is that it?"

"Yes. Explain the forms. Tell me who on them is still employed. Who's working now. That kind of thing."

"Okay," Megan said, nodding. "Are you going to bring the stuff here?"

"I have it downstairs. I'll go get it if you've got time to do it now."

Megan's glance drifted to her stove. The clock showed eight twenty-five. If she didn't start her TeleSurv calls now she'd have no time until tomorrow afternoon. "Would it be okay if you left it and came back tomorrow? I have a lot of telephoning to do tonight."

"That'd be fine." McMurphy stood, pocketing his dog-eared notepad. "I have to have the material back inside the house by Friday. Her executor takes possession of her things then, and I can't keep anything except what could be evidence."

"Her executor? Who is it?" Megan asked. Gladys had never mentioned having family alive. The one story she'd ever recounted of relatives concerned her only child, a son who'd been tragically killed in a boating accident years before.

"I don't know his name. A nephew. He's coming to walk through her property. His attorney called the captain today, asking if we were done with our investigation."

"Oh. Well, I'll have to go down and introduce myself. I'll have a new landlord." She began to worry about all the repercussions associated with that, particularly higher rent.

McMurphy nodded and went out the door. He returned with two cardboard boxes, which he deposited next to the sofa bed as Megan advised. He shook her hand as she walked him back to the door.

"We really do appreciate everything you're doing for us, Mrs. Summers. I'm real sorry about what happened to you last night, too. The captain ordered two patrol cars to stick close to this neighborhood at night, so if you see any uniforms around, don't let it scare you."

"Thank you, sergeant." Megan noticed for the first time the odd color of McMurphy's eyes. Pale brown, nearly yellow, they looked like glass in the evening shadows.

"And be sure to lock up, now."

"I will." A sudden thought struck her, and she stopped McMurphy in his tracks. "Oh, sergeant?"

"Yes?"

"Do you think it would be all right to sort of warn my other employees about this Reaper thing? Not scare them or anything, but just tell them to be careful?"

The cop shook his head vehemently. "No way. Do not do that. You could be jeopardizing our investigation, as well as their lives. Besides, I thought you said the employees had to remain unknown? The first word from them would bring the press running and you'd all be on the front page."

"And out of a job," Megan finished for him. "Okay, I see your point."

"Good night, Mrs. Summers." His eyes glittered. "Now, remember, not a word to anyone."

"Good night." She bolted the lock and pushed the door to be sure it was closed, then turned her back and leaned against it. The boxes McMurphy delivered sat there like stray dogs begging for a handout.

On the table beside them sat her bulging briefcase of police reports she'd promised Sandy Royal she'd summarize. Next to them was a pile of mending.

Megan sighed and crossed to the dinette table. She pulled the phone over to it and took a thick stack of TeleSurv paperwork off the counter. She called her six interviewers to be sure they'd received their work, then contacted Michelle Jones to see if she was still interested in doing some interviewing.

She wasn't. "Damn," Megan muttered when she hung up. Now she'd have to call Jack's scan-ads herself along with her own work.

Suddenly she lost her strength to confront any of it. She checked the kids, kissing them softly, then went into the bathroom and turned the shower on full blast. The kids' McDonald's toys from their dinner were sitting on the sink. She picked up a plastic McNugget and smiled, remembering how Jack had teased Thomas that he was going to eat it.

Stripping off her clothes and throwing them into the hamper on top of the kids' shorts and shirts, Megan smiled. Jack was her silver lining in these poison clouds. Surely the worst that could happen had happened.

She stepped into the shower, stunned by the stream of cold water. Despite her efforts with the hot faucet, the water remained icy.

Megan began to laugh. She heard the tiny edge of hysteria in the sound and took a deep breath. It was time to get a hold of her emotions and get to work. She stepped from the shower and dried off, then put on her nightie and sat resolutely back at the table.

The first person she called answered on the third ring.

"Hello." Megan forced a smile into her voice. "My name is Ann Davis. I'm with TeleSurv Surveys. Your household has been randomly selected as a representative in a nationwide TV survey—"

"—Don't watch TV, hon. Hate the bad news, murderers, drug addicts and such. Too old for that nonsense now."

Megan sighed and hung up the buzzing receiver. It was going to be a long night.

Chapter Eight

"So what did you come up with, Megan? Anything I can use?" Sandy Royal leaned back in his swivel chair and aimed a handball to bounce off the wall of his office. A package of slim black cigarettes lay by a full ashtray, and the air was thick with smoke.

Megan decided to sit, even though he had not asked her to. She retrieved a folder from the briefcase at her feet and took out the stack of police reports on the Reaper victims, and a lined sheet on which she'd made her notes. The rude thump, thump, thump of the black rubber ball was making her tense, but she knew it would be fruitless to comment on it.

"I made a few notes. The single most obvious thing I could find in common was the fact the victims all worked for a living at small, local businesses. Maybe the Reaper is a disgruntled customer. If we could get the sales records, we could compare—"

"—Take too long. Besides, no one knew the Schultz woman worked at TeleSurv, right?"

"Right." Megan felt deflated. "But Dr. George felt—"

"—You're helping me, Megan." Sandy tossed the ball with more zeal than he needed and barely caught the ricochet. "Now, what else did you come up with?"

"Well, all the victims lived in the same zip code area and all were killed in the late afternoon."

"Except Gladys Grokowbowski."

Megan nodded. "Right. Has your source at the department given you any other information that will rule Gladys out as a Reaper victim?"

"Nah. Uptight little..."

"Let me go on." Megan interrupted. "Neighbors of the first and fourth victim remembered hearing doorbells ring at the dead people's homes during the general time frame of the murders."

"Doorbells?"

"Number one and four lived in apartments, so the neighbors heard the doorbells. It might bear out the theory that the murderer poses as an official of some kind and the victims invited him in."

"Great lead, Megan. Maybe our man is really a demented Avon lady." Sandy chuckled at his remark and threw the ball in a wide arc.

Her face burned with the implied put-down. She kept her voice under control, though her stomach was jumping. "Also, there's the murder weapon. It might provide us with a lead if we could get the forensics guys to open up a little," Megan continued. "The wounds were made by a 'short, sharp tool.'"

"Tool? Not a knife?" Sandy stopped bouncing the ball and turned to face Megan. "I thought the Reaper used a knife."

"No. The reports are specific on this one item." She pushed her queasiness aside and kept her voice businesslike. This was one of the reasons she was never attracted to journalism, Megan realized. She was too empathetic to ever keep her distance emotionally.

"So who do I call to talk to the forensics guy? McMurphy?" He reached for the phone.

"I doubt he'd let us interview any of the police. But maybe if we went to the coroner's office, we could talk to whoever did the autopsies."

Behind Megan the door of Sandy's office opened.

"Sandy! I want to talk to you, boy."

Sandy jumped to his feet, nervously slicking back his hair. He slipped quickly into his sports coat that he'd tossed across the chair next to Megan. "Of course, Daddy. Megan, get right on that for me. I'll see you later."

Megan stood and faced Sherman Royal. A big man with a pot belly and a bald head, Sherman was chomping down on the wet end of a cigar as he leaned against the door. He had the air of someone who owned the place. Which he did.

"Hello, honey," Sherman said, giving her a quick head-to-toe appraisal. "You must be that little gal Sandy's helping out. I'm Sherman Royal."

She returned his smile, then glanced at Sandy. He was watching his father intently. "Should I call ahead to the coroner?"

Sandy stared at Megan for a moment. "No, we'll surprise them. It'll be a much more effective interview that way." He smiled at his father. "I noticed in the police reports that the cops let slip the Reaper is using some kind of weapon other than a knife to kill his victims. Darren George has overlooked this, but I think it might be a solid lead to the guy's identity. I'm going to check it out with the pathologist who did the autopsies."

"Good work, boy. You going to tell Darren about this?" Sherman puffed deeply on his cigar, filling the office with fresh fumes.

"It's my report, Daddy. I don't need to tell Darren anything."

"That dog will hunt, boy." Sherman laughed aloud, then gave Megan a cunning look. "You listen up to my boy here, honey. You'll learn yourself a lot. Play your cards right and maybe your pretty little face will get on my broadcast."

Megan, trying not to breath too deeply, inclined her head stiffly and marched out of the office. So much for staying up until 2:00 A.M. last night, she thought. Instead of impressing her co-workers with her research and logic, she'd handed Sandy Royal a bone to toss at his daddy.

"Oh, well," she muttered aloud. It went with the territory. Spoiled kids in jobs way over their heads, desperate for approval from their arrogant, rich daddies, populated every company. It was too bad, though, Megan thought. Sandy was a bright kid. If his father had not dropped him into a job he was so unsuited for, he might have been able to make something of himself.

Megan headed for the newsroom. She had planned to call Sergeant McMurphy to tell him two things she'd noticed last night when she'd gone through Gladys's TeleSurv files. All the staff lists and assignment ledgers for last fall's survey were missing. She'd wanted to see who had been assigned to call the area where Eva Merritt lived, but that lead would have to wait.

There would surely be copies in the headquarters office, and she needed to call and get a set for the police. But it was curious that Gladys didn't have them with the others, since everything else for the past four years was there.

The second thing that was missing was the phone bill file. It would list everyone's expense vouchers and the survey homes each had called. Where that was, was anyone's guess. The bad part was, Gladys kept the only copy. Jack's theory about the fall survey being "fixed" shot through her mind. If Gladys had had something to hide, maybe she would have destroyed the documents.

Or if Jack's other theory, that Gladys's murder was tied into the TeleSurv scam, was correct, maybe whoever killed her took the information to cover his tracks.

A chill went down her back at this thought. and she shook it off. She wanted to warn her TeleSurv co-workers, but had been ordered not to. Maybe if she just paid them all a visit, she could casually caution them? The difficulty of that was clear to her, and she gnawed the inside of her lip. Maybe she should just keep mum. It was McMurphy's job to worry about them. Not hers. Not Jack's.

"Megan!"

She turned, her hand on the newsroom door. Darren George was walking toward her, a glower once again darkening his handsome features. "Good morning, Dr. George."

"Is it? I think it's a damn mess of a morning!"

Megan winced as his bony fingers grasped her arm.

"Come with me, young lady." George steered her away from the office and further on down the corridor. He flung open the door to Mitch Kostos's office. "Kostos! I'm not happy about what's going on around here!"

The executive jumped up, knocking his glasses onto the floor and spilling a half-empty cup of coffee onto his desk. "For heaven's sake, Darren. Calm down." He mopped up the brown liquid with some tissues he pulled from a box and frowned at Megan.

"Don't tell me to calm down, Mitch!" Darren George slammed the door behind him and pointed to a chair at the other side of the room. "Sit down over there, Megan. And take some notes."

Her heart was pounding. She tasted a sarcastic reply on her tongue, but swallowed it. Crossing the room quickly, she sat down. It was hateful to be treated like a piece of baggage by two men in the space of a few minutes, but she reminded herself it was for a good cause. She could put up with these egos for a couple of months if she only remembered that at the end of that time she would be better off. And that much closer to a full-time job.

"What's wrong, Darren?" Mitch asked, tossing the sopping mess of paper into the trash can beside his desk.

"What's wrong? Everything. I've got the network people interested in my special on the Reaper. I've got commitments from New York to do a feed into 'Nightline.' But I've got no crew. No damned camera crew ready to go with me to the murder scenes beause some idiot sent them to cover the Vice President of the United States and his speech!"

Megan didn't know what she should write down from this little tantrum, so she drew a circle around the Vice-president's name. Kostos was turning red and leaning on his hands, which were gripping the back of his desk chair.

"You'll get your camera crew back this afternoon, Darren. But it just so happens that when the vice president of the United States comes to Melbourne, the 'idiot' in charge of budgeting reporters thinks that's of more importance than furthering a certain newsman's career."

"Really?" Darren's finger jabbed the air. "Well, maybe you need to remember something else Mitch. What furthers *my* career furthers a lot of other careers. Just like what screws up my career screws up a lot of others, too!"

Before Kostos could answer, Sandy Royal stuck his head in the door. He cocked his finger and beckoned Megan, ignoring the two furious men by the desks. "Let's go, kiddo. News waits for no man."

"Wait a minute, Sandy," Darren demanded. "I need Megan to do some background calls for me."

"Sorry, buddy. You gave her to me, remember?" he turned back to Megan. "Come on."

"Don't you ever knock, Royal? This is a private meeting," Mitch Kostos asked, his hands on his hips.

Sandy playfully knocked on the door. "Can I come in?"

Megan got up and crossed the room. She felt like a trained pup, responding to the shrillest whistle. Her jaw tightened as she hurried out the door, ignoring the furious glances of Kostos and Darren George. She nearly had to run to keep up with Sandy Royal. He was bubbling on about scooping Darren, oblivious to her mood.

I am going to stay calm and not let these jerks get to me, Megan told herself. In six months this will all be a bad dream.

MEGAN DROPPED THE FISTFUL of junk mail that had clogged her mailbox into the garbage and headed for the kids' room. She picked up an armload of dirty clothes and carried them into the bathroom, dumping the mess into the hamper.

She was seething and humiliated. The meeting at the coroner's office was a disaster. They'd learned nothing and had been told in no uncertain terms to go through Sergeant McMurphy for information. Then they had nearly been bodily thrown out by the assistant pathologist, Li Chin, when Sandy called him a "surly little man" to his face.

Sandy had not offered her a lift back to the station but had stormed out of the morgue like a three-year-old. She hadn't had the right change for a bus and had to walk two miles in high heels, then another two in stockings when her feet began to blister. After throwing out her soiled hose filled with runs, she gently tapped down a Mickey Mouse bandage on her heel, then laced her tennies back up.

Think of June, Megan told herself. Just get through this. She lugged the hamper into the kitchen, retrieved soap and bleach from the cupboards, then headed downstairs. Gladys Grokowbowski's ancient wringer-washer was a pain to use, but the gas dryer hooked up next to it made doing the wash in the garage under her apartment more attractive than a trip to the laundromat.

Using her fanny to push open the door, Megan walked uneasily into the gloomy garage. The door swung closed behind her. It was darker with the door closed, and she stood for a moment letting her eyes adjust. Finally able to see, she walked toward the machines on the opposite wall.

All around her, vague, bulky shapes stood soundlessly. Relics of Gladys's other homes—shadeless floor lamps, legless chairs and drawerless bureaus—were grouped like skeletal remains of past lives.

Megan's throat tightened. She never did like coming in here, especially alone. It reminded her too much of a time when she was a kid forced to play hide-and-seek in the dark with the older kids. They always scared the devil out of her, and one part of her mind half expected someone to jump out from behind something and yell "You're it!"

A single bulb with a pull chain hung above the washing area, and she put down the load and reached for it. The bulb exploded with a loud pop, making her jump and knock over the wash onto the dusty, oil-stained floor.

"Damn it." She peered around the garage, looking for something to prop open the side door of the garage and let in a little light. She found a grimy fireplace poker in the corner and walked across the garage. She opened the door and wedged the steel shaft into place, mentally reminding herself not to trip over the thing on her way out.

Above her head the roof creaked once, then again. Megan glanced up apprehensively at the roof, then returned to sort her clothes.

When she pulled out Roxie's shorts, something shiny fell to the floor with a ping. Megan bent to retrieve it. It was a badge, heavy and plated with chrome. Fire Inspector was engraved on the face of it, with Pompano Beach, Florida, inscribed in blue metallic script on the bottom.

Where did Roxie get this? Megan wondered. It looked like the real thing, not a toy her daughter would have picked up somewhere. She stuck it in her pocket and tossed the shorts on the dark pile. A hard shape inside Thomas's jeans made her pause, and she withdrew a second badge.

This one was a police ID. POLICE was engraved in capital letters, and Miami Beach, Florida, was spelled out under Shield 619. Suddenly the memory of Claude Hawkins handing her kids candy and toys through Jack's car window yesterday leapt to mind.

Megan's skin grew hot, then clammy. The badge Thomas had was knicked badly in one corner, and a thick steel pin was soldered on the back. Her baby could have cut himself with this, she found herself thinking. But then her mind screamed out a much more urgent message.

Claude Hawkins had badges. Hadn't the paper said the Grim Reaper might be using badges to gain entry to people's homes? "Good God!" Megan breathed, covering her mouth with a trembling hand. A clear explanation of how Mona Hawkins had come by the list Gladys Grokowbowski left for her spelled itself out. Mona got the list from her father. A father who probably murdered Gladys!

She had to call the police. Megan raced across the garage to the door, but then stopped. The noise she'd heard earlier came a second time. A deliberate creaking of boards, then a squeak and a soft thump. In the distance a lawnmower hummed on the warm afternoon breeze, but Megan felt ice cold. The noises had translated themselves into a recognizable pattern heard a thousand times before. Someone had opened her front door and gone inside her house.

For a moment panic squeezed all the air from her chest, but she took a gulp and swallowed. Stepping quietly from the garage, she looked down the driveway. It was empty. Across the street the postman was walking quickly away from her neighbor's house, his sack bulging and his head down as he sorted through a stack of letters.

Should she call out for help? Or run?

It was two o'clock in the afternoon for God's sake, she thought. Suddenly she was awash in self-doubt. Maybe she hadn't heard anything. Could she stand it if the cops came out for the third time in as many days to lend assistance, only to find an empty house? They'd think she was nuts if she was wrong.

Cautiously she walked to the front of the garage apartment and looked up at her house. The double windows glared back at her, reflecting the bright sunlight.

For several moments she stood, shading her eyes with her hand. Then her eye was drawn to the corner of the porch. There, crouching under the broken beach chair, was Sally, her neighbor's huge yellow cat. Megan felt like giggling as the muscles in her neck and shoulders relaxed.

The cat, all of twenty-five pounds and playful as a kitten, jumped at a bug at that moment, and the porch creaked loudly. Megan turned and went back into the garage. She started a load of wash, then bounded up the stairs and into her house. For a moment she stood and let her eyes take in the room. Everything was just as she had left it, and the last vestiges of fear left.

She began to sing along with an Aretha Franklin record blaring from the kitchen radio and put on a pot of water to boil for the kid's macaroni supper. Her mind considered the option of calling Jack and inviting him to come eat with them. She wanted to tell him about the missing lists, and also discuss what the police reports had said. And the badges. She pressed her hand against her shirt pocket, wondering what Jack would make of them.

Jack always stayed so cool. She knew he would have some ideas about how all these little facts tied together. I'll do it, she thought, crossing to the phone. Then when he gets here I'll ask him what he thinks about calling McMurphy. She took the metal trinkets from her pocket and laid them on the table, then dialed Jack's number.

After eight rings she gave up. The clock on the stove read ten of two. Megan went into the kids' room to strip off the sheets, measuring out increments of time she needed to complete her chores before the kids got home at three-thirty. As she pulled off Thomas's pillowcase, a piece of paper lying on the table between the two beds caught her eye.

Megan reached for it, the pillow clutched tightly under one arm. It can't be, she thought, panic welling up inside of her.

But it was. The list Mona Hawkins had showed her yesterday was now in her children's room. Wildly Megan turned, backing up to the bed. At that instant terror filled her and she screamed and fell forward, her balance thrown off by the steely grip of a hand on her ankle.

"Let me go!" she screamed, kicking and pulling against the force of her unseen attacker hiding under the bed. She grabbed for a weapon of any kind, settling on a foot-long metal fire engine on the floor. The skin on her ankle was burning from the grip of her assailant. She pulled again as she flung the toy at the bare arm, hoping to knock herself free.

It wedged itself against the bed frame and the attacker gave a sudden jerk on her foot. It sent her sprawling on the floor, face first into the toy truck. With an exploding flash of color and pain, Megan struck her head against it and felt her consciousness snuffed out as a black pit of quiet sucked away all thought.

JACK LEANED AGAINST the fence and watched the kids streaming out to meet their mothers. Roxie and Thomas were walking together, the blond boy docilely holding his redheaded sister's hand. They stopped at the end of the walkway and looked at him. He waved, and Roxie returned his greeting, but Thomas dropped his hand and turned away.

His small face was serious as he searched the busy street for his mother. Jack turned his eyes to the milling group of women, concerned that Megan was still nowhere in sight. He'd arrived early, fully expecting to find her here and waiting. He wanted to walk her and the kids home, maybe buy them dinner again.

Most of all he wanted to find out how she was coping with all that had happened. His efforts to talk to Mona or Claude Hawkins were unsuccessful. His neighbor's house was locked up and dark when he had gotten home last night, and Claude's truck had never returned.

He had spent the day working on his Grim Reaper story, but his thoughts had been consumed by a redheaded woman. Jack glanced back at Megan's kids. As he watched, a stoop-shouldered man in a suit walked up and stood with them. All three of them were looking at him.

Jack walked over to them. "Hi, Roxie. Hi, Thomas. Where's that mother of yours?"

The man put a hand on Roxie's shoulder and looked hopefully at Jack. "I'm the principal, Mr. Butz. Are you a relative, sir?"

"No. Jack Gallagher. I'm a friend of Mrs. Summers and the children. I can walk the kids home for Megan. She must be stuck on the phone or something."

"Oh." Mr. Butz frowned. "I'm sorry, but we can't release Thomas and Roxie to anyone without Mrs. Summers's approval."

"He's our friend," Roxie offered. "He bought us Mc-Donald's."

"Where's Momma?" Thomas asked, tears filling his voice. His hand was clenched around Roxie's skirt.

Jack leaned down and put his hand on the boy's hair. "Hey, buddy. Don't worry about your momma. She'll be right here, I'm sure. Let's go into the school office and call. Maybe she'll let me walk you two home."

The principal nodded, and Jack took Roxie's hand and followed them inside. Jack kept a smile on his face as the telephone rang on and on, but his pulse began to speed up. He didn't know a whole lot about Megan Summers, but one thing he was sure of.

She would never be late to pick up her kids. Come hell or high water, the woman took her role of mom very seriously. Which meant something had happened.

Something had happened to keep her away. He tasted the sour bite of panic in his mouth. Megan was working side by side with Darren George. Surely she had not said anything about Jack's suspicions, he reasoned. Surely she was okay.

"You guys stay here for a couple of seconds and I'll run up the street. Your mom is probably on her way now." He looked at Butz and nodded. "Keep them here, please. I'll be right back."

He raced out to the VW and jumped in. Megan was nowhere on the block, and a minute later he pulled into her driveway with a screech of tires and dust. What he saw made him want to throw up.

A paramedic van was parked in front of the garage apartment, and Megan's front door was standing open.

"JACK, I'M ALRIGHT." Megan removed the cold compress from her head as the paramedics packed up. "Please, give me the phone and I'll call Mr. Butz. We'll go get the children." She stood, but swayed with dizziness, and Jack firmly pushed her back onto the couch.

"Stay down. I'll bring you the phone. I can go get the kids and bring them back."

"I can go get them," Pollard Finch offered.

Jack looked at the little man, pale in the soft light of the room. Megan's neighbor had arrived thirty minutes before to deliver Neighborhood Watch stickers, and had found Megan's door open and her lying unconscious in the bedroom.

"Thank you, Mr. Finch. But I told the kids I'd be back for them."

"Thanks anyway, for everything," Megan chimed in.

While Jack went for the phone, the young paramedic captain gave Megan some pills and told her to see her doctor tomorrow. "You're sure you won't reconsider and come in for an X-ray?" he asked.

"Yes. I'm fine, really. But I'll see my doctor."

"Okay. And you be careful about where you're walking. Kids' toys cause a lot of accidents. Some very serious."

Megan's mouth tightened. She hadn't told the paramedics what had really happened. She didn't want the police. Not until she talked with Jack.

"I'll be sure she does," Jack added, handing her the receiver.

While Megan called, Jack walked Pollard Finch to the door. "Thanks a lot for calling for help, Mr. Finch."

He peered at Jack closely, obviously looking for an explanation for the young man's concern. "I'm a good neighbor, Mr. Gallagher. Mrs. Summers and her children are well known to all of us as law-abiding, tidy citizens. Of course I called."

"Thank you again, Mr. Finch," Megan called out from the couch. "I really appreciate your help."

"You take care of yourself, my dear." He pointed to the stickers lying on the dinette table. "Be sure and put those up. One on your mailbox. One on the front window here. And keep your doors locked."

"Can I give you some help nailing up the signs?" Jack asked, nodding to the pile of metal placards lying on the porch.

"I'm not so old I need help for that, young man," Pollard replied stiffly.

Jack watched him lug the signs down the stairs, then he turned back to look at Megan. "I'll run over and get the kids."

"Come here first, Jack. I want to tell you something."

He did not like the tension in her voice. Quickly he crossed the room and sat beside her. She was pale, and her blue eyes were red-rimmed. A huge knot had risen above her left eyebrow, and a greenish bruise was glimmering beneath the surface of her skin by her lip. Gently he moved back her bangs and inspected her face.

"You sure you don't want to go to the emergency room?"

Megan put her hand on his, feeling a surge of comfort from his warmth and strength. "No. But I want to tell you what really happened."

Quickly she explained about her attacker, adding in a rushed breath about finding the TeleSurv staff list. Jack's face hardened into anger, and his hand tightened around hers.

"Are you crazy!" he asked furiously. "Why didn't you have Finch call the police?" He started to get up and check the bedroom, but Megan held on to his hand.

"I didn't tell Mr. Finch because I didn't want the police, Jack. I think I know who was under the bed. And I don't think that person *meant* to hurt me."

"I can't wait to hear this explanation, Megan." He leaned back and crossed his arms across his chest. "I am taking you to the hospital when you're finished. Hitting your head has knocked your reasoning ability out. Some madman hides under your bed and grabs you, but doesn't mean you any harm?"

"First off, I don't think it was a man. I think it was Mona Hawkins, Jack. And I think she panicked when I came in the house, and hid, then grabbed me to keep me from calling the police."

He sat forward. "Mona Hawkins? Did you see her? How the hell did she get in?"

"I left the door unlocked when I was doing the laundry," Megan replied sheepishly. "And I'm not sure if I saw her, but I am pretty sure it was her." She pulled the list out of her pocket. "I think Mona came here to bring me this. Jack, I'm afraid the girl's in trouble. She came here to get my help."

Jack looked askance at the list, then grabbed the phone off the table and started to dial. "You're damned right she's in trouble. I know the girl's mentally disabled, but she can't go around breaking and entering, for heaven's sake."

Megan pressed her fingers on the phone, breaking the connection. "We need to talk to her, Jack. I think she may know something about what happened the other night."

He stared at her. Slowly he put the phone down. "Tell me exactly what you mean, Megan."

Megan swallowed and tried to keep her hands, which were suddenly trembling, still. "If my hunch is right, Mona Hawkins knows her father killed Gladys Grokowbowski."

Chapter Nine

"You think Claude Hawkins is the Grim Reaper?" Jack's stare was disbelieving.

"The police think whoever killed Gladys might not be the Reaper, remember?"

Jack sat down beside Megan. "But why would Claude Hawkins kill Gladys? Why would he kill anyone?"

"I told you Mona had walked into someone's house last year and the police were called out. I remembered today that it was Gladys's house, and she made a real ugly deal out of it. I'm sure her reaction didn't put her in favor with Claude."

"So you think Mona broke into Gladys's house again?"

"Maybe she did. And if Claude followed her and found out—"

"—He may have gotten into a fight with Gladys? Then killed her?"

Megan heard the skepticism in Jack's voice. "I know it's a weak scenario, but how else would Mona have come up with that TeleSurv staff list?" There was also the thing with the badges, Megan remembered. She told Jack about those.

"But his having badges only points to Claude being the Reaper."

"I know, Jack. And before you ask me, no, I don't know how Claude or the Reaper might be connected to TeleSurv and the ratings scam." She threw up her hands. "Look, we're not detectives. I know none of these pieces fits together, but I think we should go see Mona and at least find out where she got the list.''

Jack stood and reached into his jeans for his keys. ''You stay put. I'll go get the kids and some dinner. Then we'll decide later what to do about Claude and Mona.''

''Okay.'' She reached up and squeezed his arm. ''Thanks, Jack.''

Suddenly he leaned toward her and gave her a kiss on the mouth. His hand rested briefly on her cheek, but before she could react he was walking toward the door. ''Stay on the couch. I'll be back in a half hour.'' He turned and flashed a smile over his shoulder, then pulled the door shut behind him.

Megan leaned back into the sofa, willing her sore shoulder to relax. The feel of Jack's soft mouth on her own and the roughness of his beard against her face lingered. She reached a hand to her face and smiled. It wasn't the time to think about what the kiss meant, but excitement and anticipation melded together, filling her body with a rosy feeling of yearning.

Jack had kissed her. She had liked it. Megan closed her eyes and felt the pain from her headache dissipate. Something was starting. Something good.

She dozed off, but was awakened five minutes later by the jangling of the phone at her feet. Wincing with pain from reaching for it too quickly, Megan answered.

''Hello.''

''Megan? This is Telly Zemeckis. What the hell is going on in Melbourne?''

''Telly! I'm glad you called.'' She wasn't glad to be talking to her operations supervisor in TeleSurv's main office, but since he had called, she filled him in.

''So that's why that cop called me today.''

She heard his anger. ''Sergeant McMurphy?''

''Yeah. That jerk. He wants to question the whole friggin' East Florida staff on the chance someone was on the take or might know something about your killer.''

''Well, maybe that'd be a good idea.''

"It's a stupid idea, Megan! All TeleSurv needs is to have their employees interviewed by cops and reporters! Before you know it Geraldo Rivera will be doing a live show in Melbourne and I'll have to hire a whole new staff!"

Megan bit her lip. No wonder Telly and Gladys always got along so well. They both cared about TeleSurv's precious rules more than their employees' safety. "Well, I can't tell you what to do, Telly. McMurphy seems like a man we can trust. He's told no one of my TeleSurv connection."

"Megan. Are you listening to me, Megan? I want you to get this nice and clear."

"I'm listening, Telly."

"Good. Now let me tell you this. I don't want any of our staff involved in any publicity. There's several hundred thousand dollars in revenue at stake here. You got that?"

"Got it, Telly."

"And one other thing. I've got a voucher here for Elaine Jones. Gladys sent the phone bills along with it. I'm going to send it back to you for the files. I'm not saying I'm giving you the permanent coordinator job, but I do want you to keep up the files for whomever I decide should take over Melbourne next survey. Understand me, Megan?"

"I understand." You jerk, she thought to herself. She was going to enjoy resigning someday. "But before you hang up, I need to ask you to send me some material." Quickly she requested last fall's staff list and some supplies so Telly wouldn't question too closely why she needed the list. He agreed to send them out express mail, and rang off.

Gingerly she put down the phone and crossed to the box of material from Gladys's house. Another idea had occurred to her while she was talking to Telly that might give her the same information. She searched for the folder she'd seen marked "employee ratings."

Megan took it back to the couch and opened it. Last fall's ratings were on the top sheet. She scanned the results, noting that Gladys had starred two names.

One was Norma Schultz. The now-dead Norma Schultz.

The other was Elaine Jones. Megan had been forced to put the woman on probation two surveys ago because of sloppy and incomplete work, and had fired her at Gladys's direction last week.

Norma's results were usually tops in the unit, but Megan was shocked to see she'd been pushed down to second place last fall. Elaine Jones had been the top performer during the survey that had cost Jack his job, with an amazing 99 percent response rate from respondents who agreed to keep the survey diaries. Even more impressive was the 80 percent tabulated rate of diaries that had actually been returned.

Megan frowned, then looked at the results from the past surveys. This made no sense. Gladys had told Megan to terminate Elaine Jones because her work was poor. And she'd done so. She'd been surprised at Elaine's flip attitude when she'd broken the news. But why did Gladys want the woman fired? With results like these she should have given her double bonus money!

Something Jack had said clicked in Megan's mind. She got up again and searched through more folders, finally retrieving the paperwork that listed the interviewer's assignments for the summer survey by zip codes. As soon as Jack returned, she'd ask him for Eva Merritt's address.

There was no way to retrieve the diary Eva Merritt had filled out. Those had been destroyed months ago, but by knowing a respondent's zip code, Megan would be able to determine which interviewer had called the woman. Called and offered money to write down she favored Darren George's news show.

Right now she had a hunch it might be Elaine Jones.

"Mommy, we've got Church's chicken!" Thomas flung open the door and raced into Megan's arms.

"And cola and little apple pies!" Roxie shouted behind him.

Jack followed the troop in, carrying red-and-white bags of food, filling the room with mouth-watering smells. He met Megan's smile with another. "How are you doing, Megan? Your head feel better?"

"Yes." She laid the folder aside and hustled the kids into the bathroom to wash. When she returned, Jack was folding paper napkins and setting them neatly beside the plates he'd laid out.

"Why don't you sit back down on the couch and put your feet up? I'll dish the kids up and bring you a plate over there."

"I can sit at the table, *Dr.* Gallagher." Megan grinned, then glanced nervously toward the room where the kids were now fighting over who got to use the towel first. "What did you tell them?"

"I told them you fell and hit your head and that they both better be extra nice and helpful to their mom or I wasn't going to take them to Disney World this summer." He bit the corner of a plastic envelope of honey and squeezed it on a biscuit.

"Disney World? Do you have any idea how much a day at Disney World with two kids would cost?"

He pulled out a chair and pointed to it. "Sit. Yes, I do. About one-third what our weekend will. But we're going. As soon as you're done with your internship. My treat."

She sat in the chair, fighting against the tears that stung behind her eyelids. Her appetite fled. Jack Gallagher was being so generous and caring it literally hurt. Despite the craziness of the murders and the pressure of her internship, Megan felt a surge of happiness unlike anything she'd ever felt. "We'll talk about this later. You don't have to do this because you feel sorry for us...."

The kids raced out and clattered to the table. A cola was knocked off the table onto the floor, but not before it drenched the napkins and Thomas's plate of food. He began to wail. Megan jumped up and mopped up soda, while Jack calmed her son down and gave him a dry plate. She went back to the sink to wring out the sponge and Jack came up behind her. He put his hands on her waist and squeezed.

"We're going to Disney World in June. It has nothing to do with me feeling sorry for anyone. Except maybe myself."

She turned, loving the feel of his chest against her shoulder. "Why yourself?"

"For missing this kind of night. For not meeting you sooner." His dark eyes narrowed, and he moved his mouth closer to her face.

"Mom! Can I have some more cola?"

Megan smiled and nodded at Roxie, then looked up at Jack and they both laughed.

"You feel sorry for yourself for missing nights like these?" She was light-headed, and she knew it had little to do with a knock on the skull.

"Absolutely. Which is why I plan to miss very few in the future." He kissed the tip of her nose, his body tensing as the front of her breasts rubbed against his chest. A flash of heat and tightness flooded his skin, and he quickly moved back toward the table before he made a fool of himself in front of two eagle-eyed kids. "Who's ready for apple pie?"

JACK TURNED THE UNLOCKED back door and let himself into his dark house. Quickly he crossed the Florida room and pulled the binder out of the bookcase where he kept Eva Merritt's letter. He opened it and scanned it for the address. Megan might well be on to an important clue, he realized. If they found the TeleSurv interviewer who attempted to bribe Eva Merritt, they would have the first solid link between the Grim Reaper and the survey workers.

Which might also be a solid link to Darren George, Jack concluded. Convincing the authorities the anchorman was involved in murder was still out of the question. For that, they needed a lot more proof.

Jack stood and reached for the phone on the corner of his desk, but stopped short. Behind him in the hallway he heard a noise that raised the tiny hairs on his neck. Floorboards under the carpet creaked.

Someone was in his house.

He put the letter from Eva Merritt down silently and considered what to do. There was no time to call the police, and even if there were, a basic male desire to do battle with whoever had trespassed into his house asserted itself over reason.

NO COST! NO OBLIGATION TO BUY!
NO PURCHASE NECESSARY!

PLAY "LUCKY 7"
AND GET AS MANY AS SIX FREE GIFTS...

HOW TO PLAY:

1. With a coin, carefully scratch off the silver box at the right. This makes you eligible to receive one or more free books, and possibly other gifts, depending on what is revealed beneath the scratch-off area.

2. You'll receive brand-new Harlequin Intrigue® novels. When you return this card, we'll send you the books and gifts you qualify for *absolutely free!*

3. If we don't hear from you, every other month we'll send you 4 additional novels to read and enjoy. You can return them and owe nothing but if you decide to keep them, you'll pay only $2.24* per book, a savings of 26¢ each off the cover price. There is *no* extra charge for postage and handling. There are no hidden extras.

4. When you join the Harlequin Reader Service®, you'll get our subscribers' only newsletter, as well as additional free gifts from time to time just for being a subscriber.

5. You must be completely satisfied. You may cancel at any time simply by sending us a note or a shipping statement marked "cancel" or returning any shipment to us at our cost.

Stealthily Jack moved across the room, flexing his right hand. He stopped to listen before entering the hallway, but heard nothing. He rounded the corner. A figure, pressed against the wall like a prisoner caught in a guard's searchlight, screamed and crumbled to the ground.

"Mona?" Jack bent over the hysterical figure, unsure of what to do next. He touched the girl's heaving shoulder gently. "Mona. It's okay. Don't cry, I'm not going to hurt you."

"No police. Mona's sorry." Her body, filled out in a woman's shape, shook while it was racked by a child's cries.

"No police, Mona. Don't worry. I'm not going to call the police." Jack sat on the floor beside her and reached out to squeeze her hand.

Mona finally looked at him, her small eyes swollen with fear and tears. She pushed her thin hair back behind her ear and watched him, as if she were waiting to be punished.

Jack wished Megan were here. She seemed to have the instincts and compassion needed to deal with this kind of behavior. His had been to use force, but he saw that with Mona, force was pointless. "Can you tell me why you came into my house, Mona?"

Tears spilled out of Mona's eyes and she shook her head no.

"Don't cry, Mona. It's okay for you to come and see me, but you should probably wait until I come home next time."

"Mona's a bad girl," Mona replied, shaking her head no again.

"I don't think so, Mona," Jack said, exhaling. He wasn't going to get anywhere asking the girl questions, he realized. She was too rattled. He wanted to ask her if she'd been at Megan's but knew that would really frighten her and would probably make her fear the police again. He also wondered why she found her way here.

Jack stood up and reached for her hand. "Come on, honey. I'll walk you over to your house now. We'll see if your dad is home."

Mona smiled, then bowed her head quickly. She nervously twisted her hair around her finger. "Daddy's not home."

"Is he at work?"

Mona shook her head. "Mona misses Daddy when he is not home."

"I bet you do." Jack stood and offered Mona his hand. "Come on, Mona. I'll walk you over, anyway."

Mona got up, still averting her eyes away from Jack. She was nearly as tall as he was, but seemed so fragile it was all he could do to restrain himself from giving her a hug.

She led the way out the back door and around the side of his house, but came to an abrupt stop. Jack saw what had caused this the second he spotted Claude Hawkins's pickup parked in the garage. Claude was standing beside it, his hand shading his eyes as he looked toward the street. "Mona!" he hollered.

"Mona's here, Daddy." Mona took a step toward Claude, who whirled around as she approached.

His dark eyes, like wet raisins, glittered at his daughter and her escort. "What the hell's going on here with my youngin, Gallagher?"

"Mona came for a visit, Claude. She gets lonesome when you're gone all day."

"Don't be mad at Mona," Mona said softly.

Claude held out his arm and Mona ran to him. He murmured to the girl as she rested her head on his shoulder.

She peeked around at Jack and smiled, then burrowed her face again into her father's denim shirt

"You go on into the house now, girl," Claude said. He had only tenderness in his voice.

"Mona cook dinner, Daddy? Peanut butter and jelly pancakes? Strawberry jelly?"

"Anything you want, girl." She went into the house, curling her hair around her finger.

Claude walked a step toward Jack. At that moment Jack noticed the stains on the older man's overalls. They were brown-red and crusty.

"I ain't telling you again, Gallagher, to stay sway from my property and my girl. She's simpleminded. Can't reason more than a little kid, so there's nothing there for a man like you to be interested in." Claude stuck one hand into his pocket and pulled out a pair of rusty scissors. They were covered with the same stains as on his work clothes. He began to clean his fingernails with the sharp point of one blade. "You understanding me?"

"I understand you want to protect your daughter, Hawkins. But I wasn't doing anything other than taking her home so she wouldn't be scared. She came into my house when I wasn't there, and when I found her she started crying. I think you need to make arrangements to get someone to stay with Mona when you're not around."

"It's my business, Gallagher."

Jack glared at the man and crossed his arms across his chest. "It's going to be police business, Hawkins. If your daughter lets herself into the wrong house, one of your other neighbors might not escort her home. I understand something like that happened before."

"You talking about that Grokowbowski woman?" Claude's tone was huskier, and his eyes narrowed. He began to wipe the scissors back and forth on his knee, as if polishing them. "How'd you hear about that?"

"That's not really the point, is it? If you care about Mona, you'll see that she gets some attention." He stopped, wondering if he should press the man to ask Mona about the list the girl left at Megan's. It wasn't the right time, Jack decided. The irritated expression on Claude's face kept him from even wanting to think Megan's name in the man's presence.

"I'll see about Mona. She's my responsibility." Hawkins turned abruptly and walked into his house, slamming the front door behind him.

Jack stomped into his own backyard and slammed the gate. He immediately felt stupid. An eye for an eye, which is what he had aimed for with Darren George, suddenly seemed the least moral motivation in the world.

MEGAN WATCHED OUT THE FRONT window as Sergeant McMurphy unlocked Gladys Grokowbowski's house and went in. A light went on and shone through the kitchen window as Megan felt her stomach clench.

McMurphy had stopped in and picked up the material from TeleSurv a few minutes before, telling Megan little about the progress in the case. He did admit that the pressure from the citizens of Melbourne was increasing and the city council was screaming for an arrest.

When she had asked him about suspects, the cop had averted his eyes and said goodbye. Whoever was executor of Gladys's estate would be there tomorrow, McMurphy added, Megan agreed to come down and meet her new landlord.

Megan now wished she had not said she would be there. At this moment she didn't feel like she could ever step foot inside the Grokowbowski house again. She ran her hands up her arms to flatten the chill bumps springing there. She could clearly see Sergeant McMurphy's profile in the kitchen, and she moved away from the window before he saw her watching.

The cop had a right to be in the house, but there was something too sad about seeing the light come on and knowing Gladys was dead. Megan crossed the room and switched on the television. She had survey placement calls to make, but for a minute she wanted just to sit and stare at a television screen and not think at all.

When Jack called with Eva Merritt's phone number, she'd get moving again. Until then she'd vegetate.

"Momma! I'm thirsty."

Megan sighed. "Get up and get yourself a drink, Roxie."

"I'm too scared, Mom."

Megan hurled herself off the couch and flipped on the bathroom light so she could see into her kids' bedroom. Roxie was sitting up clutching Jumbo Love, her favorite bedmate. It was totally unlike Roxie to say she was scared at night, Megan thought. It must be all the mess going on around her. "What are you scared of, sweetheart?" Megan asked, taking her daughter onto her lap.

"I don't know, Mommy." Roxie sobbed heartily now, and Megan eyed the other bed where Thomas was stirring in his sleep.

She carried Roxie out to the kitchen and got her a drink, then took her to the couch and sat down. She hit the mute button on the remote control. "Tell Mom if you're worrying about anything, sweetie. I might be able to help."

Roxie nuzzled closer. "Am I ever going to see Daddy again, Mom?"

Stunned, Megan swallowed hard. "Of course, honey. Remember when he called a couple of weeks ago to wish Thomas happy birthday? He said he'd be out soon to visit."

"But he never comes when he says that. He didn't come at Christmas."

"He had to take a different job, Roxie." She hugged her little girl to her, wishing she could ease the pain, berating herself for not realizing how much the kids missed their father, even if they didn't talk about him much. "He loves you and Thomas. Very much. But when you live far away, sometimes it's hard to see the people you love as much as you'd like."

"Is Mr. Gallagher going to be my new daddy?"

Megan stiffened. "No, baby. Your daddy will always be your daddy. Mr. Gallagher is a new friend, that's all." She ruffled Roxie's bangs and glanced at the clock. "Come on now, scooter. Let's get back to bed. You've got school tomorrow."

Roxie took her hand and let her lead the way back to bed. She gripped her stuffed animal and snuggled under the light covers. Megan sat and rubbed Roxie's back until the child's even breathing told her that she had fallen asleep. Quietly she closed the door and returned to the living room. Jack should have called by now, she thought, then reached for the phone.

It rang as she touched it, jarring her already-bruised nerves. "Hello?"

"Megan. It's Jack. Are you all right?"

"Yes. The phone just startled me."

"I dug out Eva Merritt's address from my notes. She lived at 239 Champagne, Palm Bay."

Megan reached for the notes she had made before Sergeant McMurphy had taken Gladys's papers. Palm Bay was in the Metro section of Melbourne. She quickly turned to the interviewer assignment page.

Last fall the Melbourne Metro section was assigned to Elaine Jones. "Bingo. An interviewer named Elaine Jones must be the one who called Mrs. Merritt, Jack."

"Elaine Jones? Does she still work for you?"

Megan filled him in on her firing of the woman, and the bizarre events leading to it. "So there was no legitimate reason for Gladys to have told me to fire Elaine."

There was a small pause. "Unless Gladys knew about the scam."

"Unless Gladys knew," Megan agreed.

"Why wouldn't Gladys have turned the Jones woman in? Would it have reflected badly on her if she had informed TeleSurv one of her employees might have bribed some viewers?" Jack asked.

"It might have. Telly Zemeckis, our boss at TeleSurv, is famous for two things. Overreacting and temper tantrums. Gladys may have wanted to avoid a scene with Telly and just fired Elaine, figuring Elaine wouldn't complain because she had a guilty conscience."

"Gladys never mentioned anything to you?"

"No," Megan snapped, then realized Jack hadn't meant to imply any suspicion with the question. "I'm sorry, Jack."

"No, I'm sorry. Why don't you get to bed and tomorrow we'll call this Elaine person and see if she'll meet with us."

"Okay."

"Does she live in Melbourne?"

"Yes." Megan smiled, remembering suddenly the exact location of the woman's home. Elaine had mentioned the last time she talked to her that she was moving to her boyfriend's trailer. "She lives at Trailer Haven, the Airstream park off Airport."

"Great. Now get some sleep, lady. And lock the doors."

Megan glanced at her front door, wondering if Sergeant McMurphy was still at Gladys's house. "It's locked. I'll see you tomorrow, Jack. Thanks again for everything you did today. Helping with the kids, and all."

Jack's voice dropped an octave lower. "I wanted to do a lot more. And I plan to, as soon as you're feeling better."

Excitement skittered across her stomach, and she tensed her arms. "I'll hold you to that. Good night, Jack." Megan replaced the receiver and felt like giggling.

At that moment her eye was drawn to the television screen. "Special Bulletin" was flashed across the picture, then the network cut to a live broadcast. A close-up of Darren George sent her to the set to turn up the volume.

"...We'll go live now to the scene with Sandy Royal. Sandy, are the police confirming the story?"

The picture changed, and Megan watched as Sandy Royal motioned to the police headquarters building behind him. "Authorities will neither confirm nor deny the report, Darren. But I'm going into a news conference in a few minutes where it's expected they'll announce that the man found tonight has been identified as thirty-one-year-old Brad Stevens. He owned Stevens Discount Water Beds, and he is indeed the latest victim of the Grim Reaper."

Megan gasped and felt her stomach twist. "No," she said aloud. "No."

"Sandy, have you been able to confirm that one of the victim's neighbors reported seeing a uniformed policeman in the vicinity right before the victim was found?"

"Yes, I have, Darren." The camera zoomed in on Sandy's handsome face. "Mrs. Beulah Smith, who lived across the street from the victim, told us moments ago that she saw a stocky young man dressed in a blue shirt standing in the victim's driveway. Mrs. Smith also said..."

Megan crumpled to the couch as the story blared on, recounting once again the terrible list of crimes committed by the Reaper. Unable to stand it any longer, she turned off the set. How could the world be this bad? How could a madman stay free and be allowed to commit this many crimes?

Megan checked her sleeping children, adjusting covers and kissing them lightly. In the dark room she felt vulnerable, and more alone than she had the entire time since the divorce. She wished Jack were here with her, and not for the seductive reasons he suggested a few minutes ago. She felt like she needed protection.

Leaving the bedroom door ajar, Megan crossed to lock the deadbolt on the front door. It slid easily. She pulled on the knob, and felt reassured by its steely coolness. She snapped on the front light and pressed her eye to the peephole, wondering if Sergeant McMurphy was gone.

There was no sign of his car, and the lights were all out at Gladys's house. But someone else was there.

Megan caught a glimpse of a man in a blue shirt and dark hat, just before he ducked into the shadows below her stairs.

Chapter Ten

Megan's arms were leaden as she reached once again for the telephone. Messages from her brain blurted short, fitful phrases. "Call 911." "It's the Reaper." "A weapon. You need a weapon."

For the second time today terror reigned, and Megan fought the numbing bitterness burning up her throat. She had to get help. With cold fingers she pressed 9, then stopped. Sergeant McMurphy told her not to panic if she saw a uniformed cop on the premises. Was that who she saw, one of McMurphy's men?

Her intuition told her it wasn't. Quickly she punched a 1. Then 1 again. After several seconds, a response beeped in her ear. The circuits to the emergency operators were busy!

Frantically she banged on the dial tone button to disconnect. Before she could redial, a knock sounded at the front door. Paralyzed with fear, Megan stared idiotically at the door, then threw the phone down and raced to the kitchen counter and grabbed the biggest knife she had.

"You could never stab someone," the voice inside her head stated coolly.

"Yes, I could," Megan replied out loud, shooting a glance to where her children slept. She took a step toward the door when a voice called out, shattering the thick silence.

"Megan? Are you okay? It's Pollard Finch."

"Thank God!" The knife skittered onto the counter, and Megan rushed to the door. She glanced through the peephole to see her neighbor's face staring directly at her. His features were contorted, as if he were on the wrong end of a telescopic lens.

She unlocked the bolt and threw the door open. "Mr. Finch!" It was then she realized he was wearing a dark blue uniform shirt and clutched a navy blue hat in his chubby fists. She swallowed the knot in her throat. Had she made a horrible mistake by opening the door? What if her neighbor...

"Megan? I'm sorry if I startled you. I had the late shift today, but wanted to drop off your stickers with the emergency Neighborhood Watch telephone number on them." He waved his hand toward the garage below. "I put them on the mailbox and on the side window of the garage for you."

The rush of receding adrenaline made her rubber-legged and giddy. She shivered and started to grin. She really had to get a grip on herself and stop jumping to conclusions, Megan chided herself silently. Before she scared herself, and half her neighbors, to death.

"Thank you, Mr. Finch. Won't you come in for a minute? I was just watching the television." Suddenly she remembered about the news report. "Please do come in for a minute. Have you heard the horrible news about the Reaper?"

Finch clenched his jaw and his small eyes widened. "What news?" He followed her into the house and closed the door behind him.

"It was just on the television. They found another murder victim, killed late this afternoon. The police are saying it's the Reaper's work."

With that, she turned the television back on, and Sandy Royal's image came into view on the small black-and-white screen. Sergeant Pete McMurphy was standing next to him.

"It's such a pity. Good God. Will people ever learn?" Pollard said, shaking his head.

Megan and her neighbor listened for a moment while Sandy asked the policeman for information. All his questions were greeted with a terse, "We have no comment about that at this time." Finally Sandy gave up and signed off, and the network cut back to Darren George in the newsroom.

"So you have all the facts we do, ladies and gentlemen. Stay tuned to Channel Six for all the latest news. And remember, please be careful out there."

Megan clicked the set off and sat down heavily on the sofa. "Dr. George is certainly doing his part to keep the hysteria down," she remarked sarcastically.

Pollard Finch nodded, then handed Megan the two stickers he was holding. "It's good advice though, Megan. The press said today the police are now convinced Gladys Grokowbowski was killed by a copycat killer. So keep your doors locked."

Her mind absorbed the new information, and she wished Jack were here. Megan took the stickers from him, remembering her terror a minute ago. "I will. Thanks for bringing these by."

"You are welcome. We must stick together to solve community problems." Pollard marched to the door, then turned and said without smiling, "I'm committed to doing my part."

"Thanks again. I'll see you soon."

"Good night, Megan. Don't worry about anything. The Reaper doesn't strike at night." He pulled the door shut and she heard his footsteps echo off the stairs.

Megan glanced toward the clock on her stove. It was nine. About the time Gladys was murdered. It was no consolation to know only one of a pair of madmen worked the late shift.

"Stop it!" Megan said aloud. She turned and put the knife away, letting her anger build and warm her as she tidied up the kitchen and made lunches for the kids. She welcomed the anger. At least it displaced the fear, though the fact that she was truly helpless against the unexpected stayed in the forefront of her mind.

"MAY I SPEAK to Elaine Jones, please?"

"This is Elaine. Who's calling?"

Megan tensed, doubting if the ex-TeleSurv employee would be very happy to hear from her so early in the morning. "It's Megan Summers, Elaine."

The silence stretched. "What can I do for you, Megan?"

Megan detected little animosity. Frankly, she admitted to herself, the woman sounded bored. "I was wondering if I could stop by and see you sometime today, Elaine. I have a couple of things I'd like to ask you about the fall TeleSurv survey results." In a rush, she decided to lie and guarantee the woman would see her. "I think we owe you some bonus money, and I'd like to get it to you."

Surprisingly, the woman on the other end of the phone laughed. "Bonus money? That's a surprise, Megan. Considering how you and old lady Grokowbowski kicked me off the survey team."

"I'm sorry if you're upset about that, Elaine. Maybe we could get you some more work, if you're interested."

"I'm not. I'm going to Bermuda on vacation later in the week. And I'm probably going to stay, if I can find a place to live."

A picture of the blowsy-haired Elaine living on the beach flitted through Megan's mind. She hoped the phone bills would arrive today from Telly, so she could ask Elaine about Eva Merritt when she saw her. "That sounds exciting. I'd love to hear more about it when I come by. What time is good for you?"

Elaine laughed drily, but agreed to see her at six. Megan hung up feeling unsettled. She probably should have mentioned to Elaine that Jack was going to be with her, but it was too late now. That may have put her off, and Megan was really anxious to speak with her. She had a hunch the woman could solve at least a few of the mysteries swirling around, maybe even Jack's suspicions about Darren George.

The trick, of course, was going to be getting Elaine to admit she tried to bribe Eva Merritt. And then admitting why. Relocation to Bermuda sounded like money might certainly have been the reason. But who paid her off? Megan shook her head. It was obvious finances had become less of a problem for Elaine than they had been before. Maybe she would be willing to spill the beans, since she was leaving the country.

"Mom! We're ready."

"Okay, Roxie. Thomas, did you find your book?"

Thomas came out of the bedroom carrying his storybook for Show and Tell. *Grover Sleeps Over* was his favorite lately, although he'd so far refused all invitations from his classmates to actually stay the night.

Megan took a swipe at her son's face with the washcloth, then saw the stickers. Rows and rows of round gold stickers glimmered from the back of the book. "Where did you get those stickers, Thomas?"

His blue eyes met hers, then cut away to stare at his tennis shoes. "I don't know."

"Thomas? Don't tell me you don't know. Did you take those from school?"

"They were on his mail, Mom." Roxie chimed in. "He's got thousands of them, and he's a selfish pig and won't share them with me."

"I'm not a pig!" Thomas shrieked.

"Selfish. Piggy. Piggy." Roxie shouted back.

"Stop it right now, both of you!" Megan ordered. "Pick up your lunch boxes and wait on the porch for me."

Her kids went out and she pulled on her shoes. Thomas had been squirreling away things from school for weeks now, and Megan feared the stickers were the latest goods. She would have to ask the teacher about it. There was no way the child could have gotten that many stickers from their junk mail!

She made a quick call to the sitter and arranged for Roxie and Thomas to stay from six to eight, then locked up and marched the kids down the front steps. They fought the entire way to school, and she was glad to kiss them goodbye at the gate. They could not pay her enough to teach elementary school, she thought as she waved a greeting to Mr. Butz. Her love for her own kids kept her from going nuts when they were bad; she had no idea what would restrain her if she had a class of twenty acting up.

She checked the mailbox, knowing it was too early for a delivery but hoping she'd be surprised. It was empty. If her ex-husband's check didn't come today, she'd be late with her rent payment. There was $27 left in her checking account. She was going to have to call Dean and bug him for her money. Frowning at that thought, she wondered why her ex chose this month to be late. *Damn, is nothing going to go right ever again?*

Then she spotted Jack, sitting on her stairs. He was wearing white shorts and a black T-shirt. His hair was still damp from his morning shower, and his muscular legs were bare. Her pulse beat a slow increase, and a smile animated her face. *Yes. Some things are going right, right this minute.*

"Good morning." Jack sang out. He lifted a white paper bag and waved it in the air. "Care for a sugar-intensive breakfast?"

"Good morning. I'd love it." She raced up the stairs and stopped.

With casual familiarity, Jack put his hand on her shoulder and kissed her lightly. "How are you feeling this morning?"

She raised a hand to her forehead. "No headache. A little stiff, though."

His dark eyes radiated concern. "Did you hear the news?"

"Yes." She picked up the newspaper he had been reading, folding closed the thirty-point-type headline that blared REAPER STRIKES AGAIN! She unlocked the door and opened the blinds while Jack filled two mugs with coffee and brought napkins to the table. She didn't have to meet Sandy at the television station until eleven this morning, and she'd planned to wash her hair and finish the week's survey calls. But the opportunity to sit, alone, and chat with Jack was too inviting to pass up.

She bit into the sugary bear claw and sighed. It was her favorite doughnut. "I made an appointment for us tonight to see Elaine Jones."

"Good. Did you get a sitter for the kids?"

"Yes. Until eight."

Jack took a gulp of coffee. "Can Mrs. Allen watch them until ten or so? I thought maybe the two of us could go to dinner at Peg Legs."

She'd heard her classmates rave about the food at Peg Legs for years. "I don't know—"

"Come on, Megan. It's Friday. Let's have a real date." Jack reached across and squeezed her hand, struck again by how lovely and soft she looked. How lovely and soft Megan was. His grip tightened as she smiled at him. Without makeup, her hair tied back into a ponytail, she was gorgeous. The turquoise terry-cloth jumpsuit she wore made her blue eyes sparkle.

Jack stood and pulled her up out of the chair against him, his hand pressing against the small of her back. "Please. Give me tonight, Megan."

She nervously licked the trace of sugar from her mouth. "Okay. You've got yourself a date."

Carefully she moved away from him and refilled their coffee cups. "How's your article coming on the Reaper? Got any hunches?"

"It's just sitting in the middle of my desk. I'm no detective, but I feel like there is a pattern there somewhere. I just can't see the victims' connection to one another."

She blew on her coffee. "They all live so close to one another. They all worked in jobs in which they met the public. They were all home in the afternoon. And they weren't killed on a Sunday."

"On a Sunday?" Jack's forehead furrowed. "I hadn't noticed that before, the days they were killed. With last night, it covers every day of the week, doesn't it?"

"Yes. But not in order. First he struck Tuesday, then Saturday, then Monday, Wednesday, Friday, then last night on Thursday. Do you think Sunday is next?"

"God, I hope not Megan. I hope there is no next time. But I think you might be on to something."

"It says to me our man is free in the afternoons, or works in the afternoons, maybe on a rotating schedule. I still have a feeling the victims' occupations play some kind of role, but just what does a pizza parlor manager, a housepainter, a gift shop owner, a tire dealer and a TV survey interviewer have in common? The last victim owned a waterbed store." She nodded at the counter. "I just got a piece of advertising from his store with a free coupon I was saving for the kids. It's near the old Sears building."

Jack shook his head and the two sat deep in thought. He chuckled low in his throat and reached across to squeeze Megan's arm. "That's pretty amazing, how you remember their occupations."

She put her coffee mug down and wrapped both warm hands around Jack's thick wrist. "Thanks for appreciating me. When I mentioned this stuff to Sandy Royal, he hooted."

Jack kissed her hands, then stood and pulled her into his arms. With one hand he turned her chin to him, with the other he touched the gold zipper that ran down the front of her jumpsuit. It was cool, but he felt the heat from her skin underneath the thin fabric. He pulled it down a fraction of an inch, then put his mouth on her throat. Her groan of surprise did not disguise her pleasure. Her hands circled his shoulders, then went to his neck and she hugged him tightly.

His mouth moved to hers, and they kissed deeply. Jack was stunned at her response: lusty, needy. A wave of passion swept over him, tightening and filling his body with want. He had imagined a scene like this with Megan, but had not let himself plan when it would take place.

He did not want to rush her, push her, make any demands on her that would cause her to recoil. But what was happening between them now seemed, and felt, completely natural. It stunned Jack that Megan seemed to want him as much as he did her.

"You are so beautiful," he said as he pulled her closer. "It's such a cliché, but it's true. I want you, Megan."

"I've got to see Sergeant McMurphy downstairs in a few minutes, Jack. This isn't the right time." She blushed at the impersonal response, and at the vulnerable look on his face. "I want you, too, Jack. But—"

"—Shh," he whispered, then pulled the zipper to its original position. "You don't have to explain. We have time. We have all the time there is."

Outside, the unmistakable sounds of car tires crunching across the driveway wafted up on the air. They grinned at each other, then broke their embrace. Megan's skin felt chilled in the breeze, and a yearning like extreme hunger gnawed at her insides.

Megan peeked out the window. McMurphy's patrol car was stopped, and the policeman was talking to a driver she couldn't see in a dark blue Lincoln Continental parked behind him. She scooted into the bathroom and hurriedly slapped on some blusher and lipstick, then brushed her hair. Jack remained at the table, watching her.

"I'll go now and get out of your way. Until tonight, that is."

"Until tonight. That has a nice sound," she replied, her voice husky.

A firm knock on the door broke the still morning quiet. Megan opened it to find Sergeant McMurphy. He seemed cross and tense, much like the first time they'd met.

"Are you ready, Mrs. Summers? I'd like to get this over with."

Jack came up behind Megan and squeezed her arm for moral support. "Good morning, sergeant. I bet you've got your hands full this morning."

McMurphy's surprise at finding Jack in Megan's apartment was tangible. "Mr. Gallagher." The cop frowned at Megan, then looked steadily back at Jack. "Yes. The police force certainly has their 'hands' full, you might say."

"Any leads?" Jack asked.

"None I can discuss," McMurphy replied. "Mrs. Summers?"

Megan had watched the exchange between the two men with apprehension. She assumed that the police had ruled Jack out as a suspect, but the memory of Pollard Finch's words made her tense. If the authorities were convinced Gladys was not killed by the Reaper, Jack might well still be a target of the investigation. "Yes, I am." She grabbed her purse and her satchel. "Please lock up for me, Jack."

"Okay. I'll be here about five-thirty tonight, okay?"

"Fine." She met his eyes, hoping he would have the good sense not to kiss her in front of the glowering cop, but of course he did not. She really did not mind.

Blushing from his tender embrace, she went out the screen door and down the steps with McMurphy. She was probably being silly, she realized. Even without the kiss, McMurphy would have to be blind not to realize she and Jack were a lot closer now than a few nights ago.

It doesn't matter, she decided. I have a right to have a lover. This remark from her subconscious colored her cheeks, but also made her smile. She caught McMurphy staring at her and spoke quickly. "Is Mrs. Grokowbowski's nephew here?"

"Yes," McMurphy snapped.

The crunching of shells beneath the leather soles of her heels sounded overly loud. "I appreciate your introducing us."

McMurphy stopped at the door and stared at her with an irritated set to his features. "Introduce you? Let's not be coy, Mrs. Summers. He's in the living room."

She turned to the cop as they walked in wishing suddenly she was anywhere but in a dead woman's house. "Who is?"

"I am, Megan. Come on in, sweetheart. We have a lot to talk about."

Megan spun around in shock at the sound of the familiar voice.

Chapter Eleven

"Dr. George! What are you doing here?"

"Signing off the nice policeman's inventory for my dearly departed aunt's possessions." Darren smiled widely showing the points of his eye teeth. "And, to my surprise, I find that my aunt's tenant is none other than you. I should have realized that when you were among those who found her body." Darren tapped his finger against his left temple. "Sloppy investigative thinking on my part."

Darren pointed to a chair beside the desk, and Megan sat down. She watched Sergeant McMurphy stride across the room and drop himself onto the elaborately carved church pew that served as Gladys's couch.

McMurphy sat and put his big knuckled hands on his knees. "You two mean to tell me Mrs. Summers lived here on your aunt's premises and worked in your studio and neither one of you knew it?"

"What was to know, sergeant? I haven't spoken to my aunt for years." He smiled at Megan. "And I'm sure Auntie never mentioned my name to you, did she Megan?"

"No." Megan's voice broke, and she cleared her throat. "No, she never did," she said too loudly, wondering why Gladys had kept that to herself. TeleSurv employees were not eligible to be hired if they had a close relative who worked at a radio or television network living with them. Maybe Gladys was being overly paranoid, Megan thought. Or maybe Jack's suspicions held a more logical answer.

McMurphy shook his head and pulled a sheet of paper out of his coat pocket. "You need to autograph this, Mr. George. At both red-checked lines."

Darren sat across from the cop and shot a look at Megan. "I was quite surprised to hear from Sergeant Mc-Murphy that you and my aunt worked for TeleSurv Surveys."

Megan's eyes widened and she pursed her lips. "There was no reason for that to come up, Dr. George. TeleSurv employees are instructed to keep their jobs confidential."

"I understand that. It would have remained that way had Auntie not come to such a bad end. Are you the new supervisor now that she's gone?" Darren's pen made a scratching noise against the paper.

"Yes." Megan felt uncomfortable admitting this.

McMurphy squinted at Megan. "I told him about your theory that TeleSurv might somehow be pertinent in the Reaper murders when I was updating him on his aunt's case. It was all off the record, though." He glanced quickly back at Darren. "Right, George?"

"Of course. I was intrigued you cared enough to do some amateur sleuthing, Megan. Though I'm sure it must have been rather scary for you. Were you worried you'd be our boy's next target?"

Megan shifted in her chair. Darren's look was a perfect parental smile but she felt the hint of a threat. She swallowed. "No, of course not. But I did think the TeleSurv connection was worth telling the police about."

"Of course it was, Mrs. Summers," McMurphy cut in. "Oftentimes cases are solved by citizens who notice something the professionals have overlooked. At any rate, George, Mrs. Summers could lose her job if you identify her as a TeleSurv employee publicly. So let's be sure and keep this conversation *private*."

"I'll take good care of the information, sergeant." Darren's hand trembled slightly as he put it to his unmussed hair. "I'm just sorry the loyal police force of Melbourne isn't more forthcoming to the press about breaks in the case.

Two victims employed by the same company is certainly an important lead—''

''—As I assured you last night, your aunt wasn't killed by the Reaper, Mr. George. Which makes it one employee.'' McMurphy stood. ''The Schultz woman was his victim, and she did work for TeleSurv. But none of the cases show a connection between the crimes and the victims' employment.''

''I'm sorry if I sent you on a wild goose chase,'' Megan offered.

''No problem.'' The cop put his hands on his hips and addressed Darren again. ''This just goes to show what a good thing it is to have restraint when releasing details to the press.''

''I think the writers of the United States Constitution might disagree that the police are the best folks to decide that.'' Darren handed the document back to McMurphy. ''But then, the press and the cops seldom agree on first amendment rights, do they? Thanks for all your help, officer. You will keep me informed as to the progress in my aunt's case?''

''Of course.''

''Particularly if the rumor that a policeman, or someone wearing a police uniform, is our culprit.''

McMurphy glared at the anchorman. ''It's not a cop in the Reaper cases,'' he replied, then stomped by Megan and out of the house.

Megan waited while Darren George read another document backed in stiff blue paper. ''I have to be going—'' she said.

''—Give me just a second,'' he replied without looking up.

The cuckoo clock began to chirp on the half hour. She wet her dry lips. ''Is your name Grokowbowski?''

Darren looked over and shook his head. ''Not anymore. Had that monstrosity legally buried years ago. Hard to picture the NBC nightly news anchored by 'Darren Milton Grokowbowski', isn't it?''

''I can't understand why Gladys never mentioned you.''

Darren shrugged. "She had no reason to. Auntie quite hated my guts, you see. It came as quite a shock to me when her lawyer called and said she had never changed her will, though he couldn't help adding that she'd intended to. The old bat's probably turning in her grave to know I've inherited all her precious doodads." A brief expression of what looked to Megan like pain worked on Darren's mouth, but vanished quickly.

"I'm sorry, Dr. George."

"Don't be silly, Megan. She can't hurt me anymore."

She stiffened at his intimate revelation. Megan had meant she was sorry over the death of his aunt, but stopped herself before correcting his misunderstanding. Darren George obviously cared little for the dead woman. Megan wondered at the rift between the two.

"I lived with Aunt Glad for ten years when I was a child," he began, surprising her that he was willing to reveal more details. "My cousin, Tad, was the brother I never had, and dear old Gladys tried hard to replace my mother." Darren's expression hardened as he looked off into space. "When Tad was killed in a boat accident, Auntie more or less lost her marbles. Didn't seem to think it was fair that I was alive while her dear boy was dead."

"It must have been horrible for you both."

Darren rubbed the bridge of his nose as if he were suddenly exhausted. "That it was, Auntie saw to that. Well, that's enough sifting about in the ashes of the past, dear girl. Tell me—" he leaned forward in the chair "—how long have you worked for TeleSurv?"

"About three years. But I really can't talk about my job, especially with someone who works for the media."

"Of course. I'm surprised they let you intern at a TV station while you're an employee."

It was on the tip of her tongue to tell him they didn't know, but she clamped her lips shut. "Accepting money equals employment with TeleSurv. As long as WABR doesn't pay me, I'm not breaking any rules."

"You strike me as someone who'd never consider such a thing, Megan." Darren pulled on his shirt cuffs and shrugged his shoulders. "So let's talk about something else. How long have you lived in that firetrap above the garage?"

"Three years. It's not so bad."

"Oh? Maybe I better think about raising the rent then?"

"It's not that nice," she retorted hurriedly. At his laugh she allowed herself to relax a bit. It was the first time Megan had had a conversation with the man that felt somewhat natural.

"Well, you don't need to worry about your rent increasing. Though, actually, I was wondering if you wouldn't be happier with your kids in a bigger house?"

"I can't afford a bigger house right now. Once I'm done with the internship and get a job I plan to look—"

"—You can move in here for the same rent you're paying on the walk-up," Darren said. He looked around and frowned. "I'm sure most of this stuff is worthless, but I'd feel better if someone lived on the premises and kept an eye on things."

The thought of living in a house where a woman she'd known had been murdered filled her with horror. She could imagine the questions Thomas and Roxie would ask, and be asked by curious kids. "I really couldn't consider it—"

"—Of course. The corpse is buried but the death lingers." Darren stood and walked toward her as he tucked the document he'd been studying into the inside pocket of his suit jacket. "Can't blame you any there. This place gives me the creeps. Let's get back to the studio."

She glanced at her watch, which read 10:50. "Thanks, I'd appreciate a lift."

"Sure. Things, as you can imagine, are jumping now that the Reaper has struck again. An assistant of NBC's news president called me *at home* last night and asked how soon my series would be ready to roll. He was really excited to hear our boy had struck again."

"Excited? That another human being was murdered?" Megan couldn't keep the distaste from her voice. "Sometimes the media's obliviousness to common decency is too much to take."

Darren chuckled and patted her arm as they walked through the kitchen and out into the hot Melbourne morning. "Now, now, Megan. In our industry, one needs to 'feed the beast,' as my journalism dean used to say."

"The 'beast?'"

The door slammed behind them and Darren turned to lock it. "The 'beast' being viewers, dear girl. Despite all that pap you hear about people wanting to hear stories about rescues and inspired good deeds, they can't get enough of the bad stuff. Give them something sordid to gnaw on while they eat their dinners, something lurid and violent and tragic to talk about at coffee break, or they'll turn the channel on you. It's my job to make sure they don't do that."

"Interesting philosophy, Dr. George. Does your station share it or is it just your personal mantra to start each day?"

Megan turned quickly and found Jack leaning against the bumper of Darren George's Lincoln. "You're still here?"

His eyes stayed on Darren George. "Yes. I thought you might like a lift in this heat."

"Have we met?" Darren George asked, his voice hard. He walked toward Jack. "Forgive me for forgetting your name if we have." He held out his hand, his gold watch glimmering in the sunlight.

Jack shook his hand. "Jack Gallagher."

"Ah? Megan's friend. You're the man who discovered my aunt's body."

The glassy calmness of Jack's gaze shattered. His eyes widened as they met Megan's glance. "His aunt?"

She walked to his side and put a hand on his arm. "Yes. Gladys Grokowbowski was Dr. George's aunt, Jack. I just found out myself."

"You make it sound like an important connection, Megan," Darren broke in. "Got another hunch about my aunt's murder you'd like to share?"

"Oh, no. That's not it at all," she replied hastily. The tension was as heavy as a tropical storm, and her head began to throb. For an instant she yearned to run up the stairs to her apartment and slam the door against the confusion these two men stirred in her. "Jack and I had discussed the TeleSurv angle of your aunt's death, that's all. And—"

"—And since I'm a newsman who lives and dies by TeleSurv results, my relation to the dead Mrs. Grokow-bowski might be pertinent?" Darren finished. "Very dramatic, Megan. You think I knocked the old girl off to boost the ratings?"

"I didn't mean anything like that!" Megan retorted.

"Don't," Jack cut in, then took a step toward Darren George, who wore a smirk on his face, "don't try to bait Megan on this. She's not the one with suspicions."

"No?" He dug his heels into the loose gravel beneath his feet. "But you have several, don't you Mr. Gallagher?"

Jack mirrored Darren's body language, crossing his arms and planting his feet firmly apart. "As a matter of fact, I do."

"Well, I'd love to hear them. But I'm feeling rather at a disadvantage here. You know who I am and what I do, but I know nothing about you. Did Megan say you're also an employee of TeleSurv?"

"No, I'm unemployed."

"Unemployed? I see. But, let me guess—" his eyes appraised Jack's muscular forearms "—you want to be a cop. So you're going to solve the Grim Reaper case and get appointed by the mayor. Am I right?"

"Not even close." Jack smiled with no trace of amusement. "I'm a journalist. My last job was as news director of WMMB."

Darren let that fact sink in, then his features contorted with surprise, followed quickly by anger. "I see." He threw his head back and made a short, barking sound of amusement. "Sorry we never met before, Gallagher. Now I understand why I smelled a grudge in the air. We beat you folks pretty good in the ratings, didn't we?"

"Something beat us."

"Some*thing*? You mean some*one*, don't you?"

"Some *scam* is the precise way I would explain it."

"Scam?" Darren swiveled to confront Megan. "Is this why you mentioned TeleSurv to the cops, Megan? Your boyfriend's sour grapes sent you jumping to conclusions?"

"I did no such thing," Megan replied sharply. Her momentary embarrassment was evaporating, replaced by indignant anger. "I would nev—"

"—Save the self-righteous act," Darren cut in. "You told us at a staff meeting that your friend wasn't the same Jack Gallagher who worked in broadcasting. Why did you deliberately lie to me? Trying to make me out as a murder suspect? What do you hope to gain by this? A job at the network?"

The threat she had felt as a whisper before was now full-blown and dangerous. "I didn't! You see, at the time I didn't know that Jack—"

"Don't talk to her like that, George," Jack snapped. "If you've got a beef here, direct it to me."

For several moments the three of them stood in a half circle around the car, locked in silence. Megan felt unable to breathe, and avoided doing so for fear of the least noise setting the argument into an explosive finale. She turned her head to look at Jack. Suddenly it was clear how little she knew about him.

His features, which only an hour before had been relaxed and loving, were hard and enraged, set in an uncompromising expression of bitterness.

"I'll see you when you get to the station, Megan," Darren said.

She blinked and turned back to her professor who had opened the door of the Lincoln.

Darren threw his suitcoat on the passenger seat. He slammed the door closed and circled behind the car, then slid onto the seat. Gunning the ignition, he threw the car into reverse and showered her and Jack with crushed pieces of shell and dirt as he sped away.

Megan jumped when Jack touched her arm. His skin was cold. She moved away and shaded her eyes to look at him. "That wasn't handled very well."

"He's involved somehow. His reaction was guilty as hell. The man knows something about the survey results, Megan, and I'm going to find out what."

"You have no proof of that, Jack. Dr. George is angry and deservedly so. You practically accused him of committing murder and mayhem."

He continued to stare at the street, a glower encompassing his whole body. "I'll walk home and get my car, then take you to work."

"Thanks. But I'd rather take a bus." She stomped up the stairs, irritated and in turmoil. She didn't like this side of Jack Gallagher. His anger and sudden implacability frightened her.

She dug in her purse for her house key, her ears straining to pick up the sound of his tread on the stairs behind her. Despite their attraction for each other, Jack Gallagher was little more than a stranger. A stranger with a personal mission that had nothing to do with her.

Or did it? a nasty little voice in her mind taunted. Wouldn't sleeping with her make getting the goods on his arch rival a lot easier?

Her face flushed warmly, and she whirled to shout down at Jack. She wanted to order him to come up and convince her that these burgeoning fears were unfounded. She wanted him to put his arms around her and make her feel like she had earlier. Whole. And very much a part of his life.

But the driveway was empty. Jack had gone without protest. Suddenly her doubts seemed as real as the harsh sun that burned away the tears filling her eyes.

An hour later Megan slid into the seat at the far end of the conference table, hoping not to catch Darren George's eye.

The newsman was talking to a group of staffers that included Sandy Royal and Mitch Kostos. The editor was busy taking notes while Darren gave orders. The Grim Reaper story was hotter than ever, and Darren wanted all the angles covered.

Kostos assigned one team of junior reporters to check into Pete McMurphy's background, implying that the cop had more than a normal share of phobia about media investigation.

When the meeting came to a close, Darren marched out of the room without giving her a glance. Reporters, writers and research personnel followed on his heels, calling out questions as they ran behind him.

Megan let a sigh escape, wondering how long it would be before she had to face round two about her friendship with Jack Gallagher.

At that moment Mitch crooked his finger at Megan. She rose and crossed to where he and Sandy sat.

"I want you to go out with Sandy and interview the neighbors of our latest victim." He handed her a page with an address near the Melbourne mall scrawled across it. "Take the Minicam crew, Sandy. See if you can get this woman on tape."

"Okay. But first Megan and I need to check out a lead on the murder weapon," Sandy replied.

"Mitch, phone call. Line 14," a reporter called into the conference room.

Kostos nodded and punched down one of the five blipping lights on the conference room telephone. "Yeah?"

Sandy took Megan by the arm and moved her to the corner of the room. "I talked to a guy I think might be able to help us identify the murder weapon! I gave him a copy of the pathologist's reports, including the autopsy pictures, and he's testing several things to see if he can recreate the type of wounds."

Megan gulped and her hands felt moist. "That sounds gruesome. Who is this guy?"

"A local hunter everyone says knows all there is to know about guns, knives, whatever. I finally tracked him down at a swap meet this morning and got him to agree to meet with us at twelve."

"But how did you get a copy of the pathologist's report? And pictures? Aren't those part of the police investigation?"

Sandy grinned. "Yes. I bought them. Haven't you learned yet that everything's for sale, Megan?"

"Sandy!"

"Don't be naive, Megan. My money has been spread all over town for the benefit of my daddy's station. Nothing I wouldn't do for that old man." He winked at her. "Why, I even helped old Darren stay in good with his loan shark. He got a heavy infusion of cash. Bought a vehicle he wanted to get rid of."

"Come over here you two."

Megan blinked and followed Sandy back to the table as Mitch slammed down the phone. "Now what's this lead you're so revved up about?"

"First give me the go-ahead for a live feed to the five o'clock news," Sandy demanded.

Kostos shook his head. "Don't be dumb, kid. You can't guarantee you're going to turn up news at the turn of a camera. Besides, we want all the Reaper stories on tape for a special airing after the eleven o'clock news tonight. You heard Darren. The big boys in New York are hot to trot on this story."

Sandy's voice rose in defiance. "This station doesn't do every damn thing Darren George wants! I'm sure my father will have something to say about my end of this story being denied air time."

Movement by the door caught Megan's eye. In walked Sherman Royal with Darren George, in time to catch Sandy's whining threat.

"What the hell is going on here, boy?" Sherman demanded, puffing away on his cigar.

Sandy took a step back, nearly tripping on the heavy chair behind him. He slicked back his hair and glanced at Megan for support. "I have a lead on the Reaper story we've been working on. Mitch is being stubborn about giving me a live feed to bring our viewers up to date on the five o'clock report."

"That true?" Sherman snarled through a foul-smelling belch of smoke.

Darren George gave Megan a smooth look and jumped into the conversation. "I'm sure we can work this out, Sherm. Sandy, I told Mitch to keep all live feeds about the Reaper off the five o'clock report."

"I know. Because you anchor the six o'clock broadcast and you don't want any of us stealing your thunder."

"Now boy—"

Darren cut Sherman Royal off unceremoniously. "—That's not true, Sandy. I'm just trying to keep the reporting coherent for our viewers. Besides, I have a rather personal interest in this crime, and since the network's interested in the story—"

"—In you, you mean." Sandy retorted. "And don't lie to us about a 'personal' interest. Your only personal interest is your career."

"Sandy!" Sherman hollered.

"That's not true, Sandy." Darren touched Sherman's arm as if to quiet the older man down. Quickly he filled them in on his relationship to Gladys Grokowbowski.

Sandy looked pale, then turned dark red during this revelation. His voice remained full of anger. "Your aunt's death still doesn't give you any right to control this story. Nor does it change the fact that I have a hot lead, a lead that deserves *live* air time."

"The damn news director is the judge of that, boy! You know that!" Sherman shouted, straining against Darren's hand that still rested on his arm.

"Let's all calm down, now," Darren replied. He smiled at Sandy. "Why don't you and I go into my office and straighten this out? Megan, you come, too. I think we need to fill Sandy and his daddy in on your involvement in this matter."

All the men's eyes now rested on her. "I have no involvement in the Grim Reaper case, Dr. George," she said in a steady voice. Her knees felt weak, but she was completely sick of being ordered around by this man and the others. It was time to stand up for herself, even if it meant risking the internship.

"Oh, but I think you do."

"Why? Because I knew one of the victims slightly?"

"Does the term 'conflict of interest' mean anything to you, Megan?"

All three men stared at her silently.

"What are you talking about, damn it?" the owner bellowed.

Darren turned smoothly to Sherman. "This is all my fault, Sherm. It seems our little girl has an interesting part-time job. She works for TeleSurv. And victim number four of the Reaper worked for her."

"Why didn't you tell somebody about this?" Sherman demanded. He adjusted his belt and hiked up his pants in irritation. He had no idea of the significance of what Darren said, but his strong suit was acting irritated, so he rarely let an opportunity go by.

"Oh, she told someone. Which is why I'm going to have to reassign our little helper to the accounting department for the rest of her internship. Can't have her conspiring with the enemy?"

"The enemy!" Megan gasped. "The police aren't the enemy!"

"No, of course they aren't. But ex-news directors of our competitors' TV stations are."

"Damn it to hell!" Sherman roared. "What in hellnation is going on here?"

Darren smiled and inclined his head toward the door. "Let's go into my office and we'll have Megan explain the whole thing, shall we?"

The urge to flee was again strong, but Megan stood her ground. She held her head up and followed the trio of men down the hallway, wondering what the devil else could go wrong in a day filled with so many reversals.

MEGAN UNLOCKED the door and herded the kids into her house, exhausted and sick at heart. The first things she caught sight of were the half-full coffee cups and empty donut package on the table. Memories of standing in Jack's arms roared back with an intensity that made her blood warm to the surface of her skin.

Amidst the complaints of her kids, Megan snapped on the oven and popped in a tuna casserole, then served up snacks. While they ate she folded up the bed, trying not to savor the hint of Jack's scent that clung to everything. She kicked over the phone and leaned over to pick it up. The dial tone buzzed, but an odd clicking sound interrupted it every two seconds.

Megan depressed the switch hook, but could not make the sound go away. She tried to dial out, but couldn't break the clicking noise. "Great," she said out loud. A broken phone was all she needed on top of the day she'd had.

"Mom, are you going out with Mr. Gallagher tonight?" Roxie asked.

"No!" Thomas chimed in. "I don't want to stay with a babysitter."

She'd lost much of this morning's anticipation over her date with Jack, but she still planned to keep it. Though what she had in mind was no longer a date but a necessary interview with a woman who might have the answer to the mystery of the TeleSurv's fall survey results. Darren George and Sherman Royal had threatened her with a lawsuit this afternoon if she told anyone the survey was fixed without proof. Their rude arrogance had made her want to find proof in the worst way.

Once that mystery was resolved, she and Jack Gallagher would have no other professional business together. He could keep his hunches about the Grim Reaper to himself.

She had other things to discuss with him of a personal nature. "Yes, baby. Mom's going out and you two are staying with Mrs. Allen. Now finish your snack, then get your homework done." She patted Thomas on the head as she passed. "No more complaining from you, buddy, I deserve a night out and you always have fun with Mrs. Allen. She said you guys could have popcorn."

After they settled down, Megan went outside and down the steps to collect the mail. She glanced at the closed-up house as she walked by, then quickly looked away. Thinking about the events that had taken place there would just depress her more, she thought.

The mailbox was full of bad news. First thing she noticed was that there was still no check from Dean. The second was that her phone bill had been returned to her. Post Office Will Not Deliver Mail Without Correct Postage was stamped in red across the front of the envelope.

"Darn it." Megan slammed the mailbox with all her strength. "Darn!" There was also a thick envelope from TeleSurv, which contained the phone bills Telly had sent. She glanced at them quickly. Elaine Jones had turned in some copies of a paid hotel's phone bill, dated November 2 of last year.

That was odd, Megan thought. Elaine must have been out of town when she made her calls. It wasn't illegal, but the interviewers were asked to get permission first. Elaine had not asked her. Had she asked Gladys? She stopped at the bottom step and stared at the first page of the bill. It was from the Miami Hilton, but the name of the room holder had been obliterated by a felt pen.

Megan stuffed the phone bill away, then glared at her payment envelope to the phone company. How could she have not put a stamp on the damned thing? she chided herself. Then the realization of the clicking on the phone sank in.

The phone wasn't broken. It had been disconnected!

"Damn!" She had to drag the kids down to the bus and try to make the phone company business office before it closed at 4:30, she realized. Megan broke into a run. If Telly Zemeckis called from TeleSurv and got a disconnect recording, she'd be fired.

As she started up the steps she heard a car move into the drive behind her. Megan turned, her heart racing. Was Jack early? she found herself hoping. A white Ford mustang with a Hertz rental tag on it drove to the foot of the stairs and stopped. The glare on the windshield kept her from seeing clearly, but she made out a blond man with dark glasses behind the wheel.

He stopped the car and got out, removing his glasses. "Hello, Megan. Surprised to see me?"

Surprised was not the word. Flabbergasted. Appalled. Irritated as hell. Those were better descriptions, her brain responded. "What are you doing here?"

"I have two children who live here. Remember?" Dean Summers replied. "And if it's not too much trouble, I'd like to see them."

Chapter Twelve

Megan stared down at her shoes, noticing the small hole in the left toe. "You should have called."

Dean leaned back against the car and crossed his arms. "I tried to. Your phone has a recording on it."

She grimaced and looked up. "Oh. Yes, I just found out there's a problem."

"You really should pay your bills, Megan," Dean said in a righteous voice. "What if something happened to one of the kids?"

"Daddy!" Roxie shrieked behind her. "Thomas, Daddy's here!"

While her kids rushed down the stairs to greet the new arrival, Megan clamped her teeth together and told herself to stay calm. She leaned into the stair railing for support, watching as Roxie jumped into Dean's arms. Thomas hung back on the bottom step, but finally went to Dean when he called him.

She looked up at the sky in rebuke. "Thanks," she mumbled crossly. A miserable day had just done the impossible. It had gotten one-hundred-percent worse.

"Okay, kids. Let's go upstairs so I can talk to your mom," Dean Summers said.

The four of them trooped upstairs. Megan put on a pot of coffee, retreating into action while she couldn't trust words. The clock read 3:45 P.M. She had to get to the phone company, but asking Dean to drive her over was impossible until she got her equilibrium back. She stuck the mail in her purse, then swept the floor and wiped the dinette table.

Dean was sitting on the sofa holding Roxie in his lap. Thomas sat beside him and openly sucked his thumb, hanging on every word his dad said.

Guilt and pain washed over her. It was quickly replaced by anger. She had nothing to feel guilty about, she told herself. Dean was the one who'd wanted a divorce. She wasn't responsible for causing Roxie and Thomas the heartache of a broken home.

"I have to get to the phone company before 4:30," Megan announced. "Do you intend on staying for supper?"

Dean gave her a steady look. "I'm in Melbourne until Wednesday on business. I was hoping the kids could come stay with me at my hotel." He smiled at Roxie. "It's right on the beach. Have you learned how to swim yet?"

"On the beach? Oh, Mommy, can we go?" Roxie wailed.

"On business?" Megan replied. "I thought you were selling life insurance in California?"

"I'm regional sales manager now," Dean replied proudly. "We're having a convention in Orlando."

"You must be doing very well," Megan retorted. "Did you forget to mail my child support check this month?" She felt like a jerk bringing it up in front of the children, but after the irritation of the day's events, she felt entitled.

"No. I have it in my pocket. I figured I'd deliver it in person," Dean shot back.

"Can we go, Mom? I love the beach." Roxie snuggled deeper into her father's lap. "Can we get pizza in a box, too?"

"Would you like some pizza, Thomas?" Dean asked the quiet little boy.

He looked at his mother with his eyes wide, then turned back to his dad and shook his head vigorously. "Yes, sir."

In the face of such joy, it was hard for Megan to refuse, but she made a feeble attempt. "But you're working. How can you work and spend any time with them?"

"Reva's here with me," Dean replied smoothly. "And I'm only working Monday night and Wednesday morning. She can watch them then. It'll give them all time to get acquainted."

Megan felt the skin on her face stretch taut. "Reva?"

"My fiancée. So, if it's okay with you, let's get the kids' things together and then run by the phone company." He smiled. "I'll get the phone turned back on so the kids can call you from the hotel."

"I'll help you pack, Mommy!" Roxie screamed, then ran like a wild thing into her room. Thomas then took a turn on his father's lap, smiling at Megan blissfully when he looked at her.

Swallowing a huge lump in her throat along with the desire to strangle Dean, Megan packed the kids' pajamas and nearly all their clean clothes and underwear. She emptied paper from book bags and rinsed out their lunch boxes and put Roxie's reading book inside.

"They need to be at school at eight in the morning—"

"—and they get out at 3:00 P.M. I remember from last time I was here, Megan. Don't worry about them."

Easy for you to say, she thought, reveling in her anger now. All he does is send money in the mail. He doesn't have to worry day and night about hurt feelings, earaches, adjustment problems. He comes and goes, like Santa Claus, always greeted with smiles.

"Come on, Daddy," Roxie demanded from the door. "Hurry up, Mom."

Suddenly Megan was overwhelmed with loneliness. She didn't want her babies to leave. She wanted to gather them both into her arms and hold on for dear life. But maybe with the Grim Reaper thing heating up, and her involvement with it, getting the kids off-site was the best thing possible. "Dean, you'll be careful around the water, won't you? And you'll call every night?"

"Whenever they want to. I'll be careful, Megan. I love them too, don't forget," Dean said, an emotion looking much like sorrow furrowing his brow. "Now, let's get to the phone company."

Megan wished she had time to put on different shorts and comb her hair, but suddenly it didn't seem to matter.

''Fine.'' She grabbed her purse and locked the door behind them.

JACK PARKED THE CAR and stared up at Megan's apartment. A single light shone through the small window, throwing a pool of yellow illumination on the splintered boards of the stairs.

The memory of the sunlight spilling across her hair the day before brought a rush of heat to his body. But the pleasure melted away as his words to Darren George echoed back to him.

He'd be lucky if Megan didn't slam the door in his face, Jack thought to himself as he got out of the Volkswagen. He'd acted like an immature teenager. A vindictive, immature teenager. And he'd allowed Darren George's attitude to bring all the resentment and bashed dreams of the past year to the surface.

His career was in shambles, and he wanted it back, Jack admitted. He wanted it back, *badly*. And he blamed Darren for part of the loss. In his heart Jack was sure the anchorman was somehow connected with viewer Eva Merritt's accusations. It was logical. Darren George benefited directly from the faulty TeleSurv report, and the checking Jack had done on the man's background had uncovered less than a sterling character.

But nailing George was not the top priority it once was, Jack realized as he stared at Megan's window. Her opinion of him, and their relationship, was of much greater concern.

This morning he had no intention of making love with the woman, but he very nearly had. And he knew the moment he admitted to himself how much he wanted to that he had stepped over a boundary of no return. He wanted her for his own. And he meant to have her.

Running through apologies in his mind, Jack quickly took the steps, covering two at a time. He rapped on the door and glanced around. A huge yellow cat lay curled in a corner of the landing and opened one eye.

"Hey, kitty, kitty," Jack called. The cat closed its eye in bored dismissal.

Jack knocked again, wondering suddenly at the silence. He hadn't heard Roxie or Thomas at all, and the lack of energetic noise that accompanied those two filled him with anxiety.

Turning at a sound behind him, he saw Pollard Finch wheeling Edna Adams out for her evening walk. He waved and faced Megan's door. *Neighborhood Watch patrol in action.*

Panic seized him as he shook off his ludicrous thought. Why wasn't Megan answering the door? Jack wondered. Where were the kids? He reached for the knob, but just then the door opened.

"Hi. You're early," Megan greeted him, smileless. "I'll be just a minute."

"I know. I couldn't wait to see you." He wanted to say immediatley how sorry he was, but he was sidetracked by how gorgeous Megan looked.

Her red hair was twisted into an elegant ponytail on the top of her head, the shining strands held in place by a heavy silver buckle. She had on a simple navy blue dress that looked like silk, deepening the shade of her eyes to violet. The low neck fell in a soft fold, and a modest glimmer of cleavage showed. But her expresion, usually one of patience and sweetness, was carefully controlled and distant.

His eyes caressed the length of her throat. "You look fabulous. Is everything okay?"

"Thanks," she responded with a smile, then turned on her heel and headed for the bathroom. "It's an old dress I got several years ago for a funeral. It fit the bill for our 'date' tonight."

Ignoring her edgy tone, Jack let his eyes drift down to her long legs. She was wearing dark stockings that had a sheen to them and spike-heeled shoes.

"Where are the kids?"

Megan stopped briefly but didn't turn around. "They're with their father," she said over her shoulder, then disappeared behind a door that closed with more force than was necessary.

Their father? Jack whistled softly. Megan's behavior suddenly made more sense. If Thomas and Roxie's dad had shown up unexpectedly, she was surely rattled. She had not said much about her divorce, but he knew she fretted her ex didn't spend enough time, money or emotional support on their children.

He took a seat at the table, glad he was wearing a tie. If he was going to have to pick up the kids from their father's, it would help his cause if he didn't look like the unemployed bum he had acted like today.

"I'm ready," Megan announced from the tiny hall. She opened a closet Jack had not noticed before and took out a short-sleeved jacket that matched her dress. Silver earrings dangled from her ears as she moved into the jacket. An armful of matching bracelets tinkled as she reached beside the sofa and retrieved a purse.

Jack followed her to the front door. The bright lipstick she wore at their first meeting was back, outlining her expressive mouth. "Megan..." He reached for her wrist, surprised when she stiffened at his touch.

Megan's blue eyes clouded, but held no trace of this morning's passion. "We better go now. I told Elaine Jones six o'clock."

Jack slipped his arm around her waist and pressed her body closer. He could not bear her aloof, controlled behavior. He knew he had acted like a sap, but not enough of a one to erase the feelings they'd shared earlier. "I'm sorry I acted like such a cretin this morning. Did Darren give you any flack about what I said?"

"Flack?" Her eyes darkened further. "Yes, I caught a little 'flack.'" Try as she might, Megan couldn't keep the tremble of emotion from her voice. "But that's no concern of yours. Now, can we go?"

Jack squeezed her arm tighter. "God, I'm sorry. I should have kept my big mouth shut."

She stared at him squarely. "Yes, you should have. But it's not important. We need to stop and tell the babysitter the kids are with their father, then get to Elaine's."

Megan pulled the door open but Jack spread his hand on the wood and pushed it closed. "What's going on here, Megan? Why are you so eager to leave? Can't you stand being alone with me?"

The pain in his voice surprised her, but she forced herself to ignore it. "Don't start, Jack. I told you, we need to go. We have to stop by Mrs. Allen's—"

"—For Christ's sake, we'll call her! And I don't care if we keep Elaine Jones waiting until midnight! I want to know what happened to you today. When did Roxie and Thomas's dad show up?"

"Don't worry about my kids, or my ex-husband. Neither he, nor they, have anything to do with you!"

His hands went to her shoulders and he brought her face next to his. "Don't say that, Megan. If it has something to do with you, it concerns me. Don't you know how I feel about you?" His voice tightened. "What did you think this morning was all about?"

His anger, and the fact that he cared, seemed to undo her reserve. Megan began to cry. She waved her arms in the air as she related the happenings of her day to him.

Starting with Darren George's snide insinuations that if the TeleSurv results had been tampered with, maybe she was the one who had done the tampering, followed by Sherman Royal's threat of legal action, and ending with Roxie's sudden attack of tears when Megan left the hotel, she hurled the stories at Jack as if they were rocks.

He opened his mouth to say something, but Megan cut him off.

"And, in between having to put up with Dean's smug remarks about my budget problems and the moron at the phone company who treated me like a criminal and couldn't 'guarantee' my phone would get reconnected today, I found a note in my son's papers when I got home reporting Thomas left school today at lunch with a little friend of his! The principal found them with their pockets full of stickers they stole out of someone's mailbox, so now I'll probably have to talk to the FBI or something!''

Jack put his hands on his hips. "Now slow down, Megan." His head was spinning with the facts. "Go back to Darren George. He's taking your internship away from you?"

"He might as well have," she replied, collapsing on the couch. She'd shed some tears but managed to keep from sobbing, though now she felt as if she might start and never be able to stop. "He assigned me to the accounting department for the next eight weeks. Nice, safe, menial labor that will keep me out from under his feet. And qualify me for nothing on the job market!''

"So quit!" Jack yelled, his mood darkening to take up the anger Megan was throwing off. "Just quit! I'll make a few calls and get you an internship at my old station."

"Quit? I can't quit. I've got a plan, and it goes like this. Internship. Letter of recommendation. Graduation. One last summer at home with my kids. Full-time job landed in September, acquired on the basis of how well I did out 'in the industry.' I can't be like you and jump from city to city to chase an internship!''

"I didn't jump, Megan," Jack countered. "I came to Melbourne specifically to find out if I could prove there was a scam involving TeleSurv. And to freelance a story on the Reaper."

"Whatever!" Megan replied. She stood and grabbed her purse off the floor. "Enough. My point is this. I have a plan, a schedule, goals. I got sidetracked by this Reaper thing, and your suspicions about TeleSurv. But now all I want to do is get the Elaine Jones interview over with, then you can go on your merry way and I'll go mine.''

Their glances locked across the silent turmoil of the small room. "That's not how I'd planned things, Megan."

She walked to the door, dabbing her eyes with a tissue. "Make new plans. I have to."

Without another word she walked outside.

TRAILER HAVEN sprawled over several acres fronting Airport Boulevard. Most of the inhabitants lived year-round in double-wides with well-manicured front lawns and flower beds. A section of the development was set aside for seasonal renters who were Airstream trailer owners from around the U.S.

Here they parked their rigs, the "Cadillac" of trailers, enjoyed the sunshine and ease of Melbourne life during the fall and winter, then journeyed home when the Eastern and Midwest weather mellowed.

There were several vacancies, Megan noted as Jack stopped the car in the visitor's section. Thomas always begged her to visit this place, he was so entranced with the Airstreams. The first time he saw them he'd marveled at the "giant silver loaves of bread."

Jack parked the Volkswagen at the curb and walked around to open Megan's door, stepping back so she had enough room to get by without having to touch him.

It was twenty past six, and the fragrance of someone's dinner of fried liver and onions assailed Megan's senses as she walked through the gate. Generally she liked that smell, but after the emotional upheaval of her scene with Jack, it made her feel like throwing up.

She wondered fleetingly what her kids were up to, then pushed thoughts of Roxie and Thomas away. She needed to concentrate and get through this meeting, then get through the next couple of days without the kids. Dwelling on how much she missed them would not make it easier.

Megan also had to get away from Jack, she realized suddenly. Despite his sympathy, his verbal and physical expressions of affection, it was clear she and her family could have no permanent place in his life. Jack lived his work, was as desperate as a fish out of water without his job.

His fierceness with Darren today proved that. Once he was "on the job," he returned to what he himself had told her was his one-track workaholic self. He'd never have time for a family.

There was no way she could allow herself to put Roxie and Thomas, or herself, through a liaison with a man who put them second. Dean Summers had put them second. Megan had promised herself years ago never to settle for that spot again.

Remember what you just told Jack, she told herself. You've got a plan. And it doesn't include him.

"What number is Elaine Jones in?" Jack asked, touching her arm gently.

She shied away from his touch. "Number D. Letter D, I mean." Megan pointed. "It's right there."

The trailer Elaine Jones owned was surrounded by clutter. Boxes were stacked outside the door, and the green-and-beige awning that had once shaded the east side was rolled up and leaning next to the trailer. Metal stairs led to the entrance.

Jack rapped on the door. Megan looked around and caught sight of a white-haired lady peering out of the window on the trailer next to Elaine's. She waved at Megan with a smile, then disappeared.

Jack knocked louder. "She might not be here."

That wouldn't be such a loss, Megan thought glumly. As much as Jack was interested in finding out about Elaine's connection with the accusations his letter-writer had reported, right now she was having a hard time caring about TeleSurv or much of anything else. She'd not taken the time to check and see if Eva Merritt's number was actually listed on the bill Elaine had turned in, either.

The door creaked open, and Megan turned as Elaine came through the door. Megan was startled at the other woman's appearance. The platinum teased bouffant that Megan remembered so vividly was replaced by a smooth, black pageboy. With a shock, Megan realized Elaine was a lot younger than she'd thought.

"Hey there, Megan. Well now, and who are you?" Elaine asked as she laid one scarlet-nailed hand on Jack's arm. "I'm Elaine Jones."

"Hello, Elaine," Megan replied, noting Elaine's expensively cut, chic outfit. If she wasn't mistaken, the ex-TeleSurv phone interviewer was wearing an Adrienne Vittadini combo that cost a couple of hundred dollars. Things,

Megan thought in amazement, have certainly changed in Elaine's life since she'd last seen her.

"This is Jack Gallagher, a friend of mine." She didn't like the strained note she hit saying the word friend, but there was little more she could do.

"Hi, Elaine," Jack said.

"Well, any friend of yours, as they say, Megan. You two come on in here. I'll mix us a little something cool, and we'll get acquainted." Elaine pushed the screen door to her trailer open and winked at Jack. "Come on, now, don't be shy."

Jack held the outer trailer door while Megan passed through. She was more and more perplexed by Elaine's overtly friendly manner. The woman had been hostile when Megan had fired her, and decidedly cool a couple of days ago on the phone. Today she acted like she and Jack were her long-lost sister and brother, arriving Christmas Eve for a reunion.

The money. It must be because I mentioned money. But Megan pushed that thought aside as she took a seat at the Airstream's tiny dinette table. Elaine's new look and her upcoming move to Bermuda suggested a small bonus from TeleSurv was low on her list of priorities. The possibility of Elaine being in on a scam seemed greater than at any time before, and Megan regretted she'd not looked further into the Eva Merritt telephone number.

Jack sat opposite her and gave her a quizzical look. Megan widened her eyes to show him she hadn't a clue as to Elaine's friendly manner.

"Now, what can I get anybody? Gin and tonic? Greyhound?" Elaine grinned, showing where her scarlet lipstick had rubbed off on her top tooth. "I can make Sex on the Beach. You had that before, Megan?"

"Excuse me?" Megan squawked.

"Sex on the Beach, sweetie," Elaine said with a laugh, a husky tinge deepening the sound. "It's a drink. Though I won't say its namesake isn't something I've experienced, too."

"I'd love a glass of water," Megan replied, her cheeks rosy. She wasn't embarrassed by Elaine's remark, only by Jack's intense gaze.

"How about you, Jack? Can I interest you in a little Sex on the Beach?" Elaine winked and laughed again as Jack grinned.

"I'm game, Elaine. If you'll join me."

"Follow my moves, luvvie," Elaine replied.

While her hostess bustled around her small kitchen work area, slipping a sharp paring knife out of a drawer, and chatting about her upcoming trip, Megan tried to reorder her thoughts.

Her gaze moved beyond where Elaine was working, toward the end of the trailer. On the back wall above a bunkbed, a small color television was mounted. Its picture was on but the sound was turned down. A tabloid magazine was tossed on the bunk below, its headline about Elvis Presley's latest incarnation as a gypsy dwarf singer standing out on the faded red bedspread.

She smiled at Elaine's choice of reading material, then glanced back at the television. The nightly news was on, and Darren George's face filled the screen. He cut away to an outdoor shot of Sandy Royal. Megan let out a startled gasp as the interview subject was silently introduced.

Claude Hawkins, a Florida State Gators cap sitting askew on his head, peered into the camera's eye.

"What's wrong, Megan?" Jack asked, reaching a hand across the table to grasp her hand.

"Nothing," Megan replied sharply, her eyes meeting Jack's. She tossed a glance toward the TV. "I was just surprised to see one of our neighbors on TV."

"Who's that, hon?" Elaine asked. She walked over with the drinks, blocking Megan's view of the TV.

Megan pointed at the back wall. "Claude Hawkins. He lives next door to Jack. He's being interviewed on the news."

"He is?" Elaine exclaimed. She rushed over to the set and snapped on the volume. "It's so-o-o exciting knowing someone on the news! I bet it must be about this murderer.'' Elaine collapsed onto the bunk and watched in rapt attention.

Jack patted Megan's arm, then stood and leaned against the counter to watch the screen.

''—So, in your opinion, Mr. Hawkins, the murderer might be using a machete of some type to kill his victims?'' asked Sandy's disembodied voice.

''Ain't saying that, son,'' Claude scratched his face, then pointed to a table he was standing behind. The camera shot tightened on the objects lying on it. ''Now, from what this here pathologist's report says, the wounds were less than one inch deep, but had a lot of force behind them.'' Claude's hand picked up a hunk of pink meat.

To Megan's horror, it was rabbit, now skinned.

''Now you see this here machete...'' he said, then went on to demonstrate the effects of different slices.

''Oh, no!'' Elaine squealed.

Megan felt like she was going to be sick and welcomed the squeeze Jack gave her shoulder.

He shook his head. ''High standards are once again met by television journalism,'' he muttered.

The camera zoomed back to Claude's face, which was smiling. ''No, sir. I'd say one-inch cuts had to be made with some kinda tool, like a painter's scraper or maybe a gardener's blade.''

The interview ended and Darren George's image replaced the graphic images. ''So ladies and gentlemen, a piece of the puzzle of the Grim Reaper brought vividly into view by Action News. Stay tuned for my live interview with Sergeant Peter McMurphy, coming up after these messages.''

''Oh, honey. You are good!'' Elaine gushed, then seemed to remember her guests. She got up and snapped the set off, then slid in beside Jack at the table.

''You like Darren George?'' Jack asked.

''He's a winner,'' Elaine replied. ''So-o-o sexy with those long eyelashes and long fingers.'' She shivered. ''Don't you think he's gorgeous, hon?''

Megan smiled weakly. ''He is good-looking.''

"You can believe it!" Elaine drummed her scarlet nails against her glass and gave Megan an appraising look. "I bet your TeleSurv interviewers are having no trouble getting their folks to keep diaries with all this going on!"

Megan stiffened. Here was her opportunity to question Elaine, but suddenly she had no appetite for it. She felt Jack's eyes on her, and so she forced herself to speak. "The survey is going well, Elaine. Our percentages for the first week were great. Of course, nowhere near as great as what you did last fall!"

Beaming, Elaine poked Jack in the arm with her elbow. "If I do say so myself, I did real good on that survey. They must have all liked my sweet voice. You think, Jack?"

"I'm sure they did," he responded easily. "Did you have any secret way of encouraging them to send their diaries back in? Promise them Sex on the Beach, maybe?"

Elaine laughed raucously and slapped Jack's arm. "Now, you can ask Megan about that Jack. We interviewers have very strict instructions to follow our script exactly like TeleSurv wrote it. No improvising." She took a big swig of her drink, then swirled the thick liquid around in her glass. "Though I will admit, since old lady Grokowbowski isn't here to have a hissy, I usually told my folks about the money."

"The money?" Megan croaked.

"Sure, honey. Money talks with folks. When I told them TeleSurv was going to include two crisp dollar bills with their survey diary, well, you could just hear their little minds whirring. Two bucks is two bucks."

"That's amazing, Elaine," Jack said. "You mean people would be more cooperative about keeping track of the programs for only two dollars?"

"Sure enough. Though I always wondered why the little darlings didn't just take the money and throw the diary out. I would have. It's not like TeleSurv was going to come knocking on the door to get the two bucks back."

"People are pretty honest, I guess. They feel obligated, once they've been paid." Megan stopped and cleared her throat. She wasn't surprised at Elaine's revelation that she veered away from the script she was trained to follow. Many of her interviewers had done that. But she was astounded at her easy manner in relating this information. Surely the woman would be nervous if she'd bribed people, Megan told herself. No one was this cool an actor outside of Hollywood.

"Speaking of honest," Megan continued, "I went over the standings from last fall and found out you finished number one in the group, Elaine. I'm going to call Telly Zemeckis in Maryland and ask him to send you $50 in bonus money. You didn't receive it already, did you?"

Elaine snorted. "From Auntie Grim? No way. That old bat was in a snit about 'irregular' results. She didn't even want to pay me for making placement calls." Elaine drained her glass. "I wasn't too upset to hear she bit the dust."

"Well, then, I'll speak to Telly about it on Monday." Megan felt at a loss for a second. "Are you going to be in Bermuda long? Should I have the money sent to you there?" she asked, hoping Jack would jump in and steer the conversation back to some topic that would help his investigation.

Elaine scooted out from the bench and began throwing the ingredients for another batch of cocktails into the blender. "I'm kind of playing that by ear, Megan. Just have it sent here, I'll get the post office to forward it if I need to."

"Are you taking your trailer?" Jack asked.

"No way! It belongs to my boyfriend, anyway. He's going to have it moved off to a hunting camp, or some such place." She pressed the mix button, and the high-speed whine of the blender stopped all conversation.

Jack winked at Megan and nodded. He must have found out something worthwhile, Megan thought. Though what it was totally escaped her.

"A little more Sex, Jack?" Elaine asked.

"I think I've had all I can handle," Jack replied, then stood. "But thanks very much for your hospitality. And have fun in Bermuda."

"You can bet on that, hon." Elaine smiled at Megan. "Thanks for coming by. That was real nice of you. Are you doing the supervising on TeleSurv now that Gladys is out of the picture?''

"Yes."

"Mrs. Grokowbowski was a bear, wasn't she, Elaine?" Jack asked smoothly. "Did you know her very well?"

"I knew her type the minute I laid eyes on her," Elaine said. She poured herself a second drink and clinked the glass against the blender. "Everything I ever heard about her is bad. Whoever killed her probably had a good reason."

Before Jack or Megan could reply, the phone rang.

"We'll leave you to your call," Jack said, holding the door for Megan.

"Thanks, hon. You two be good tonight. Don't do anything I wouldn't!" She closed the door and grabbed the ringing phone, removing her heavy crystal earring. "Hell-o-o-!"

A big smile formed on her face. "Well, hello, sweetheart. I saw you on television. You sure handled yourself well!"

The smile faded a bit as the man on the other end replied sharply. Elaine took another swallow of her drink. "Okay. Okay. Yes, I'll be sure and bring it with me. Don't worry." She hung up the phone and gulped the last mouthful, then poured another. If he was in a nervous mood, worrying about dead Auntie Grim and the TeleSurv lists, tonight would be no fun at all.

"Come to Momma, baby," Elaine murmured and grabbed for the blender. "Probably the only sex I get tonight."

Chapter Thirteen

"What did Elaine say to make you smile like that?" Megan crossed her arms acorss her chest as Jack opened the car door for her.

"Get in. I'll tell you on the way to dinner."

"No, tell me now," Megan demanded. His high spirits made her feel dense. And that was one feeling she had had enough of from smug newsmen and tight-lipped cops the past couple of days to last a lifetime. "What did I miss?"

"She called Gladys '*Auntie* Grim.' And her 'boyfriend' owns the trailer. It's got to be Darren George! Don't you see, Megan? All I have to do is check the registration on the Airstream, and we've got him!" Jack gave Megan a bear hug, nearly lifting her off the ground.

"You think Darren seduced Elaine, then got her to skew the survey?" Megan's voice held the doubt her heart felt. She couldn't imagine a woman less Darren George's type than Elaine Jones.

"Sure. It's simple and obvious. Most cops say that's usually the case. He met her on purpose or accidentally, thought up the scam, and now he's probably sending her off to Bermuda until the heat dies down."

"What heat?" A chill raced down her arms. "You mean from the Reaper? Other than Norma Schutlz being a victim, there's still *no* connection at all between him and TeleSurv."

"I agree. But Sergeant McMurphy knows, thanks to you, that Norma and Gladys both worked for TeleSurv. My hunch is that Darren panicked at the thought McMurphy is looking at TeleSurv for any reason, so he's sending Elaine out of town to keep the cops from interviewing her."

"So you don't think he's the Reaper?"

"I don't know. But I'm sure he's not legitimately number one in my survey area!"

Megan frowned. Now he was disregarding mass murder for the sake of his business goals! "But what about Gladys? The cops are convinced the Reaper didn't kill her."

Jack's expression changed. "Right . . ."

She didn't want to ask the question, but Megan forced herself to. The words came in a rush. "Do you think Darren killed her because she found out what he was up to?"

"I don't know, Megan. I really don't. Even for a while there when I figured Darren was connected to the Reaper murders, I had trouble picturing the man capable of cold-blooded killing. Especially since Gladys Grokowbowski was his aunt!"

"There wasn't much love lost between them," Megan offered. "He didn't grieve at all."

"Dry eyes are no proof of anything, Megan. But let's check out the registration at the DMV. If Darren's name is on the trailer, it's a direct link to TeleSurv. We'll know more once a few of those links are joined." His eyes were shining with excitement.

"It's nearly seven. And Friday night. They are closed until Monday morning, Jack."

"God, I hate state agencies."

"Monday is soon enough," Megan said, relaxing for the first time tonight. "Now, did you **say** something about dinner?"

"Yes. But maybe we could check in the rental office. . . ."

Megan watched Jack turn and look in the direction of Trailer Haven's administrative building. Jack Gallagher was tenacious, and single-minded when it came ot his career. She'd seen that fact borne out several times today. It was an admirable trait that was probably necessary for success, she realized, but a sadness that felt like loss stung her senses.

Her earlier intuition was right. Jack the newsman consumed Jack the private person. "Wait and call the DMV Monday, Jack. Then let McMurphy take it from there."

"Maybe." He turned back to Megan. "You could do a little snooping yourself at the station, you know. Check out the phone logs, maybe. See if Eva Merritt's number showed up last November. Ask around if Darren's been seen with Elaine."

"No," she snapped. "This is a police case. If you think Dr. George is a suspect in his aunt's death, let them nail him."

Megan was right, he knew it. But the newsbound in him was straining at the bit, wanting to track a story. Scoop-happy he'd always been. Jack pointed to the Volkswagen. "Get in, gorgeous. Let's have dinner and drink and a dance or two."

"I need to call Mrs. Allen and tell her the kids won't be coming before I do another thing."

"Okay. Then you're all mine for the rest of the night." Jack hugged her again. She didn't return his embrace, but he refused to let that worry him. "When do we have to pick up Roxie and Thomas?"

"They're staying with Dean until Wednesday," she said, then clamped her mouth closed as if trying to keep other words from escaping. She turned and slid into the car.

Jack closed the door. He crouched down to look into her eyes through the open window. "Great! Then you're all mine until Wednesday." He gave her a quick kiss, loving the soft feel of her mouth on his. "Maybe we can take a picnic down to Indialantic and swim tomorrow. Get in the mood for a little Sex on the Beach? Elaine gave me the recipe."

He laughed, but she looked pained and turned away.

Jack hurried around the car and got in. Megan was probably jumpy because her ex-husband had her kids, he told hmself. She would be okay if he gave her a little time. He started the car and turned up the radio, singing along with Mick Jagger on "Under My Thumb."

Megan cringed at the saucy lyrics Jack was so energetically belting out, suddenly wishing she were home alone. This man just admitted he was glad to have her to himself for a few days. What further proof did she need that the responsibilities of her kids had weighed on him, despite his kind treatment of them? After all, he hadn't seen his own kid for ages.

"You okay, Megan?" Jack suddenly interrupted.

She took a deep breath. "I'm fine, Jack. But I'm not really in the mood to go out. Could you please just take me home?"

"Megan—"

"Please, Jack. I don't want to argue."

They stopped at a light, and Jack made a U-turn out and headed in the opposite direction toward her house. "Okay. Home it is."

She heard the confusion and disappointment in his voice, but hardened herself against it. Jack Gallagher was a big boy, she told herself. He would get over his hurt.

What she needed to concentrate on, Megan thought closing her eyes, was getting over hers.

THE WEEKEND FELT like it lasted three months, Jack thought as he dressed Monday morning. He had dialed Megan's number twenty times on Saturday, and got busy signals each time.

Unable to believe she had that much TeleSurv work to do, he finally called the operator to check the line. The tinny voice had reported back "no trouble," and Jack had been forced to accept the fact that she was busy and didn't want to talk to him. He gave her all of Sunday without another try, burying himself with work on his Grim Reaper investigation.

But today he was going to see her. And find out what the hell was going on.

She had not invited him in Friday, and had offered a cool cheek to kiss goodbye. Whatever had gone wrong had gone wrong fast. Well, as far as she was concerned, Jack told himself, they could right things just as quickly.

He pulled the back door closed with a slam and locked it. His glance shifted next door to the Hawkins's. Claude's truck was parked in the drive, but he had not seen Mona for days. He wanted to get her alone again, try to find out how she came by the TeleSurv list, but knew he had to wait for Claude to be out of the picture.

"Good morning, Mr. Gallagher!" a female voice sang out, interrupting Jack's thoughts.

He spun around and saw Edna Adams and Pollard Finch parked across the street. "Good morning, folks. Everything okay with you both?"

"We're fine, Mr. Gallagher," Finch hollered back.

Jack walked to the end of the drive and crossed over to them. "Things were pretty quiet all weekend. Looks like the Neighborhood Watch programs have done well by us."

"They have, they have," Edna agreed, rustling comfortably in her wheelchair. She was wearing an enormous straw hat with a faded orange sunflower. Its long green leaves cast shadows over the edge of the brim and across her face. "We're having another meeting tonight." She waved at the Sissler's house. "Right across the street from you. Hope you'll join us."

"Is your neighbor coming?" Pollard asked, pointing at Claude's house. "If he is, I hope he has the decency to be embarrassed about his abominable appearance on the tube a few nights ago."

Jack grinned at Pollard's peevishness. "I don't know if Claude's coming tonight or not. What's the meeting about?"

"I'm getting a committee together to help with a billboard we're erecting at the end of Country Club Drive, Mr. Gallagher," Pollard Finch said. His bald head glistened in the bright, cool morning. "Can you make it?"

"Sure. What's the billboard all about?"

"Pollard's working with the city on an antilittering campaign to make Melbourne beautiful," Edna explained. "It's his pet project you see. People littering the environment, giving no thought to the future."

"Very commendable," Jack replied, noting the stern look on Pollard's face. If the man's expression was any clue, litter was more than just a pet peeve to Pollard. "I'll see you both tonight."

"Be sure and bring Megan with you, too," Edna said.

He smiled at the older woman's tone of voice. Everybody loves a lover, he thought. "I'll call and let her know about the meeting, Miss Adams. Thanks."

Jack crossed the street and glanced at his watch. It was a little past seven-thirty. Since Megan didn't have to walk the kids to school, it was a good bet he could get to her now. He unlocked the house and went back in, but got only a busy signal for his efforts.

"Fine," he muttered aloud as he started the Volkswagen and pulled out of the drive five minutes later. If she wanted to leave the phone off the hook, there was nothing he could do to reach her now. But as soon as he was finished with the DMV, he was going to go to her house and sit on the front porch and wait for her to turn up. A weekend was enough time for her to get over whatever was bothering her. It was time to talk it out, and get past it.

It was time, way past time, to finish what they had started.

That thought brought a smile back to his face, and he roared down the street, looking forward to everything the day promised.

"GOOD MORNING, BABY. Did you get ready for school?" Megan listened to the phone receiver with a lump in her throat as Thomas gave her a glowing report about his weekend.

"Yes. But mom, you know what? Daddy got us real poles and real little fish to hook and catch the bigger ones. Mine got eaten off, Momma, but it was okay."

"That sounds like a lot of fun, Thomas. Now, you be a good boy at school today. Be sure and take your raincoat." Suddenly she remembered the note crushed inside his lunch box. Trying for a little more authority than she felt, Megan lowered her voice. "And listen, young man, I don't want another report of you leaving the school yard. Mr. Butz sent me a note saying you and another boy in your class left and took some things out of someone's mail box on Friday.''

"Uh-uh, mommy. I didn't take nothing. Mona gave us her stuff.''

"Mona? Mona Hawkins?'' Megan's heart began a faster, skipping rhythm. "You left school with Mona?''

"No. Me and Robert saw her on the playground. We just walked around the fence and she gave us her extra letters. Honest mum, we didn't steal them.''

Megan could see a trip to the school needed to be included in her day's agenda. The specter of Mona Hawkins stealing things out of mail boxes was as worrisome as Thomas running off. "Okay, Thomas, Momma believes you. But you and Robert are not to set one foot off the playground! I don't care who is on the other side of the fence. Do you hear me?''

Before Thomas could answer, Dean took the phone. "Megan? What's wrong? I've got to leave now or the kids are going to be late for school because of this rain.''

"Nothing. Thomas and I were just having a review of the rules.'' She realized she didn't want to tell Dean about the trouble, mostly because of an insanely possessive feeling that was devouring her right now. "How's it going? The kids making you nuts?''

"No. They're wonderful. You've done a great job with them, Megan. Reva and I have enjoyed every minute. We can't wait to have them for a longer visit.''

Longer visit? Megan felt herself stiffen. She told herself to keep her voice calm, although she knew Dean well enough to know he was up to something. "Great. May I speak with Roxie for a minute, please?''

"Hang on. Reva's french braiding her hair. Roxie's very impresed she knows how. I think she wants to lord it over her friend, Carrie. Hang on.''

Megan paced in a small, tight circle, hearing the giggles and voices over the phone wires and feeling more alone than ever. Finally her daughter picked up, breathless with excitement.

"Momma? I've got a french braid, and a new pink ribbon, and new sundresses! And a tiger stripped bathing suit. It cost $30.00! Daddy bought them!"

Megan gnawed the inside of her mouth raw. "How are you, sweetie? I can't wait to see you."

"I love you, Momma. See you sometime!" Roxie laughed and hung up, leaving a buzzing phone receiver in Megan's hand. She put it back on the cradle carefully, then went and stood underneath the shower. Her eyes stung with tears, but she refused to give into her feelings of self-pity. She washed her hair, then rubbed her body furiously with the washcloth, as if she could remove the ache and need she felt for Jack off her skin. It left her frustrated and jumpy.

She dried off and dressed, wrapping her wet hair into a tight bun and pinning it off her neck to dry. She had to be at the television station in two hours, so she might as well organize her checkbook. The bank draft from Dean fluttered out of her hand and to the floor when the sound of a car engine sent her running to the window.

"Jack?" she said aloud. Through the glass she recognized Darren George's Lincoln, and the disappointment was so real she felt a physical ache. A steady drizzle was picking up, and a crack of lightning brightened the dark sky to the east. Megan stepped back so the newsman couldn't see her and watched. He got out of the car and strode over and unlocked Gladys's house. He glanced in her direction once, then the door slammed behind him as he disappeared inside.

Megan frowned. There were at least a hundred good reasons why Darren was in his dead aunt's house, but something about his body language told her the anchorman was nervous about being there.

She picked up the folder of phone bills she'd lifted from the box of documents Sergeant McMurphy had given her to go over. She'd found Eva Merritt's number twice on the November bills Elaine Jones had been reimbursed for, which certainly proved a connection between Elaine and the woman who'd complained she'd been bribed.

Briefly she wondered what Jack was going to discover about the ownership of Elaine Jones's trailer. If Darren did own it, and they got Elaine to admit she bribed people... "Stop it!" Megan ordered herself aloud. In disgust she threw the phone bills into the box. It was time to call Sergeant McMurphy. Let the cop shuffle through this labrynth of clues.

Megan again looked out at the Grokowbowski house. At that moment Darren George emerged from the doorway, carrying two full black plastic trash bags. He unlocked the trunk of the Lincoln and put them inside, then slammed the lid closed. Shielding his eyes against the rain, he looked toward Megan's apartment.

She shrank back against the wall, fear suddenly chilling her. She was alone, the screen door unlatched. Had Darren George cold-bloodedly murdered his aunt a few nights ago? Wiping her clammy hands against her shorts, she hurried toward the door. With a flip of the latch she locked the screen, then tensed silently and listened for Darren's step on the stairway. The rain was louder now, and thunder rumbled from the ocean with increased menace. The temperature felt as if it had dropped ten degrees in the past five minutes.

Megan shivered and wrapped her arms around her body. Several seconds later she heard a door opening beneath the porch, then a minute later a dull thud. The hair on the back of her neck rose as another sound drifted up from the ground floor garage. A human sound? Had she heard a cry for help?

She unlatched the door and walked out onto the landing. The rain had stopped, but the ominous fullness of the black clouds above her warned of an imminent donwpour. What was Darren doing in the garage? Megan wondered. Had Gladys stored anything of value in there?

What noise had she heard?

Hesitantly she walked down six of the fourteen stairs and bent down to peer through one of the dusty windows running in a row across the top of the garage door. "Dr. George?" she called out. Silence followed, save for the sounds of a trash truck a block away. "Dr. George? Are you okay in there?"

There was no light on in the garage, but Megan suddenly remembered the burned-out bulb she had never replaced. The image of Dr. George stumbling around in the dark, possibly knocking over some of the junk piled to the ceiling came to mind. Without another thought, Megan hurried down the remaining steps and around to the side entrance.

The door was closed. "Dr. George?" Megan called. The knob was cold in her hand when she turned it. The door was stuck, swollen with the humidity and years of neglect. Using her shoulder to push, Megan banged the door open. As she did the storm broke above, dumping sheets of rain, which obliterated the house a hundred feet away.

"Dr. George?" she asked again, cold and shaking, her heart thumping faster from the spookiness of the garage and the exertion of getting in. A movement to the right caught her eye and Megan turned toward it. Before she could scream the man lunged for her, gripping his hands around her throat and hurling them both to the filthy cement floor.

Dark eyes glared through the eyeholes of the ski mask, outlined in the garish purple that seemed to floruesce in the murky shadows. Megan gagged and writhed beneath her attacker, fighting for breath.

A glimmer of remembrance from a self-defence course shimmered to mind. "Move your hands," a voice scolded. "Hit him back!" As her consciousness began to slip into the spinning pit of fear her mind had become, Megan stabbed her fingers at the madman's eyes. The mask was soft against her skin, but a tiny thrill of victory skittered through her as she recognized skin and the curve of an eyelid. The monster holding her groaned, then slapped a sickly smelling cloth against her nose.

Megan fought the urge to gag as the fumes burned along her nasal passages. Then blackness descended while her scream of rage died with her consciousness.

"MEGAN. MEGAN. TRY TO OPEN your eyes." Jack leaned over the hospital bed and stroked her forehead.

"Let her rest, Mr. Gallagher. She'll wake up soon enough. She's still in shock," the nurse ordered in clipped tones.

Jack turned and stared at the woman, then glanced at the doctor standing on the other side of the bed. Sergeant Peter McMurphy frowned as the doctor shook his head.

Jack kissed her bruised mouth gently and went out into the hall with the doctor and the policeman. "Why the IV?" he asked the doctor.

"Standard procedure on concussions. We don't want her to get dehydrated."

"Why isn't she awake yet?" Jack demanded. It seemed like hours since he'd found her on the floor of the grimy garage. His pulse raced at the memory. For a second he'd been paralyzed with fear; he'd thought she was dead. When he touched her neck to feel for a pulse he had nearly cried with relief.

"It takes time, Mr. Gallagher. Trust me, she's going to be fine." The doctor walked off and Sergeant McMurphy motioned Jack to join him in the small lobby two doors down from Megan's room.

The cop looked as bad as Jack felt, Jack found himself thinking.

McMurphy's face was heavily lined with fatigue. He took out a leather notebook and read quietly for a moment. "Tell me why you looked in the garage for Megan."

"Her laundry basket was dumped next to the front door. It was full of clean clothes. I thought she might have gone back for something," Jack replied.

"And you saw no one?"

"No one." Jack shook his head.

"But what's your hunch? You're a newsman, after all. Give me an educated guess."

Jack locked eyes with the cop, anger flaring. Obviously the cop had checked him out. But he couldn't do anything about that now.

What was important was Megan. And finding and punishing the animal who'd attacked her so viciously. Quietly he began to tell McMurphy the story behind his leaving WMMB and his theory on the TeleSurv scam.

"I looked into that Merritt woman's death. Nothing odd about it at all," McMurphy interjected gruffly. "You never did get any proof that the survey was stacked, despite her letter, did you?"

"Not yet. But I'm working on it."

"Humph. And while you're working on it, you're thinking whoever killed Gladys Grokowbowski and attacked Megan might be involved, right?"

Jack's nerves zinged. The cop's voice grated nearly as much as his doubtful attitude. "It's possible."

"What would be the motive for ruining a survey?"

"Age old reason. Greed. To get ahead."

"I see." McMurphy made another note. "You mean it had to be someone in the news business who'd stand to profit."

"You understand me, sergeant."

"I think I do, Mr. Gallagher. Got any likely candidates?" His lip quivered. It was obvious he knew Jack had someone in mind, but he was going to make him name names before he listened any further.

Jack took a deep breath. "Darren George."

The cop surprised him by showing no surprise whatsoever at the mention of the anchorman's name. "Got any proof?"

Jack recounted how Megan had been told by Gladys to fire Elaine Jones, and that Elaine Jones was the interviewer who had called Eva Merritt. He then told McMurphy about visiting the woman's home, and pulled the slip of paper from his pocket. "I think Elaine implied she knew Gladys Grokowbowski was Darren's aunt. And she said her boyfriend owned the Airstream."

McMurphy took the piece of paper, then his tired eyes darted back to search Jack's face. "Where'd you get this information?"

"DMV."

The cop tucked the note away in his pocket. "You know this George fellow personally?"

"No."

"Ever hear any rumors in the business that he was a gambler with a lot of debts to the wrong kind of debtors? Someone he works with told me he unloaded some big-ticket items lately just to raise cash."

Jack's heart pounded. He had heard some talk that Darren lived way over his head, but had discounted the comments as envy. "A few. Why?"

McMurphy smiled. He was not about to answer any of Jack's questions. "But you didn't see him today at Mrs. Summers's house?"

"No." Jack felt excitement churning through his veins. Though the cop hadn't said so, he must have been investigating Darren all along. "Did your guys get any prints from her apartment?" The place had looked like a tornado had passed through it, Jack recalled. Books, papers, kids' toys, food from the cupboards dumped all over the floor. Whoever had searched her house had been thorough, as well as savagely messy.

"Thousands. Do you know where her kids are?"

"They're staying with their dad until Wednesday." Jack filled the cop in on the pertinent details. "I know Megan will want to talk with them and reasure them she's okay as soon as she wakes up."

McMurphy raised his bushy eyebrows. "You don't want me calling them, is that it?"

Jack smiled. "It's just that I know how Megan is about her kids. She'd be furious if we scared them."

At that moment the nurse came to the waiting room door and crooked a finger at Jack. "Mrs. Summers is awake. She's asking for you."

Jack hopped to his feet and jogged to her room. He was at the bedside in seconds. "Hey, lady. How are you doing?"

The nurse had cranked the bed to a sitting position. A glass of ice chips and a straw were sitting on the table next to Megan. Though still unnaturally pale, Jack thought she looked better than a few minutes before.

When he kissed her, Megan's eyes filled with tears. She swallowed, wincing with pain. Her voice was a rough whisper. "Jack, will you call Roxie and Thomas for me? Tell them I'm okay, and I'll be at school to pick them up Wednesday.''

"Of course. I'll call them as soon as they get out of class." He gently pushed back her hair from her forehead.

"Mrs. Summers. Are you up to answering a few questions?" Sergeant McMurphy walked up next to Jack, still clutching his notebook.

"Yes," Megan whispered.

The cop moved to the other side of the bed and sat down. "Take your time, Mrs. Summers."

Megan glanced at Jack, then swallowed slowly. She recounted her morning's activity. When she told them she had watched Darren George come out of his aunt's house, then disappear in the direction of the garage, both men's expressions changed.

The cop looked deadly serious, Jack murderous. After a minute of talking her throat felt as if it were bleeding, and she asked Jack for some water.

He gave her the glass, holding the straw in her swollen lips. His face had drained of all color at her story, and he was finding concentration difficult. He wanted to leave and find Darren George. If the man had laid a hand on Megan, Jack swore to himself, he'd live, but only long enough to regret hurting her.

"Did you see Darren Geroge inside the garage?"

Megan shook her head no. Then, in halting phrases, she told the cop about the ski mask. "It was the same one as the man's who attacked me at Jack's. He was the same size. I think it was the same man."

"Was he dressed the same?"

"No." She paused a few moments and took more water. Her head was aching and she felt nauseated, but she knew the infomation was crucial and forced herself to go on. "Differently."

McMurphy's pen made scratching sounds across the paper. "What did he have on?"

"Dark pants and a blue shirt." Megan said. "And a badge. I think it was a Melbourne police uniform."

Chapter Fourteen

"A police uniform! My, my, my, my, my! Won't the viewers eat that little tidbit up!"

Megan gasped and Jack swung around at the sound of Darren George's voice. "What are you doing here, George?" Jack demanded. He took a step toward Darren.

The newsman, holding a pot of pink azaleas, retreated.

"Hang on, Mr. Gallagher," Pete McMurphy called out from the other side of the room.

Darren bobbed his head around Jack's menacing figure and flashed a smile at the cop. "Sergeant! Didn't see you when I first came in. How's our girl doing? You coppers run down the perpetrator yet?"

"How'd you hear about Mrs. Summers?" McMurphy asked.

"I have one of the reporters monitoring police calls at all times." Darren flashed a sharkish smile. "We wouldn't want to miss it when you bag the Reaper. Or Mrs. Summers's attacker, either. Especially if they're one in the same and he's a cop. Care to comment on the record with a hunch about the crimes?"

"Get the hell out of here, George," Jack bellowed, clutching his fists at his side.

"What's your problem, Gallagher? Got a Rambo complex?" Darren said. He walked around Jack and stood beside Megan's bed, waving the flower pot. "You don't mind my showing my condolences, do you Megan? Call off Rover here, so we can talk.''

"Jack," Megan rasped. "Please don't make it worse—"

"Why don't you come outside with me, Mr. George?" McMurphy cut in, his arm out in invitation. "I have a few questions I need to ask you."

Darren blinked, then rubbed a spot below his eye that was swollen. "Just a minute. I want to see how Megan is."

Looking close, Jack saw the anchorman had on the pancake foundation makeup he wore on screen. "What happened to your eye?" Jack asked, moving closer. His anger was beginning to boil.

Darren smiled and patted his cheek. "Got smacked by an oleander bush this morning when I was carrying out trash crates. As a public figure I've got to do my civic duty." He set the pot of flowers down on the table and sat on the end of Megan's bed.

"Sorry I didn't come to your rescue, Megan. I can't for the life of me figure out how I didn't see you go into that garage. I was right outside the door, behind the shed. If it hadn't been storming, I'm sure I would have heard you."

"You didn't hear a thing, I suppose?" Jack asked.

"Of course not, Gallagher. Or I would have helped! It's outrageous," Darren continued, staring at McMurphy. "First my aunt, now sweet little Megan! If it turns out this guy was the Reaper, you're going to have a revolt on your hands if you don't arrest someone soon."

"I agree," offered McMurphy, his tone mild. "But don't worry, we're working on it."

"I'd suggest working a little harder, sergeant." Darren's voice had a sharper edge to it then before. He looked at Megan as he stuck his hand inside his navy blazer and pulled out an envelope. "Here, sweetheart. Your first check. It's only minimum wage, but I figured you'd be needing it."

Megan licked her lips. She began to tremble and had a flash of hot followed by a chill. "What are you talking about?" she replied, seeing the blank look on Darren's face. "I'm not entitled to get paid for work. I'm an intern!"

"We pay all our interns, sweetie. Didn't I mention that? It's a bonus for working at the number one rated news station in East Florida."

"I can't accept it—"

"—Why?" Darren interrupted, then patted Megan's arm. "Oh, come on, now. Don't worry about my little fit of temper last week. I've worked all that out. I don't really care if you're dating the *ex*-news director of a second-rate competitor." He turned on his heel and met McMurphy at the door. "Take care, Megan. Let me know if I can help out."

McMurphy opened the door, and the two men left.

Jack felt himself flush hot at Darren's words, but put his own anger on hold. Megan began to cry. "Hey, don't be upset, honey. I won't let that baboon near you. And neither will McMurphy."

"It's not that," Megan said. She picked up the white envelope Darren had dropped on her blanket. "This money is going to cost me my job at TeleSurv! I can't be paid for working at a television station, for God's sake!"

Jack pushed the envelope aside and sat beside her on her bed. "It's okay. Don't worry about this. It's probably just another trick of Darren's. It might even prove to the cops how interested he is in fouling up TeleSurv and covering his tracks. He might even be trying to blackmail you—"

"—But Jack—"

"Visitors' hours are over!" A nurse announced from the door. "Time to leave, sir. Mrs. Summers needs her rest."

"Trust me, Megan. It's going to be okay. Rest." He leaned down and kissed her.

Megan watched him leave, then closed her eyes in exhaustion as the nurse strapped the blood pressure belt around her arm. Trust me, he'd said. She wanted to, Megan realized. This last miserable two days without him had proved that.

But should she?

Could she trust *any* of them?

"Good girl," the nurse cooed. "Your pressure's all back to normal." She disconnected the IV and handed Megan her glass. "Now, drinks lots of fluids. After a shock, you have to keep lots of liquid in you."

"Okay," Megan replied. She downed a couple of ounces of water then tossed off the blanket. She winced at the sound of the envelope hitting the linoleum floor. That check proved that forces somewhere were trying to trip up her plan for success. Maybe it was time to be a little more active on her own behalf, Megan realized.

"Can I get you something, hon?" the nurse asked, alarm coloring her voice.

Gingerly Megan moved her legs over the side of the bed and stretched her toes. "Yes, thank you. You can get me to the cashier so I can check out of this place."

JACK CAUGHT UP WITH McMurphy in the hospital parking lot. The cop was sitting in an unmarked sedan, calling in his report over the radio. Darren George was nowhere in sight.

"...And tell the captain the search warrant needs to cover the contents of the trunk of the car as well as the inside of the home."

The dispatcher's voice came out of the car radio with a burst of static. "Roger. Dark blue Lincoln, william allen baby robin, number one. Right, sir?"

"Correct. I'll be back in the station within the hour, so tell Barnes and Martinez to be ready to go right out." McMurphy looked up and caught sight of Jack. The policeman frowned.

"We'll get the judge's signature and the warrant will be ready in an hour, sergeant." the radio voice crackled.

McMurphy clicked the handset off and looked up to meet Jack's stare. "What do you need, Gallagher?"

Jack slipped his hands into his pocket and nodded at the radio. "Sounds like a good idea. I'm sure there's something interesting inside those trash bags George ferreted away before Megan's attack."

"Yeah? You wouldn't also think he kayoed your girlfriend in there?" McMurphy leaned back against the cracked vinyl seat, slipped a pocketknife out of his pocket and began to clean under his thumbnail with a lethal-looking pick attached to the knife.

Jack stiffened. "If he did, he's going to have more than a search warrant to contend with. Did you see his eye? It looked like something scratched it—"

"—Dr. George said a bush clipped him." McMurphy didn't look up.

Crossing his arms, Jack leaned against the unmarked car. "Convenient."

"We've got a skin sample from under Mrs. Summers's fingernail." McMurphy smiled a rare smile. "Isn't technology great?"

Jack wanted to say more, but bit his tongue. The cops were investigating Darren George, that much was obvious. They didn't need Jack sounding off any more. He'd told McMurphy about Elaine Jones and the TeleSurv connection. If George was a suspect in his aunt's death, that fact alone was enough to keep the anchorman in the hot seat. Jack straightened up and extended his hand to McMurphy. "Thanks a lot for showing up so fast today, sergeant."

McMurphy cast his eyes toward Jack. He folded up his knife, then slowly reached for Jack's hand. "Mrs. Summers is going to be fine, Gallagher. You take care of her. *We'll* take care of the sicko who attacked her."

"You think it was the Reaper?" Jack asked, his tongue moving slowly over the fearful words.

"You think Darren George is the Reaper?"

"No. I don't know."

"Neither do I."

"What about the fact the guy was wearing a uniform?" Jack pressed.

A strained look passed over the cop's features. "What about it? Right now it's just a fact. What it means remains to be seen. I'm late, Gallagher." McMurphy pulled his door shut and gunned the engine.

Jack watched the cop turn left out of the parking lot, then he jogged over to his Volkswagen. The memory of a news story he'd worked on years before flashed through his mind. A cop in Kansas City turned homicidal maniac, knocking off five friends of his before anyone caught on he was the guilty party.

Jack glanced in the direction of McMurphy's car. It was headed north, toward Trailer Haven. Was Elaine Jones still home or had she left on her trip to Bermuda? Jack rolled his head around to get rid of a crick in his shoulder. McMurphy's little trick of cleaning his nails with the jagged tool on his pocketknife was making him paranoid. The cop didn't act creepy enough to be a serial killer, Jack told himself.

Then he thought of the cool good looks of Ted Bundy, and the elegant calm of the Kansas City Killer cop he'd seen close up. His brain's rationale did nothing to dissipate the unease he felt in his gut.

"Mr. Gallagher."

Jack turned, shocked to hear his name. He spotted Pollard Finch getting out of his vintage Plymouth, and in surprise watched as Claude Hawkins limped out of the passenger's side, holding a small bunch of yellow daisies.

"What in the hell . . ." Jack swore under his breath. "Hi. What brings you both out here?"

"We heard about Mrs. Summers." Pollard Finch called out. "This is dreadful. Unbelievable! The authorities are even more moronic and inept than we thought!"

Jack's stomach turned over. "How did you hear about Megan?"

"It's on the television," Claude offered.

He was wearing his trademark overalls, which looked as grimy as usual, but Jack noted that the man's hair appeared to be combed. "The television? The news?" Jack asked, walking up to Pollard's car.

"Yeah. I was home watching one of the soaps 'cause Mona's at school. That news fellow what came out to the house the other day asking about knife marks cut right into 'All My Children' with a 'Special Bulletin.' Said Mrs. Summers was attacked, maybe by that Reaper character."

"What!"

"It's reprehensible!" Pollard thundered.

Jack looked back and forth between the two men, more furious with each passing second. *Thomas and Roxie.* The possibility that Megan's kids could have heard about her attack in such a ghoulish manner set him into motion.

"Are you going to see Megan?" Jack asked.

Pollard nodded. "Yes. Edna insisted I come and tell her we'd watch the children for her if she needed us."

"And I'm sure Mona's going to want to come," Claude offered, then glanced away. "She likes Mrs. Summers a whole big much."

"Well, give her my love. I've got to leave but I'll be back in an hour or so." Jack ran back to his car and gunned the motor, laying down three yards of rubber as he left the parking lot. It was only one o'clock. He would swing by Elaine's and still be at school when the kids were picked up by their dad.

The thought of meeting Megan's ex-husband gave his stomach another lurch, but he pushed his personal concerns aside. Right now he had to check and make sure Elaine Jones was okay.

His pulse pounded over what he regarded as the less-than-ethical way Darren's station had broadcast news of Megan's attack. They showed absolutely no restraint in broadcasting half-truths and speculation, all in the hopes of garnering a bigger viewing share.

Had he ever been that ruthless? Jack asked himself. He cruised up to the intersection at Trailer Haven and looked both ways. There was no trace of McMurphy's faded brown sedan, proving that his paranoia had been unfounded, Jack realized. He turned in the driveway, absorbed by a second question that was unavoidable.

Could he be that ruthless in the future?

For the past few weeks, working on his story of the Grim Reaper murders and the TeleSurv scam, his priorities had shifted. The redheaded woman who monopolized more and more of his thoughts was partially the reason for this change.

But a basic uneasiness with how he operated, had to operate, as a newsman was part of it, too, Jack realized.

Chasing news stories was a lot like chasing ambulances. You felt empathy for the victims, but also a kind of hyped-up excitement at being close to tragedy. At the time, it always seemed justified to ask questions like, "How did you feel when you found the body?"

Jack cringed at memories that rushed through him, and tried to make his mind go blank. He firmly believed a free press was the backbone of a free country. But right now, weighing what he'd done and what he'd planned to do made him wish he had never started his private investigation of Darren George.

Jack turned off the engine and got out of the car. He walked toward Elaine's, remembering Friday's conversation. She'd been hospitable and open, and he'd hidden the truth, both of his profession and his reason for being in her home.

Maybe now was the time to present Elaine Jones with the whole truth, Jack thought. Lay it all out for her, see if she'd nail Darren George on the scam. He grinned, liking that possibility. It wasn't a wise reporter's move, but he knew Megan would approve of the direct approach.

His knuckles rapped sharply against the metal door. After several seconds, he knocked a second time. But Elaine didn't answer. He looked around, then caught sight of an elderly lady in the next trailer peering at him through the curtains. She was a Slavic-looking woman of about eighty, with a thick bun of white hair topping her regal head.

Jack waved back, then crossed to her lawn and knocked on the door.

The woman answered immediately. "Hello. Can I help you, young man?"

"Hello. Yes, maybe you can. My name is Jack Gallagher. I'm looking for Elaine Jones, your neighbor. Have you seen her today?"

"Elaine's gone, young man," the woman replied with a smile. "She and that boyfriend of hers carted out three big red American Tourister suitcases late last night. Looks to me like Elaine is going on a long vacation."

Jack grinned, noting how detailed the woman's observation was. "Do you know her boyfriend's name?"

The woman gave Jack a feigned look of shock. "We stay pretty much to our own business here, young man. Elaine never did say his name, even though several other people asked her." She laughed, a girl's lilting giggle. "Mrs. Yablonski, who lives behind me in the Airstream with the New Jersey tag said he was a news reporter on TV. I never did see him clear, but I did see his car once. Big, dark Lincoln with the radio station call letters on the tag."

Jack's pulse sped up, and his throat tightened in excitement. "Is Mrs. Yablonski home, do you know?"

"No. She went to Mobile. Her second daughter is having a baby and she's looking after the children for her until the baby's due. Should be back next month, though, if you'd like to come back."

"Thanks very much, ma'am." Jack grinned, knowing he was being flirted with. A sudden thought made him risk pushing the woman's curiosity to a nervous level. "Is anyone picking up Elaine's mail or watching the trailer for her? I'd really like to get in touch with her about a business matter as soon as possible."

"Check at the office. Beulah McKinney will have the information. She's the rental agent. Tell her Anne Babba sent you."

"Here's my card if you should hear from Mrs. Yablonski. And thank you, Mrs. Babba—"

"—It's Miss, young man. And you're welcome."

Jack hurried toward the rental office, the news Miss Babba yielded lightening his step. Despite his earlier feelings about his job, he was pumped up with adrenaline again. He could see the story unfolding, the shots of Darren George intercut with interviews of TeleSurv officials, even old Sherman Royal himself.

It was a great story! And it was his!

POLLARD FINCH CRUISED up to the curb in front of the elementary school and looked over the top of his glasses at

Megan. "Are you sure you wouldn't rather go straight home, dear? I could come back for your children."

"No, thanks, Mr. Finch. I'm just going to get out and wait for them, then walk up the block." She touched her head. "I feel like I could use a little exercise after a morning in the hospital."

"Think you should have stayed put, little lady," Claude Hawkins said from the back seat. "Bumps on the head can be pretty bad stuff. You might be getting the blackouts, throw up and stuff."

"I'll be fine, Mr. Hawkins." She smiled and unlocked the car.

"I'm going to drop your flowers by your house for you. I could come back," Pollard said.

"No. Really, please go on. And thanks again for bringing me home. You showed up at just the right time." She slammed the heavy car door and waved, unwilling to admit that she felt weary and a touch light-headed. The doctor had thrown a fit when she checked out, but Megan hadn't cared. She wanted to see her kids, assure them she was okay, then go home and sleep for the next two days.

A brief thought of Jack flitted across her mind, but she pushed it aside. Slowly she walked up to the school office and sat stiffly on the stone bench outside it. The sunshine felt good in her face, and she closed her eyes. Immediately the image of her mask-clad attacker loomed into her consciousness, and her body began to tremble.

The second attack had been more vicious than her first encounter. It had also been more frightening. Something about the man was familiar. Not only familiar from the earlier meeting, but a smell, a body shape, something about the man had rung a bell. Did she know him? Megan opened her eyes and stood, rubbing her hands up and down her arms to keep warm. If only she could think what it was, who it was . . .

"Megan! My God, what are you doing here?"

Megan blinked, then swallowed. Dean was standing five feet from her, his hands on his waist. The look on his face told her he'd somehow heard what had happened. "I'm fine, Dean. I just came to see the kids and tell them I'll be here Wednesday.''

He stomped across the asphalt and crossed his arms on his chest. In his navy jacket and white slacks, he looked the epitome of a salesman. "Shouldn't you be in the hospital? The news bulletin I heard said you'd been attacked, for Christ's sake!''

"I'm fine." She looked around in a panic as kids began to stream out of the classrooms from all directions. "Please keep your voice down and don't act so alarmed. You'll scare Roxie and Thomas to death!''

"I'll tell you what's going to scare them to death! The fact their mother was attacked where they live, possibly by a mass murderer! Really, Megan, we need to talk about making some other living arrangements. I can't allow—''

"—It's not up to you to *allow* anything, Dean. I have sole custody of the children. I'll take the very best possible care of them, just like I have for the past *several* years since you dropped out of their lives. So don't lecture me!''

Her quick response seemed to cool Dean's temper, but he thrust his chin out as if he didn't like what she said. "Fine. This isn't the place to discuss the children. But I do want you to realize that I've decided to modify the custody arrangements in the near future.''

"*You've decided*. Are you practicing family law on the side?''

Dean flinched, then softened his tone. "I miss the kids, Megan. And Reva wants a family—''

"—So tell her to have one," Megan snapped.

"Mommy!''

Megan clamped her teeth together and turned as Thomas came running toward her, his chubby face wreathed in a smile. She leaned down and hugged him, covering his face with kisses as tears burned in her eyes. She blinked them away quickly, not wanting him to see anything but her usual controlled self. "Hey, big buddy. How are you? Mommy just wanted to come by for a kiss.''

"Hi, Daddy," Thomas said, then wrapped his arms around his mother. His bright eyes widened as he spotted the bandage across Megan's scalp. His fingers reached and touched it. "What happened to your head, Mommy?"

"I just bumped myself, baby. I'm fine."

"Mommy! Daddy!" Roxie ran up and threw herself at her mother, strands of red hair streaming around her face. "You're both here! Are we all going back to the hotel? You'll love it, Mommy. They bring food to your room!"

Dean's face contorted at the happiness in his daughter's voice. He glanced nervously at Megan, not sure of what she was going to do next. "Mommy's going to her house, honey."

"I want Mommy to go to the hotel, too!" Thomas chimed in, his arm tightening around his mother's neck. "I don't want you to leave!"

Gently she unlaced her son's arms from her neck and stood up, forcing her voice to sound cheery. "I can't come today, kids. I've got TeleSurv calls to make and homework from school. But how about if I come see you tomorrow night?"

"That'd be great," Dean cut in. "You can join us for dinner and meet Reva. She's anxious to discuss some plans she's making for the children this summer."

"Oh?"

Dean's jaw quivered. "Now, don't get your back up. She's very anxious to be a good stepmother, Megan."

"How nice." Stepmother. Her kids were going to have a stepmother. She shuddered internally at this less-than-pleasant thought. Struggling to keep her tone light, she smiled. "Well, I'd love to come have dinner at the hotel tomorrow. Now, you guys run along, Momma wants to talk to Mr. Butz for a moment." She kissed them both quickly and turned away. Dean must have already talked to them about her mishap, because they hadn't brought it up. If they did by tomorrow, she already had an explanation in mind.

Megan hurried into the principal's office without a backward glance. She closed the door behind her and stood with clenched fists, forcing herself to regain control.

After a moment she walked to the front counter. No one was in sight, but she heard movement from the small room used as the nurse's office. "Mr. Butz?" she called.

There was on response from the next room, but Megan was sure she heard the floor creak. She glanced through the floor-to-ceiling windows at the bustle outside, willing her chill bumps away.

The Grim Reaper was not waiting in the next room, she told herself. And she better get a grip. Slowly she pushed the gate to the office open and walked toward the dark room. "Who's in there?"

Something bumped against the wall, and Megan flicked on the light. Mona Hawkins was hunched in the corner on the floor. Her head was hidden inside her arms, and her shoulders shook with silent crying.

"Mona? Honey, what is it?" Megan knelt beside the girl and put her arms around her. "Don't be afraid, Mona. Tell me what's wrong. I'll help you."

"Mona is sorry," the girl said in a strangled voice. She was crying out loud now, and banged her forehead repeatedly against her knees.

"It's okay. Don't cry. What are you sorry about, honey?"

The girl picked up her head and looked at Megan. Fear made her eyes huge. "Mona killed the lady. Mona is going to jail!"

Chapter Fifteen

The blood drained out of Megan's face. Her head began to throb when she squeezed Mona's hand. "What lady, Mona?"

"Mona doesn't know her name. The mean lady."

"Mrs. Grokowbowski?"

Mona stared at her blankly.

"Gladys? The lady who lived in the house in front of my apartment?" Megan asked, dread, liquid and hot, churning through her.

Mona shook her head yes, then returned to the silent sobbing, her head buried against her knees.

"I'll be right back, honey." Megan hurried into the outer office just as Jack burst through the door.

"Megan, my God, what are you doing here?"

"I wanted to see my kids."

"I was coming to tell them you were okay. I guess I was a little late. Elaine Jones—"

"—You went to see Elaine Jones again?"

"Yes." Suddenly he flushed. For some reason he felt like he had let Megan down in some basic, important way. "Her neighbor saw her leave last night. I checked the airlines, and she had a ticket booked. But she never boarded the plane."

Megan had a knot in her throat equal to the one on her head. "Elaine's missing?"

"It's a little early to say that, but it doesn't look too good."

"You'll have to tell McMurphy," Megan replied curtly. Jack, the bloodhound, had good intentions, but it was clear to her his pursuit of Darren George had top priority. Hearing a low sob from Mona, she forced her mind back to the present and picked up a nearby phone book and began thumbing through it. Claude Hawkins better be home, she prayed. His daughter needed him.

"What's going on?" Jack's voice was full of concern. He watched Megan scribble down a phone number, then turned toward the dark office where Mona sat sobbing. "I came up here to find you when the hospital told me you'd checked yourself out. For what my opinion is worth, I think you better let me take you back."

"I'm not going back to the hospital." Megan looked away and dialed Claude Hawkins's number, then held up her hand for Jack to be quiet. "Mr. Hawkins. This is Megan Summers. Could you please come up to the elementary school right away? Mona is here, and I think we've got a small problem."

Jack crossed to the door of the second office and frowned at the distraught figure huddled beside the small cot. He looked back at Megan, meeting her eyes as she hung up the phone. "What's happened?"

Megan ignored him. "You better tell McMurphy about Elaine. Even if it blows your scoop. She could be in trouble."

Jack flinched, then followed her into the room where Mona was hunched on the floor. He went into the room, kneeling beside the girl. "Mona. Are you all right, honey?"

Mona sobbed and sniffed, but gave Jack a weak smile.

He patted her hand and rose, crossing back to where Megan was dialing a second telephone number. "Who are you calling now?"

"Pete McMurphy."

Jack put his hand on the phone. "Wait a minute, is Mona connected to this thing somehow? Tell me what's going on, then—"

"—Stop it, Jack. We're not investigating this anymore on our own. This is police business."

"Megan!" Jack sighed in exasperation. He knew she was right, but if he could get the jump on the police with what Mona had to tell, phone his old station... Suddenly Jack stopped his mind's race through the facts. What was wrong with him? he questioned himself silently. It was reprehensible to take advantage of this situation. He was acting no better than Darren George.

"Sergeant McMurphy? This is Megan Summers. Could you meet me at the Melbourne Lower School as soon as possible?" She paused a frown creasing her brow. "I understand how busy you are, sergeant. But this is urgent." Cut off by the cop a second time, Megan chewed her lip. A school bell filled the air with a deafening noise, then stopped to eerie stillness. Megan let her impatience show. "You have to come. Mona Hawkins may have seen who killed Gladys Grokowbowski."

THE STORY WAS PIECED together after two tortuous hours of stressed temper on Claude Hawkins's part and half-sentence answers and tears from Mona. When they convinced her she hadn't killed the older woman, she calmed enough to give a straighter version.

Megan stayed through the ordeal at Mona's request. Jack refused to leave without her. McMurphy and Officer Judy Barnes had arrived within minutes of her phone call and explanation marching in with the flustered-looking principal in tow.

McMurphy, after Hawkins had come to be with his daughter, agreed to conduct Mona's interview in Mr. Butz's office instead of taking the girl into the precinct. The principal and Jack had been asked to wait outisde, but Megan was allowed to sit with Claude and Mona.

The sergeant nodded to his officer to read back Mona's statement one last time so they they could all go home.

Judy Barnes licked her thin lips. "I changed it to using 'I' instead of 'Mona' like we agreed." Clearing her throat, she read in an emotionless voice. "I, Mona Hawkins, entered the home of Mrs. Gladys Grokowbowski the night of March 8, without knocking or gaining approval from Mrs. Grokowbowski. I wanted to see the clock, and thought the woman was not at home.

"The kitchen was dark, and a glass of liquid was spilled on the floor. When I went into Mrs. Grokowbowski's living room, I heard voices from the bedroom. A man and a woman were arguing about something. I heard the man say, 'We're changing the plans.' The woman made a sound like a cry. I was scared and hid behind the green-flowered couch. A little while later a person walked out of the bedroom.

"I did not see this person.

"When the person was standing in the living room, I heard Mrs. Megan Summers call Mrs. Grokowbowski from the back door. The person in the living room went back into the bedroom.

"When Mrs. Summers left, the person went to the front door and went out. When the person shut the front door, I went into Mrs. Grokowbowski's room. She was staring at me, and had blood on her clothes. I ran out of the front door and hid in the bushes. I found a piece of paper there, which I kept and put in my pocket. It said Megan on it.

"When I heard the police cars coming I ran home."

Officer Barnes stopped and stared at Mona. "Did I get it right?"

Mona stared at the policewoman, then turned to her father.

"Tell the truth now, gal. Don't be being afraid of nothing. Your daddy's here," Claude urged.

"Yes," Mona asnwered.

"And you didn't see anyone or anything else when you ran home? Are you sure about that, Mona?" Pete McMurphy asked.

Mona stared at Megan. Megan smiled her encouragement. "It's okay, Mona. You're doing really well."

Mona looked at Sergeant McMurphy. "Mona did see a car. The car almost hit Mona. A man with yellow hair was driving."

"What kind of car was it? Can you tell us what it looked like?" McMurphy asked.

The girl dropped her head, and the adults in the room exchanged tense glances.

"It was black. A long, black car."

"Are you sure it wasn't blue, Mona?" McMurphy questioned. "Dark blue, like your daddy's overalls?"

Mona darted a glance at her father, then shrugged her shoulders. "Mona don't know."

Judy Barnes made more notes, a tiny smile of satisfaction on her round face.

Megan looked through the glass out to the waiting room. Jack was pacing; Mr. Butz was staring into space. Both men seemed to be wrestling with private demons, so engrossed were they in their thoughts.

Megan stared at Mona, a sudden thought leaping from her mouth before she considered the consequences. "Have you ever seen the man driving the black car before, Mona?"

"We'll ask the questions—"

"It's okay, Judy," McMurphy barked. He looked at Megan and winked. "Go ahead and answer, Mona. Mrs. Summers asked a very important question."

Mona sat for a moment and stared at the floor, then spoke. Her eyes remained downcast, but her voice sounded relieved, as if she were at last done with a worrisome secret. "Yes, Mona has seen the man in the car."

"Do you know his name?" McMurphy asked quietly.

Megan's stomach clenched and her hands gripped the hard wooden arms of the chair. It had been terrifying to listen to Mona's halting description of hiding in Gladys's house with a murderer, especially when the girl revealed the man had been there when Megan was in the house!

The seconds ticked away. Finally Mona answered, "No."

"No?" McMurphy replied, his exasperation clear as he slapped his hands agaisnt his legs. "Are you sure, Mona? Please think hard, child. This is very important."

Mona looked up and the cop and spoke clearly. "Mona doesn't know the car driver's name. But Mona knows his channel."

Megan gasped, and Judy Barnes gave her a vicious glare. Claude moved uncomfortably in his chair.

McMurphy came closer and leaned down in front of Mona. "His channel? Do you mean television channel, Mona? Was the man someone you see on television?"

A beaming smile lit Mona's face, and she shook her head vigorously. "Mona sees him on Daddy's television. 'News Center Six . . . Alive with all the stories Melbourne wants to hear.'"

Megan felt sick at the girl's parroting of the promotional catchphrase used by Sherman Royal's station. Could it be true? she wondered. Darren George was a murderer?

Sergeant McMurphy smiled broadly, then turned to Officer Barnes. "Did you get that?"

"Yes, sir."

McMurphy sat down behind the principal's desk. "Thank you all," he said, then picked up the phone and dialed. He pressed the receiver to his ear. "Mr. Hawkins, you can take Mona home now. We may have to ask you to bring her down to the station in a few days to sign this statement. Thank you, Mrs. Summers. Mona, you did a great job."

They all stood. As Megan opened the door she heard McMurphy say into the phone, "Pick him up. I'll meet you when you book him. Give me thirty minutes."

"I need to speak with you, sergeant," Jack called out from the door. "It's about Elaine Jones."

McMurphy pointed to the chair. "I'll be right with you."

JACK COULDN'T STOP SMILING. He was bustling around Megan's kitchen, heating soup, making coffee, straightening up the remaining havoc Darren George had committed when he'd searched Megan's home.

Megan was lying on the couch watching the news that was rocking all of Melbourne.

He glanced over at the small screen. Sandy Royal was reporting live outside the sunny police department headquarters. Darren George had been booked a few minutes before for the murder of Gladys Grokowbowski. Royal also announced that George was under suspicion tonight as a possible suspect in each of the Grim Reaper killings.

In a serious tone the young man in dark glasses added that "reliable sources inside the police department" were investigating a possible scam involving TeleSurv Ratings that Darren George may have instigated.

Jack listened as Sandy answered carefully posed questions from a reporter in the anchor booth, questions designed to distance the ownershiup of WABR from Darren George as much as possible.

It looked to Jack's professional eye that the Royal family was making a big play to paint Darren Geroge as a boogey man.

"The kid looks scared," Jack crowed.

Megan studied the young man, then turned away. "I'm sure he is. It's his career, his father's reputation, scandal, ruination, he's reporting. Wouldn't you be?"

"What goes around comes around."

Megan looked at him sharply. Jack smiled and took her a bowl of soup, which she accepted without a word as he sat on the floor beside her. "It's pretty funny, you know. After all this, WABR will probably blow all the other channels off the map in the current ratings sweepstakes."

Megan kept eating as the faces of the Grim Reaper's six victims flashed across the screen. She felt drained, exhausted, disgusted and, oddly, removed from all that had happened around her. She wanted Jack to leave. It was unbearable, having him excited and happy. Whichever way you sliced this story, a tragic piece remained behind.

"Do you want some more soup?" Jack touched her leg.

"Thanks." She handed him the empty bowl and leaned back and closed her eyes. She heard him click off the television. Night was falling, and the neighborhood sounds of dinner and folks returning from work echoed up from the street. Something about the normal feel of the night made her want to weep.

Megan squeezed her lids together, wishing she'd accepted the prescription for codeine the doctor had waved at her.

"Megan, what's wrong?"

"Wrong?" She opened her eyes. "Wrong? Let's see, my neighbor, Mrs. Grokowbowski is dead. My instructor, Darren George, is a suspected murderer. My ex-husband, who has shown no interest in Roxie and Thomas for over a year, suddenly wants joint custody. I not only don't have an internship, but when the TeleSurv brass hear I've earned money from a television station, I won't have a job. Is that enough, or would you like some more?"

He chewed on his lip as if to keep from speaking. Finally he turned and got her more soup, then silently returned and handed the steaming bowl to her. "Drink this."

"Thanks." Jack was staring at her with concern stamped on his face. She took a lungful of air, then plunged into a speech, praying the right words would come. "I really appreciate everything you've done, Jack. But why don't you go on home and get some rest? I'm going to shower, go to bed early, whatever."

She averted her eyes, unable to keep talking without wincing from the hurt that flashed in his dark eyes. Megan sat forward and put the bowl down on the floor. Her eyes fell on the box of phone bills she'd found on which the calls to Eva Merritt from Elaine Jones were found. "Really, Jack. Go on home. You've done enough here."

Jack's voice was frigid. "You mean I've done too much, don't you Megan? Or is it that I haven't done enough?"

"I don't know what you mean."

He sat down beside her. "I think you do. Ever since Friday night you've been pushing me away. What's happened? Can't you see how important you are to me? How much I care about you and Roxie and Thomas?"

"What is 'caring' to you, Jack?"

He looked taken aback. "Feeling involved. Thinking about you night and day. Wanting to be with you."

"Until when? The next mass murderer? The next local scam?" The tears, so long held in check, rolled down her cheeks. "You don't even realize how absorbed you are in your job, Jack. Even now. Right this minute you're helping me, concerned about me, but your focus is on a news story, and how it's going to help the competition!"

"Hold on, Megan. Are you ticked off at me because of my push to tie Darren George and the TeleSurv scam together?"

"No. I'm ticked off at you because you have a one-track mind. And it's set on your career. For God's sake, Jack, you've already admitted that that attitude cost you your marriage! Why do you think I would willingly get more involved with you? I've been in a relationship that went bad once before. Why do it again?"

Jack looked flabbergasted. "I can't believe this. Why are you taking two disparate issues and playing them one against the other? I care for you. I'm falling in love with you! Yes, I have a career. One that's ready to take off again. But that's good news for us, not bad!"

Megan was stunned at his declaration, even though its delivery was unromantic, at best. To cover her shock she grabbed the phone bills and tossed them at Jack. "Here. Take these. Let it be the last little assist I give you before you go on. But don't sit there and tell me to be happy you're turning back into the workaholic you once were." Megan knew as she spoke that she was blowing it, but she felt unable to contain the sudden anger in her heart.

His hands clenched the paper. "What are these?"

"They'll let you scoop Sandy Royal's report. It's proof Elaine Jones called Eva Merritt."

Jack looked down at the bills, then reached for Megan's arm. "Don't push me away, Megan. I don't blame you for being angry right now, a lot has happened. But I care about you. And your kids. The past week I've felt like a part of your family. Don't put an end to all of it just because I have other interests. No man can give you a hundred percent of his time and attention."

"I know that. But I sure as heck need more than the little bit your life allows. Can't you see? You're pressing for more from me, but you have no intention of giving me more!"

He reached a hand toward her, but dropped it just as quickly. "You're making a lot of decisions here that you shouldn't. You're assuming things you're wrong to assume."

Megan put a hand to her head and sighed. "Let's drop it for now. Jack. I—" The ringing phone cut her off and Megan stomped to the counter. "Yes?" she yelled into the phone.

"Ah, hello. This is Gary Martin from Station WMMB. Is this Megan Summers?"

"Yes, but I can't comment now—"

"—Hold on, Mrs. Summers. I'm a friend of Jack Gallagher's. Is he there, please?"

Megan whirled around and held out the receiver to Jack. "It's for you. A business call. I'm going to take a bath. When I'm finished, I may need to nap."

With that she handed him the phone and ran into the bathroom, slamming and locking the door behind her.

WHEN MEGAN CAME OUT of the shower thirty minutes later, Jack was gone. She sat down at the dinette table and let herself have a good, draining cry.

Whatever was blossoming between her and Jack was now ruined, of that much she was sure. The hollow, painful feelings registering in her numb brain told her how much she wished it could be different.

Standing quickly, Megan threw herself into cleaning up the apartment. Activity was always a good antidote for pain. She piled all the information she'd brought home from Sandy Royal on the table, placing the envelope with the check Darren had left with her at the hospital at the top.

She heaped a second stack for Pete McMurphy, including the phone bills from Elaine Jones. Megan rubbed her fingers across the photocopied reports, wondering again who rented the room from where Elaine made her calls. Earlier she had called the Hilton and found out there had been a network convention in Miami during the same time Elaine was there, but they couldn't give her any other information.

"Who cares?" Megan said aloud, but stopped, wondering where the ex-TeleSurv interviewer was now.

An odd excitement surged through her. If she took the material down to the televisvon station tonight, she might be able to check out the file cabinets contining expense reports. If this sheet of phone calls matched some Darren George turned in, it would be more proof of the newsman's guilt.

The prospect of taking a bus downtown did not delight her, but then she thought of Pollard Finch. Her neighbor had been such a good Samaritan lately. Maybe he wouldn't mind driving her down.

Megan crossed to the phone, a light bounce to her step. Maybe this was just what she needed. Actively try to resolve some loose ends, then the thing would be over. Pollard had been preaching to them all to do their part in the Neighborhood Watch program. He would surely be delighted if she hinted their errand might assist the police.

Pollard agreed to come right over. Megan slipped on her shoes and ran through what she had to do. She would leave the files in Darren's office, then take a look around. Suddenly she pictured Sandy Royal. The kid had looked scared. Well, they were all scared, Megan thought. And the best way to fight fear was to act against it.

She didn't believe Darren George had killed his aunt. Nor did she believe he was the man in the mask who'd twice attacked her. While there was something familiar about the assailant, it was nothing connected to Darren George. "Damn," Megan muttered as she ran a comb through her hair. "What is it?"

Outside the low growl of an approaching car in the drive sent her racing to the window. She grabbed her purse and the stack of material and waved to Pollard from the porch. The clock on the stove red 6:26. "I'll be right down."

THE GRIM REAPER RUBBED his stubby fingers against his temples and sighed. It was nearly six-thirty. So much to do today, and so little time to do it in. But, onward he must press. His persistence was necessary, if anything good and pure was to remain in the world.

The voice inside his skull had commanded this, and he trusted the voice. It had never betrayed him, nor let him down like the humans around him did so consistently.

The Reaper frowned and looked around. If only the voice had warned him sooner. He could have taken care of Megan Summers weeks ago. Could have cleansed the soul of the girl before she spread any more of the toxic waste among the people, polluting their thoughts and minds.

He sighed again as he got comfortable in his seat. His fingers reached inside his pocket for the badge he always carried with him. Slowly he put his lips to it, his breath clouding the engraved officialness. With reverence he rubbed it against his faded denim pant leg, appreciative of the ease with which it had helped him enter each and every offender's house these last six months.

"Don't worry about this girl," he mouthed without a sound. Tomorrow he would take care of Megan. Tomorrow the cancer would be stopped before it spread any further among them.

Tomorrow, when Megan Summers was dead, he could rest easier. And wait for the next perpetrator to be unmasked.

"THANK YOU, MR. FINCH," Megan said as Pollard drove the beamy white Plymouth up in front of the television station office. "You were a real help to bring me here tonight."

Pollard eyed the huge sack of papers Megan held on her lap. "You sure I can't help you with those? Or wait until you're finished and drive you home?"

"No. I don't know how long I'll be. Besides, you need to get to the Neighborhood Watch meeting, don't you? You've got that billboard project to worry about."

Pollard blinked. "You're right, dear. Well, take it easy tonight. Go straight home and get some rest. You still look a little peaked from your experience this morning."

"Thank you, I will." Megan jiggled the door open and stepped out. Impulsively she squeezed Pollard's arm. It was surprisingly solid. "Thanks again. You're a dear man and a wonderful neighbor."

Pollard looked serious. "It's my fondest wish, Megan. I do my best."

"Well, we're all lucky to have you." She slammed the car door and waved, then headed into the building. Her neck felt slightly stiff, but otherwise the burst of adrenaline revived her.

Megan's thoughts returned to Jack as she made her way into the station, but she brushed them aside. She was doing this for herself, and in a strange way for Darren George. With the lynch-mob attitude in Melbourne and the indictments she heard murmured throughout the hallways of the station, she was the only one who seemed to feel he might be innocent.

"Megan."

She stopped and turned, a chill skittering down her arms at the familiar voice. Sandy Royal was standing in front of Darren's office, a set of keys dangling from his hand. His thumb was hooked into his jacket, and the garment was flung over his shoulder. With his dark glasses, he looked the picture of yuppie journalism.

"Hi, Sandy." Setting the bag of matetrial on the floor beside Darren's door, she reached for the keys. "Here, let me open it for you. I have some things to leave in here, too."

He allowed her to take them and unlock the room, then he hit the light switch and closed the door behind him. "What's all this?" he asked, pointing to the sack.

"I wanted to return the material we put together on the Grim Reaper."

Sandy tossed his jacket into the chair. "Great! I was going to come to your house tomorrow to pick this stuff up. I need those files, since it looks like I'll be covering this story now."

"Really?" She couldn't read the young man's eyes because of his sunglasses, but she heard the triumph in his voice.

"Sure. You didn't think my daddy would let a murderer roam the hallways of his business, did you?"

"No, of course not. But I assumed Dr. George would be allowed to come back to work," Megan added lamely. "Until the trial, I mean." The chill bumps reappeared, and Megan rubbed them away. In the corner of her mind an

larm was jangling. She sniffed the air, unable to concen-
ate on what Sandy was saying.

"Did you hear me, Megan?"

She inhaled again and blinked. "I'm sorry. What?"

"I said, there's no way Daddy is going to let George back
↓ here," Sandy answered. "That jerk's ticket has been
unched. I filled the cops in on his gambling. They'll find
ut the rest."

Megan stiffened, not liking the smug hostility in his voice.
Well, I'll be going now."

"Aren't you going to keep working on your internship? I
ould use you to run down some small details."

Megan sighed and sat on the chair, moving Sandy's coat
side. Her nostrils filled with the scent of the slim, black
garettes he favored, and the warning inside got louder.
Small details," she said softly. "That's what I came in for
night. To run down some small details. Do you know if
arren went to the broadcasters' convention last Novem-
r in Miami?"

Sandy rocked backward in his chair. "Yeah, several peo-
e did. Why?"

A twinge of disappointment tweaked in Megan's heart.
andy's words proved Darren was in the same town as
laine Jones when the incriminating TeleSurv calls were
ade. "Did he stay at the Hilton?"

He paused several seconds. "I have no idea. Why are you
king, Megan?"

She flushed, not wanting suddenly to appear to be the
nateur sleuth she was. "No reason." Suddenly the mem-
y she'd been coaxing into her consciousness loomed full-
own, and her hands went rigid. She remembered what was
miliar about her attacker. It was his smell. A tobacco
nell.

Keeping her voice smooth, she glanced outside the of-
ce. No one was in sight. "Do you really think Darren did
, Sandy?" Megan racked her brain for a distraction,
nowing she had to keep the young man talking until she
w a way to escape.

"Which 'it'? Figures he took out his auntie. The old biddy was loaded. And no treat at all in the relative department. She hated Darren. But I don't really think he's the Grim Repaer, do you?"

"No. No, I don't." Megan stood. "Well, I need to catch my bus. Give me a call if you need some help reading my notes—"

Her voice tipped him off. Sandy put his foot out and blocked her path. "Sit down, Megan." He leaned back and took his sunglasses off as he stared up at the ceiling.

The jacket next to her fell onto the floor, and Megan reached for it. The corner of the bulky-knit shape fell from the inside lapel pocket. Megan retrieved it and absently began to stuff it into the pocket. A garish stripe of purple caught her eye, and her hand froze in midair. She looked at Sandy.

"What have you got there, Megan?" Sandy asked softly.

Feeling paralyzed, she clamped her lips shut and again looked outside just as the outer office lights went off. She was alone with Sandy. Completely alone with a man who had nearly killed her twice before.

He leaned forward, his hands in his lap. It was then that she noticed his left eye. It had a scratch on the eyelid, and was bleary and bloodshot.

Megan let the ski mask and the coat slip to the floor. Her hand covered her mouth as a scream of panic caused a spasm in her throat. "My God . . ."

Sandy raised his right hand above the table. It clutched a stubby silver gun, which was pointed at her abdomen. "Keep it down, kiddo. Hand me the coat. And the mask."

"You . . ."

"Yeah, me." Sandy stood up. "You've got real bad timing, Megan. I nearly had to waste you the other night at Gladys's house. Then again at that creep Gallagher's. And now today in the garage. You know, I had every intention of leaving that incriminating little clue on Darren's dead body for our good friend McMurphy to find. Too bad you found the mask first." He came around the table at her, his eyes gleaming with a feverish light.

"You killed Gladys?" Megan rasped, unable to move. "Why?"

"Because she was a fool. She hired me to jimmy a survey for her own reasons. I did it for some reasons of my own. But she tried to back out of our deal. The biddy got cold feet, so I gave her a cold body to go with them."

"What? But why would she want to fix a survey to make Darren look good? You said she hated him."

Sandy stood and grabbed Megan. He draped the coat over his arm and glanced through the glass window. "She did. She was going to jimmy this month's survey the opposite way and make it look like his station dropped by several thousand viewers. He'd get the ax, which was what she wanted."

"And you'd get the anchor job," Megan whispered.

"Which is the job I deserve," Sandy replied angrily. "But Gladys was getting worried her boss in Maryland was going to find out just because that dingbat Eva Merritt sent Daddy a letter. Lucky for us, I got the letter when Daddy was out of town."

"And you killed her, too..."

"She was old. She was due, the damn busybody."

Megan felt like she'd gag, but she knew she had to keep him talking. Someone might come by and help her. "But why did you kill Gladys?"

"She fired Elaine. Tried to back out."

At the mention of Elaine Jones, Megan started to calm down. She had to proceed carefully. Mabye she could buy herself some time until she could formulate a plan that would get her away from this madman. "Did you kill Elaine, too?"

"Not yet." Sandy grinned, a hideous and mirthless expression. "She's waiting for me in that junkie trailer I bought last month from good friend Darren, wondering what's next." He motioned toward the hallway. "Let's go see her and put her out of her suspense, shall we?"

"You can't get away with this. The cops have samples of the tissue from under my nails." The false assumption McMurphy had made about Mona's identification of a newsman flashed through her mind. "And the police know of someone who saw you leaving Ms. Grokowbowski's house. Any moment they're bound to see their mistake. They'll release Darren, and start looking for you."

"No chance." Sandy's features contorted in rage and what looked to Megan like naked fear. "You see, I had a police uniform that conveniently has your bloodstains on it in Darren's house. Along with some TeleSurv information I took the night I killed Gladys. No, sweetheart, the pressure's been too hot on McMurphy for him to let Darren loose. They'll fry the bastard before they ever look for anyone else."

Megan detected a shake in his voice, and she pressed harder. "You know that's not true. Darren's got too much clout. He'll have an excellent attorney. You better run now. Without me, Sandy. It's your only chance."

"Shut up," he hissed, then waved the gun. "Walk in front of me. Now. Or I'll shoot you on the spot."

Chapter Sixteen

Sandy's dark blue Lincoln was parked by the rear entrance of the news station. Megan read the plates as the horror of her predicament pumped through her system. WABR 2. Of course, she realized, staring at the trailer hitch. There were three Lincolns. Mona had seen one the night Gladys was killed, but it belonged to Sandy, not Darren.

Sandy's breath warmed her icy neck. "Slide in."

Megan reached for the door handle mechnically, pressing against it to get away from him. "Where are we going?"

"I told you. To visit Elaine."

The headlights from an approaching car shone over them, and Megan held her breath. When the car drove by without stopping she felt panic bite at the base of her spine. She allowed herself a glance at Sandy. The fact he looked as scared as she felt helped her equilibrium a little.

"Why don't we go back inside and talk this over some more, Sandy? I really think you're making a tremendous mistake—"

"Get in! Now, Megan." Roughly he pressed the muzzle of the gun into her ribs.

She slid across the seat. When she rested her hand on the handle, the snap of the automatic door lock sounded like the crack of a pistol.

"Put your seat belt on. I wouldn't want you to get hurt," he ordered. He was left handed and kept the firearm pointed at her while he clumsily maneuvered out of the parking lot onto the road.

The Monday night traffic was light. Megan kept her face averted from Sandy's as her eyes searched the oncoming traffic for help. Though what she could do if she saw a police car, or someone she knew, she did not know. Suddenly Jack's face flashed into her mind. A physical stab of fear and longing shook her. If only she had been less defensive with Jack. If only she had admitted how much she cared, and how vulnerable the depth of her feelings for him made her. If only she had called him to take her to the station....

Megan slid her eyes in Sandy's direction. The young newsman appeared relaxed, though his knuckles where he gripped the steering wheel were white. He made a left onto Airport Boulevard, and the Hilton Tower glittered with lights against the dark sky. Megan's mind felt like mush. She knew she had to do something to get away, but jumping out of a car going forty-five down a busy street offered little hope of anything other than instant death.

Sandy began a slow brake and hit the blinker. Quickly he made a left into Trailer Haven's parking lot, coming to a jolting stop in front of Elaine Jones's Airstream. "Let's go."

"Elaine's not here," Megan replied, realizing how absurd a response it was, but desperate to buy some time.

He pushed the gun against her ribs. "Out. Slide your butt this way and don't try anything like screaming. The old folks around this joint are pretty hard of hearing."

When he grinned, Megan wondered how anyone had ever found the man attractive. He looked like a rodent, all teeth and snout. Without a word she undid the seat belt and scooted out of the car. Walking quickly, Megan glanced at the trailer next to Elaine's, praying the nosy lady she'd seen before was on the lookout, but the interior was dark.

Stifling a sigh, she continued as Sandy directed her toward Elaine's door. Sandy pulled out his keys and unlocked the heavy aluminum inner door, then pushed the screen open. Bits and pieces of past conversations skittered across Megan's mind. A co-worker's remark that Sandy liked "older women," Mona's identification of a "news-

**Journey with Harlequin into
the past and discover stories
of cowboys and captains,
pirates and princes in the
romantic tradition of
Harlequin.**

man" with blond hair, the odor of black cigarettes. Dear God, she thought, they had all jumped to conclusions, overlooking the obvious every time.

"Have a seat," the young man ordered with false cheer. "I'll get Elaine."

She sat where he pointed the gun, in the seat at the small dinette she had occupied during her visit with Jack. Numbly she watched as Sandy opened the door to the tiny lavatory and pulled Elaine Jones out of the closet-size room as if she were a bag of laundry. He carried her over his shoulder and deposited her with a slam of flesh against leather onto the dinette seat opposite Megan.

Elaine was wearing the same outfit as last time, and was bound and gagged. Her eye makeup had been cried off into smudges all over her face and neck, but it didn't hide the bruises.

"Elaine!" Megan gasped. Both women turned rage-filled eyes to Sandy.

"You two know each other, I understand," Sandy shot back. His forehead was shining with perspiration. "Now, ladies. We're going for a little drive. Y'all can ride here, like nice girls, or in the potty, which should be very uncomfortable." He reached above him into one of the storage cabinets and pulled out a length of rope identical to the one binding Elaine. He also held a strip of wide tape.

"For God's sake!" Megan cried. "Don't be a fool!"

In response Sandy grabbed her by the hair and snapped her head back against the seat. He pressed the gun against her temple. "Shut up, Miss College Girl. I'm in charge here!" He slapped the piece of adhesive across her lips, then jerked her arms behind her and wrapped the length of cord tightly around her wrists.

With a triumphant look he hurried out of the trailer, leaving the two women staring at each other while he locked the doors outside. For several moments they both sat still in shock. A huge tear rolled out of Elaine's swollen left eye, and the woman crumpled down into the seat. Megan yearned to comfort her, but the minty tasting gag kept her from saying anything.

Megan flexed her legs, then carefully scooted out from behind the table. Whatever reason had caused Sandy to forget to bind her ankles, she was grateful for it. Being mobile gave her the only chance to escape.

Megan backed up to the drawers she'd seen Elaine remove a knife from. Slowly she slid the drawer open, then used her fingers to feel for something to cut her bindings. Her skin zinged with the touch of a razor edge. Gingerly, with her thumbs and index fingers, Megan lifted the knife out of the drawer. Now, if she could just get Elaine to buck up enough to help hold the knife, she could saw the rope off.

Just as she had a good grip on the tool, Megan heard a noise across the room that made her grow cold with fear. It was the scrape of a key against the metal lock. Sandy was back!

Megan hurried back to the dinette, but dropped the knife to the floor just as the trailer door flew open.

JACK PACED FOR THE TWENTIETH time the ten feet of linoleum in his Florida room. He stopped in front of the phone, glared at it, then resumed his prowl.

He had left Megan's and gone to the police precinct, but Pete McMurphy didn't have time to talk. So Jack had come home and tried to work on writing his piece on Darren George that his old boss Gary Martin wanted tomorrow. His dark eyes scanned the desk top for the pages he had poured over, but he turned away in disgust and walked off the twenty-six squares of tile again. He couldn't think of anything but Megan, and how badly he had let her down.

She had her priorities and had made no bones about them. Megan was a woman who lived up to her obligations, never letting ego or personal needs interrupt the responsible way she led her life. Jack sighed. She had been willing to let him into her life, of that he was sure. A woman like her never considered making love with a man without serious intentions. The image of her in his arms, a smile of longing and need on her lips, punished him.

He had blown the trust she had put in him. He hadn't seen how his ego ruled his priorities. Hadn't realized he'd lost her until she had told him in no uncertain terms to leave tonight. "Damn," Jack muttered aloud, his muscles taut.

The phone shrieked beside him, and for a fleeting instant he felt joy. *What if it is Megan?* "Hello?"

"Hello. May I speak to Mr. Gallagher, please?"

The woman's voice was youthful, and vaguely familiar. But it wasn't Megan. Jack had to force himself to answer. "This is Jack Gallagher."

"Hello, Mr. Gallagher. This is Anne Babba. We met Friday at Trailer Haven. Do you remember?"

He pictured the feisty lady and answered in genuine tones. "Yes, ma'am. How are you? Did Elaine Jones ever show up?" He hated himself for asking the last question, but it had slipped out without thinking. An image of Megan's face flashed in his mind, and he felt lower than ever.

"No. But I saw your young lady friend. I was concerned when she arrived with that other man. The poor child looked very tense. And they never turned the lights on in the trailer."

A rush of panic made Jack's ears ring. "What are you talking about, Miss Babba? You saw Megan at Elaine's trailer? When?"

"She arrived about an hour ago. The young man with her is hitching his car up to Elaine's trailer right now, and I haven't seen your friend since." She coughed uncomfortably. "It's not that I sit and spy on people, but I was concerned when I didn't see her come outside."

"I'll be right there, Miss Babba." Jack slammed the phone down and ran out to his car. Five minutes later he was sitting with his blinkier on to pull into the Trailer Haven lot when the sleek blue Lincoln turned across four lanes of traffic in front of him, towing the Airstream behind it. His jaw dropped. How the hell did Darren George get out of jail? Jack wondered. And where was Megan?

Damn. He should have had Miss Babba call the police! Pushing the accelerator all the way to the floor, he swerved back into the fast lane in pursuit of the shining silver vehicle several hundred yards ahead. The Lincoln was traveling east on 192, heading for the four-lane A1A connector that ran east from Melbourne across the Indian River.

Jack pressed the Volkswagen harder, but he was losing ground to the Lincoln. Approaching the intersection leading to the marina at the Front Street Park, he finally got a chance to catch up. The car and trailer stopped for a red light, giving him time to zigzag in and out of traffic, gaining a half block on them when the light turned green. When the Lincoln sped through the intersection, Jack was now only two cars back.

It was at that moment he spotted the woman. In the rear window of the trailer, a pale face with a swirl of red hair appeared. She was gagged, and a slash of color stained her cheek. *Megan!* Jack's blood raced as he recognized her. The driver in a car directly behind the trailer saw her at the same time, and began to furiously honk his horn.

"Idiot!" Jack screamed. Couldn't the man guess whoever was driving the trailer knew about the woman in trouble? He sped up and cut the man off nearly crashing him into the retaining wall as he braked to avoid hitting Jack.

Jack waved his arm at Megan. "Sit down! You're going to get hurt!" He took advantage of the slowing traffic to nose into the lane beside the Lincoln. Anger, potent and red-hot, spurred him to draw recklessly close to the sedan. Through the dark-tinted glass he saw the silhouette of the driver, but he couldn't be sure it was Darren George. The driver looked over, then sped up.

As the bridge over the Indian River flashed into view, he took desperate action. Turning the Volkswagon's tires sharply to the right, he bashed the side of the Lincoln. His move took the driver by surprise, and the luxury car veered off the concrete and down onto a sandy strip running next to the river. Jack turned and followed it, bumping up and down sharply over the hilly terrain leading to the water. Several picnic tables sat empty, and for a fleeting second Jack was sure he had boxed him in.

But the road went further than he realized, and it looked like the Lincoln could follow it and get back up to 192. Desperate to stop them, Jack rammed the back of the trailer, hoping the jolt didn't hurt Megan worse than she already was.

The trailer swayed with the impact, but the biggest damage was to his own car. As the fender bent over his front wheel, the Volkswagen began to shudder. In desperation Jack floored the accelerator, knowing he had one more try before he lost the Lincoln to its superior power.

He took dead aim at the trailer and rammed it again. The force of the impact sent the car and trailer careering into the water, where they jack-knifed and the trailer fell on its side. Jack jumped from the car and ran toward the wreckage. The trailer was being pulled further into the river by the current, but the car seemed anchored by some tree stumps it had rammed into. The wheels on the Lincoln were still spinning when he approached.

Jack waded into the water, hollering over the hum of the tires. "Megan! It's okay. I'm coming to help!" He knew he had to get to Megan before the trailer filled with water and plunged to the murky depths on the river bottom. Finally he reached the door and pulled himself up onto the silver skin. "Megan! Open the door!" He screamed.

He thought he could hear pounding from inside, but there was so much noise around him he could not be sure. A white helicopter hovered nearby, the call letters of Darren George's television station stenciled on the side. The steady whappy, whappy, whappy of its blades cut the air above. In the distance Jack heard the scream of police sirens mesh with the traffic congesting on the bridge above. Miss Babba, bless her heart. More help was arriving by the second, but it would be too late if the trailer went any deeper into the dark water.

"Megan!" Bubbles gurgled all around the trailer, and a wrenching sound of tearing metal rang out from the car. In terror Jack realized the trailer hitch was being sheared off the car. If that happened, the trailer would float further into the channel.

Pain bit into his shoulder, and he whirled around, and the mistake he had made came plainly into view. Darren George was still in jail.

But Sandy Royal stood ten feet away, his arms pointed out straight from his body, a gun in his hands. He fired again as Jack ducked. The shock of seeing the young newsman instead of Darren George slowed his reactions, but he managed to avoid the bullet.

"Down on the beach!" a voice through a loud speaker blared. "Drop your weapon!" Sandy whirled toward the voice, firing wildly.

Jack heard the quick retort of a shotgun and watched Sandy Royal crumple to the ground. He turned his full attention away from the policeman crawling down the embankment and climbed up onto the trailer. "Megan! If you can hear me, pound on the door." The trailer was now half submerged. Jack clung to the frame of the outside door, unable to force it open. In desperation he screamed to the men on the shore to help, and one man in uniform ran toward him. Then he heard the noise. Pounding.

Megan was alive!

As the man ran toward him, Jack spotted the pop-up air vent at the top of the trailer. The waterline was within inches, but with the door locked, it was the only possible escape hatch. He inched toward it. It wasn't closed all the way. "Megan!" Jack yelled. "Can you crawl up here?" He panicked that he couldn't hear her voice, but then he remembered the tape. With slippery hands he started to pry open the vent, praying the trailer hitch would hold.

"Can you pull it off?" the cop yelled, jumping onto the side of the car and shouting out to Jack.

"I think so. Can you get some people down under here to anchor this thing? The current's pulling it apart."

"I'll get a tow truck. Jump off if it starts to go or you'll be in trouble."

"Hurry!" Jack ordered, turning away from the man. He had no intention of letting the river take what he now acknowledged as the most important part of his life.

INSIDE THE TRAILER Megan finally worked the knife through the last of the rope holding her hands. The way the trailer was tipped forced her to lie on the sink and stove, but that angle afforded her clear access to another knife. She felt the bindings give way and gasped as the circulation returned to her numb fingers. She tore the adhesive from her mouth and gulped the air.

As carefully as possible she crawled across the jumble of pots and pans and reached Elaine, then went to work on her bindings. The woman was unconscious. Her face was a horrifying shade of greenish white in the dank light of the trailer.

"Elaine, Elaine. Try to wake up. We have to get out of here," Megan pleaded. At that moment the trailer pitched further to its side, hurling her headlong into an open cabinet door. She felt blood ooze from her eyebrow, and swore for all she was worth.

Above her out of the night she heard Jack's voice. "Megan! Megan, come to the air vent."

She blinked and tried to raise herself up, but was trapped by the closets. The water seemed to be rising faster, and she heard a rushing noise from the window over the bed. A stream of water was bubbling up from the bunk, probably from a gash in the trailer's skin.

Megan took several breaths and made her way back to Elaine. "Jack!" she screamed with her hands cupped around her injured throat. "Hurry, the trailer's filling up with water." She had no hope he could hear her; to her ears her voice sounded like a whisper.

"Megan! Hang on. Help's coming." Over the roar of the water and the noise outside, Megan heard Jack. Hot tears poured from her eyes and she started to shake.

She could hear him prying off the air-vent, and her eyes searched wildly for something to help. Lying on its side just out of reach was a knife block, its polelike sharpening rod rolling free. Megan waded two steps and grasped the cabinet door, finally grabbing the instrument she sought. Slowly she pulled herself back up on the sink and banged on the ceiling. "Try to reach down and grab this, Jack. Put your arm in as far as you can."

The vent was two feet away from her, but if Jack helped she could get the tool to him. Like a disembodied animal, his arm dropped through the six-inch clearance as his hand grasped empty air. Megan balanced on her knees but couldn't reach. Water was pouring through the sink drain hole and out of the bathroom. She stretched as far as she could go.

Wiggling the instrument to the tips of her fingers, she managed to slap the thing into his palm before she lost her balance and pitched back into the cold, dank water. Megan came up sputtering, but heard the renewed efforts above and in seconds saw the air-vent rising.

Elaine was still unconscious, but Megan refused to believe the woman was dead. "Come on, Elaine. Try to wake up," she yelled, carefully moving to where Elaine was wedged against the bunk over the dinette.

Under her the trailer shuddered, and she felt it move as a grating sound of metal assailed her ears. The water was nearly to her chest, and it smelled like gasoline. Megan leaned over Elaine and shook the woman.

Elaine's eyes fluttered, then opened. "Megan?" she rasped.

"Don't try to talk, Elaine. We've been in an accident. Hang on." She tired to keep the hysterial edge out of her voice, but something cold slithered against her calf and she yelled and kicked at it in the liquid darkness.

"The water's nearly got us," she screamed into the darkness above. "Hurry, Jack!"

In answer to her scream the top of the trailer vanished with a wild ripping sound and Jack's face instantly appeared. "Megan?"

She flailed both hands. "Here. We're here."

"My God, Elaine's with you?"

"Yes. And she's hurt."

Jack shouted behind him. "There are two of them. Get some more rope!" Suddenly he dropped into the darkness with a splash and she felt his arms around her.

"Jack!" Megan allowed one sob to escape as she clutched at him, but then pointed to Elaine. "You'll have to carry her out of here first. She's almost unconscious."

A few minutes later, Megan felt herself tugged into the air then pulled roughly out of the watery nightmare below. A blanket was wrapped around her. She refused to move until she saw Jack's head clear the trailer. Elaine was carried off in a stretcher strung on wires and ropes leading to the shore, where every conceivable type of vheicle, headlights glaring, waited to help. Megan felt Jack's strong hands and arms on her as he helped her toward land.

He kissed her and spoke into her hair. "Megan, I'm so sorry. I love you. I was so afraid."

She knew he said several other things, but the gurgling sound from the trailer sinking below the surface blotted out all sound. She was safe. She was with Jack. Nothing else at that moment mattered.

AT TWO-THIRTY the following afternoon, the trash truck came, startling Megan from her drugged sleep. She lay, disoriented for several seconds while her mind took inventory of her body. Her throat ached, her head throbbed, and the new stitches in her arm and eyebrow hummed with hurt.

She shifted under her covers, comforted by Jack's presence beside her. The all-too-real nightmare slowly came into focus, and she shut her eyes against the memories.

Sandy Royal was dead.

Darren George had been released and had announced he was suing the police department for five million dollars.

Elaine Jones was going to make it.

And the gossip Jack had overheard from the cops and news people milling about outside was that Pete McMurphy was probably going to be fired for arresting the wrong man.

All those bits of information fused into a whole, and Megan shuddered. The pain Sherman Royal must now live with was greater than he'd ever done to his son, but she was sure the man would gain no comfort from that fact. He'd failed his son, and now his son had failed in life in the ultimate manner.

"Megan." Jack's voice was soft and full of worry.

She rolled over toward him and put her arms around his neck, wincing from the physical pain but wanting to feel his warmth. He had a row of black stitches in his shoulder where a bullet had grazed him, but appeared not to even notice them.

"Good morning," she said. "If I didn't say it last night, thanks."

He kissed her hair and hugged her tenderly. "You're welcome." They lay there several moments, both content in each other's arms.

"I should call the kids," Megan said. To her amazement she suddenly felt like anything but sleep, her body soothed by the nearness and heat off Jack's skin.

"No, you shouldn't. You should let me love you."

He rolled closer to her and kissed her, rising up on his arm and looking down into her face. "Are you too tired. Because I can wait. I just wanted you to know how much I need you—"

"—Sh-h-h." She pressed a brusied finger to his lip, arching her back to fit more snugly against him. Suddenly she remembered that he'd stripped her clothes off and stood with her in the shower last night, then carried her to bed, where he'd slept without making a single demanding move. "You've seen me naked."

His dark eyes glowed, and a smile tugged at his mouth. "I have."

"No fair. I haven't seen you."

A muscle tightened in his jaw. With a flick of his wrist he tossed back the sheet, then casually relaxed, arms behind his head as he lay back on the pillow. "Now you have."

Megan blushed, but looked without blinking. He was as gorgeous as she had dreamed, despite the black-and-blue and green-and-yellow bruises and scrapes covering his body. "Turn over."

Her impish suggestion surprised him, but he grinned, turned over, then back again to face her. "Do I pass?"

Her shoulders ached as she sat up and pulled off her T-shirt, her hair tumbling around her shoulders. She settled herself against his chest, an inch away from his mouth. "You pass. Come here, Jack Gallagher."

An hour and a half later a sharp rap roused her from a dreamless sleep. "Damn," she whispered, rising slowly as every muscle in her body complained. Jack said Dean was going to bring the kids home after supper. It was only a little after four o'clock.

Megan pulled on her T-shirt and peered through the peephole to find Sergeant Pete McMurphy waiting. She glanced at Jack, then smiled. She was no longer worried about propriety where Jack Gallagher was concerned. Nothing was settled between them, and yet, everything was.

The future looked brighter than she had ever planned on. She pulled on her jeans and stepped into thongs as she opened the door.

"Good afternoon, Mrs. Summers. May I come in?"

"Certainly." She held the door open. "Excuse our appearance, but we're still recovering from last night." She nodded at where Jack was sleeping deeply. "Should I wake him up?"

"No. I'm sure you can answer my questions." McMurphy settled into one of her dinette chairs and wearily retrieved his pad. They had gone over her account of being kidnapped by Sandy and his explanation of the TeleSurv scam he pulled with Gladys the night before.

Megan sat across from him at the dinette table. Her legs ached with the small amount of walking she just did, but the sleep and Jack's lovemaking had left her mind clear.

"I authenticated the phone bills Elaine Jones turned in. We've checked with the Miami Hilton and the calls were made from Sandy Royal's room. We also found a hunting knife and some bloodstains in the back of his car. I'm betting they match Mrs. Grokowbowski's blood type." The cop turned his watery eyes to Megan. "You were right about TeleSurv being a connection to this case."

"Do you have any proof yet that Sandy paid the viewers off to list WABR in their diaries?"

"Yeah. Elaine Jones told us to check out a bag of paperwork Sandy had at his condo. It was full of cancelled checks for $50 from folks who cooperated. Cocky little punk paid them himself out of a personal account. A hundred and ten viewers. Hard to believe that many dishonest people in a small area." The cop shook his head. "Doesn't take much to buy people off these days."

Megan reached her hand out and squeezed the cop's arm. He was clearly exhausted and depressed. "I think you've done a great job, sergeant. You've certainly helped me several times. Every time I was attacked, you were on the scene to help almost instantly."

McMurphy frowned. He shut his book and removed a small leather case from his pocket, slapping it down on the Formica table. It fell open to reveal his Melbourne Police badge and identification. "See that? I've worked hard for this town for twenty-five years. Started as a rookie the week I got back from Nam. Never took a bribe or fixed a ticket, did all I could to clear the scum out of the path of law-abiding folks." He leaned forward, his face tense and drawn. "But what's it gonna get me, Mrs. Summers? It's gonna get me fired. Without my thirty-year pension, too."

"Surely they can't fire you just because—"

"—They can fire a good cop for any damn reason they like," McMurphy shot back bitterly. "I'll be lucky to get a job as a security guard at Harris once the press is through with me."

"Maybe I can talk to Darren George."

"Don't bother." The cop grinned mirthlessly. "It just don't matter anymore."

Behind her, Megan heard Jack stir. She turned and smiled at him as he sat up, looking disoriented. "Hi. We've got company."

McMurphy stood suddenly. "But don't get up on my account. I'm going. Just wanted to check and see you were okay, Mrs. Summers. I thought you'd be alone." He inclined his head toward Jack, then hurried to the door.

"What was that all about?" Jack asked as he got up and came to the table. Like most men, he was unembarrassed by his nakedness, a thought that she let herself enjoy.

He kissed Megan on the top of the head, then sat down with a groan.

"I'm not sure. Poor man, I think he's still in shock that Darren George was the wrong man to arrest."

A second, sharper rap sounded from the door. Megan and Jack exchanged looks, then she rose and crossed to the door. It must be Sergeant McMurphy again, she thought. Maybe he forgot something. She opened the door wide.

Dean stood there, white-faced and obviously scared to death. "Is Thomas here?"

The room began to spin as her already frazzled nerves seemed to snap apart. "What are you talking about? He's at school. Isn't he?" she demanded, not feeling Jack's firm grasp on her arms.

"What's happened?" Jack chimed in as Dean grew paler still.

"I went to pick up the kids at school," Dean replied. "But Thomas isn't there. No one has seen him for three hours!"

Chapter Seventeen

Jack immediately got on the phone with the police.

Megan sent Dean back to the school to man an information post in case Thomas showed up there. She also gave him a list of telephone numbers to call. They were her son's friends, and Thomas might be with one of them. "Pull yourself together," she admonished her ex-husband. "Don't let Roxie see how scared you are. I'll be up at school in about an hour, after I search between here and there."

As she watched Dean drive away, her heart pounded, and every inch of her body ached with fear. To not know where Thomas was, to imagine the worst fears a parent must ever confront, obliterated all other feelings. "I'm going now," she hollered to Jack.

He gave her arm a squeeze and continued arguing with the police dispatcher. "Look, the kid is only five. Surely the twenty-four-hour waiting period makes no sense for kids that little!"

Megan slammed the door and raced down the steps. "Thomas! Thom-as!" Her throat burned with the effort, but she continued her call, sure if her son was within hearing distance that he'd reveal himself. Dean said he'd last been seen at lunchtime. Her mind sped back to the note the principal had sent last week.

Had Thomas left school again? she worried. Had he been hit by a car? Fallen and hurt himself? Gone off with a stranger?

The last thought made her trembling worse. "Thomas! Thomas, it's Mom! Thomas! Thomas Summers!" she called out. The first three houses she found empty. The next four were occupied, but no one had seen her son. She crossed the street, trying unsuccessfully not to cry.

She hurried to the intersection across from her children's school, dismayed as she recognized a car heading slowly in the opposite direction. "Damn," she swore aloud at the disappearing Plymouth. She'd been hoping to recruit Pollard Finch into helping her with the door-to-door.

Megan crossed the street without waiting for the light and ran onto the school campus. In the office Mr. Butz and his secretary were on separate phones. Dean was in the small office where only a few days ago she'd comforted Mona Hawkins, and Roxie was coloring at the desk.

"Mommy!" her daughter sang out, a huge smile wreathing her face.

"Hello, baby," Megan replied, hugging her daughter to her. "Are you okay?" she asked, hoping Roxie wouldn't be frightened by her tear-stained face.

"I'm fine, Mommy. But Thomas is really in trouble, isn't he?" Roxie's voice filled with tears. "Are we ever going to find Thomas? Is he lost, Mommy?"

Megan hugged Roxie more tightly, catching Mr. Butz's pained look of pity. "He's not lost, baby. He just forgot to tell us where he went. But don't worry, we'll find him."

Dean hurried out of the office at the sound of Megan's voice. "Did you call the police?"

"Jack's handling that. I've started a house-to-house search, and I'm going to work my way back there now. Any news?"

Dean glanced at Roxie, then shook his head. "No. No one has seen him since lunchtime." His voice wavered.

Megan glared at him. "Keep calling. Call everyone in his class. I'll be back in a few minutes." She hugged Roxie fiercely then raced out the door. Skipping Edna Adams's house, she rang the bells on five more houses. No one had seen her boy.

"Thomas!" she screamed, her throat feeling like it was bleeding. "Thom-as!" At the end of Country Club Drive a car honked at her. She looked up to find Claude Hawkins's pickup truck parked at the curb.

"Mrs. Summers? What's wrong?" Claude called.

Megan ran up to the truck and told Claude the story, a thought suddenly jogging her memory. Thomas had said Mona had been the one who had enticed him to go off campus the last time. "Did Mona go to the elementary school today?"

Claude stared at her, his eyes narrowing. "She wasn't supposed to, but she might have. I been gone up to the swap meet since nine o'clock. We can check with her." Claude opened the door on the passenger side. "Hop in and I'll drive you to my house so's we can check."

Something made her hesitate a second. She felt uneasy around Claude Hawkins, ever since that bit Sandy had filmed with the man demonstrating how to butcher small animals. But she shook off her apprehension and got into the car.

"You doing okay?" Claude asked as he gunned the pickup. "Saw yous on the news last night, and you looked pretty banged up."

Megan grimaced. Last night's horrors now seemed a million years away, so terrifying were today's. "I'm fine, Mr. Hawkins."

"Shame about that Royal boy," Claude said. "Who'd a thought by looking at him that he was a cold-blooded murderer?"

A chill raced down Megan's back at Claude's words, and her mind registered for the first time the dark brown stains on the man's jeans. Had he been butchering things again? she wondered. Bile, bitter and hot, seeped into the bottom of her throat, and she swallowed hard as Claude turned into his drive.

"You're right there," she replied. Suddenly she wanted out of the car and away from this man. She threw open the door and jumped out into the drive. "I'll wait out here," she said nervously. "You go ask Mona."

Claude limped around the car, his eyes unreadable. "You can come inside, Mrs. Summers. You look like you should sit down a bit." He reached out and touched her, and she moved back as if his hand sported fangs.

"No. Please, I'm going to keep calling for Thomas. I'll wait here."

Claude shrugged and disappeared into the house. Megan walked to the end of the drive. As she did so, Jack's Volkswagen came screaming down the street. He pulled over when he saw her.

"Why did you leave the house? Are the police looking for him yet?" Megan cried.

Jack shifted the car into neutral and got out. He put both arms around her. "Hey, calm down. McMurphy picked up the call. He's at your house himself, manning the phone. The patrol cars are beginning to look now. They're using your apartment as the command center."

"Oh, God, Jack. Where is he?" Megan felt herself losing control as she buried her face into Jack's solid chest. Guilt washed over her, and helplessness. She was the mother. Good mothers didn't let things like this happen to their children.

"Calm down, sweetheart. We're going to find him," Jack soothed. "Why don't you let me take you back to your house now? The police want a picture of Thomas to show around the neighborhood. And I called the television stations. They want a picture, too."

"You did what?" She felt like hitting him. "Why? Is this just another scoop for you, Jack? Honestly, how could you even think about your career at a time like this?"

"Whoa!" Jack held up his hand, but his face flushed dark. "I called them so we'd get the word out and have some help finding Thomas. Don't read the wrong thing into this, Megan."

She heard the pain in his voice. "I'm sorry, Jack. I'm just nutty right now and..."

He hugged her closer and refused to let her go on. "It's okay. Believe me, I understand. Now, let me take you home. You look exhausted."

"No." She pushed away from him. "Give the police and the media the picture on the kitchen bulletin board. It's the most current one. I've got to keep looking, Jack. I'll go crazy if I sit around and do nothing."

"Okay. But then I'm going to come back and help," he offered. He looked over her shoulder as Claude Hawkins walked toward them. The gun trader had a scowl on his face.

"Can't help you much now, Mrs. Summers. Mona's no-where around here. I'm always home with her by about three o'clock, except for Sundays when I need to be at the swap meet till late. She must have got mad with me and run off. But when she shows up, I'll ask her about your youngin."

"Thank you." Megan felt hysteria moving up a notch in-side of her but she fought to keep it out of her voice. She dug her fingernails into Jack's arm. Sunday. Claude Hawkins was home every day but Sunday. She considered for a moment rushing him and barreling into his house to check for Thomas. But she fought her hysteria, and nod-ded. "Let's get going. You start across the street. I'll meet you at the elementary school in half an hour."

"Okay," he said, kissing her lightly. "Now, just remem-ber. We're going to find him."

Megan turned away, hoping to hide a new wave of tears. She cupped her hands around her mouth. "Thomas! Thom-as!" Please baby, she prayed. Call me if you can hear me!

THOMAS SAT HUDDLED behind the towering stack of enve-lopes and wiped his chubby fists across his eyes. He had heard his mother calling him a few minutes ago, and he'd called back to her, but her voice had trailed off. Momma had not heard him, and she had not come to rescue him.

Mona had not come back, either. She left a long time ago, Thomas knew, before he heard his momma. Mona went away after the little door got stuck. Mona said she was going to get him out, but Thomas was worried she'd forgotten.

The small boy wiped his nose on his shirt and stood up. The pockets of his jeans bulged with stickers. Mona had shown him the garage with the millions and millions of letters, and he'd helped himself to some of the stickers.

Thomas lied to his momma about leaving school the other day, and now that thought made him feel like crying. He was never going to lie to Momma again. But now Thomas was worried that Momma would be mad. And the man who owned the garage, too. If he came back, Thomas decided he would hide. It would be better to wait for Momma.

Thomas looked up at the dirty window way above his head. The sky seemed to be getting dark. He was sure school was over, which was why he was so hungry. Too bad he hadn't brought his lunch box with him. There was still an orange and a package of peanut butter cheese crackers Daddy had let him buy.

Thomas sighed. Was Momma going to come back? Where was Mona? he wondered.

MONA HID BEHIND THE OLEANDER bushes and watched Megan Summers come up to the door of the house next door. She chewed on her bottom lip and wound her long hair around her finger. What should Mona do? the girl wondered. Daddy was going to be mad at Mona.

Mona had promised not to go into any person's house without being invited. Was a garage like a house? she asked herself. If it was, then Mona was in trouble. But if it wasn't, then maybe Daddy wouldn't be mad at her.

"Thomas! Thom-as!"

Mona wound her hair around her finger tighter as she heard Thomas's mother call for him. She sounded very sad. This made Mona even more afraid. Daddy would be mad at Mona, she suddenly knew. But then Mona thought of Thomas, and wondered if he was okay. He was little. Real little. He was probably even more afraid than Mona.

Mona parted the bush in front of her and looked up the street. Two ladies were talking and pointing at Mrs. Summers. That made Mona come out of the bushes. Mona would tell Mrs. Summers about Thomas, she decided. Mona knew it felt bad to have people point at you.

She hurried after the red-haired woman.

Megan turned, surprised to find Mona on her heels. The girl put her head down. "What's wrong, Mona?" Megan asked. She hurried up to the girl and put her arm around her neck. "What is it, honey? Do you want me to take you to your daddy?"

Mona cried a little harder. "Mona is a bad girl."

"No," Megan soothed. "Mona is a good girl. Come on, sweetheart. I'll walk you home. I wanted to ask you a question, anyway, so I'm glad to find you."

Mona stopped dead and looked at Megan full in the face. "Mona knows where Thomas is."

Megan nearly screamed with relief, and held the girl across from her to keep her fully concentrated on the task at hand. "You do? Where? Where is he, Mona?"

"Mona will show you." She took Megan's hand and cut through the backyard of the vacant house next to Edna Adams's house. She felt so glad to be of help. She even smiled and didn't worry about her daddy being mad. At the fence dividing the vacant house from Edna's, Mona pointed to a big hole near the bottom.

"That's the way."

"But can't we go around?" Megan replied. "There's a gate."

Mona shook her head. "Big lock. This is the way." The girl fell to her knees and crawled through the fence.

Megan followed, then hurried after her as the child raced to a small, padlocked door at the back of Edna's garage. Her pulse raced and her mouth was dry as a sudden feeling of danger struck. "Wait, Mona. Are you sure Thomas is in there?"

Mona turned. "Mona saw him go through the kitty's door." She pointed to the flap at the bottom of the door, barely big enough for a small animal to negotiate. A sheet of plastic used to seal the door up with hung halfway down over the flap, making it impossible for a cat to use.

Megan knocked on the door and put her ear against it to listen. "Thomas! Thomas, are you inside?"

Time seemed to stop while she waited for a reply, then, in a tiny voice, she heard her son cry out.

"Momma! I'm in here, Momma! Let me out!"

"Baby, it's okay. Don't cry, Thomas. Momma will get you out." Megan turned toward Mona, stunned to find the girl gone. Mona must be scared, she realized. Well, she'd go see her later and straighten everything out.

"Thomas, are you hurt?" She began to shake with anxiety and relief, though the frightening sense that something was very wrong stayed with her as she rattled the door.

"No. But I'm hungry," came his reply.

Megan let the tears fall. She didn't know why Thomas had gotten locked in the garage, but right now it didn't matter that he'd disobeyed her. She tried to pull the plastic out so Thomas could crawl through the hole, but it was wedged tight. "Hang on, big boy. Momma will be right there to get you."

She went around to the back door of the house and tried the knob, but it was locked. Without another thought she picked up a metal sprinkler lying in the bushes and smashed it into the small pane of glass beside the knob. Apologizing to Edna Adams and Pollard Finch would be a small price to pay to get her baby out of the garage.

The lock was easy to undo, and she was in the house in seconds. The porch she broke into led to a small utility room with an ancient wringer washer similar to the one Mrs. Grokowbowski kept in her garage. A door was in the wall next to it, and Megan bet it led to the garage. It, too, had a small animal door cut into the bottom, and the smell of a cat box assailed her nostrils. She tried the knob and was surprised: it turned in her hand.

The sight that met her eyes made her gasp. The garage, nearly two stories high, its high dormers covered with white cotton curtains, was completely crammed with mail!

Thousands and thousands of rubber-banded bundles, stacks and loose letters were piled row upon row throughout the barnlike structure, covering nearly every inch of space. "What in the world?" she gasped, then looked around the gloom for her child.

"Thomas?" she called. "Thomas. Come here, baby." A second later her boy threw his arms around her leg. He'd been concealed in a tiny crevice within a massive mound of letters beside the door.

"Momma!"

Megan hugged the little boy to her. Never had anything felt so dear and precious. She kissed him several times and squeezed his warm little body against her. "Baby, did you get locked in? Are you okay?"

Thomas began to cry. He burrowed his head into her chest and nuzzled her with his head. "I heard you, Momma. But you didn't hear me!"

"It's okay, sweetheart. Don't cry. Momma is here. Come on, now. I'm going to take you home."

"I can't let you do that, Megan. Sorry."

The man's voice sliced through the darkness behind her and hit Megan like a bucket of ice water. She whirled around, holding Thomas in her arms. Pollard Finch blocked the doorway, obliterating the dim light behind him. A sliver of illumination from the dormers reflected off his glasses and the silver badge that was pinned to his dark blue postal worker's uniform. She could read nothing from his voice, or the expression on his face.

"I don't understand," she began, hugging Thomas to her.

"I know you don't," Pollard replied wearily. "None of them did. All the purveyors of debris and waste and trash and destruction in the world never seem to understand their sins. Never seem to see how they have to be stopped."

Her pulse pounded loudly in her ears, and she squeezed Thomas against her chest. "Stopped? What do you mean, Mr. Finch?"

"Cleansed. Released from their sinning ways. Eliminated, my dear. And by me." Slowly he removed a metal instrument with a huge blade, then ran it down the tall cardboard box next to him filled with catalogs. The cardboard split like an old flour sack and spilled the contents at his feet. "For you shall reap what ye have sowed," Pollard intoned. "And the junk mail despoilers of the earth reaped me."

Her mouth went completely dry. Several bits and pieces of memory from working with Sandy and Darren congealed into one thought. Badges. A doorbell ringing. No question of admittance. We all answer our door and open wide for the mailman.

Megan stepped back and moaned. She had been right that the victims' professions linked them together. Their businesses sent out sacks and sacks of third-class mail. Including Megan. As a TeleSurv employee she had instigated the third-class mailings of hundreds of diaries for viewers. In so doing, she, and those poor people, had attracted the wrath of Pollard Finch, psycho postman.

Pollard Finch was the Grim Reaper. "My God..." she gasped.

Pollard's maniacal laugh echoed up into the rafters. He crossed his arm across his chest, and his eyes rolled back in his head. The laugh died and a huge sigh erupted. "Yes, I am the Grim Reaper. I am the punishment people like you, and your coconspirators in sin, must face. I was so very, very sorry to learn of your connection with TeleSurv, my dear. Norma Schultz was one of your foot soldiers, wasn't she? One of those who caused the burden of hundred-pound bags of filth to be carted from house to house on the backs of unfortunate government workers like me."

Megan took a step back, sanity returning to her numbed brain. She had to get out of here. Get Thomas out of here. If she kept him talking, she might have a chance. If only Mona went for help! "I'm so sorry if my work caused you problems, Mr. Finch. But Thomas isn't involved in this. Let's send him home, then we can discuss it."

"No, my dear. Let me have an audience to explain how I vindicated myself with that pizza man, and the tire-store owner who sent out catalogs four times a year! And you people at TeleSurv! Packages and packages of trash and debris, riding on the backs of men like me, bowing us down, killing us!" Pollard's glasses flashed and for a moment he appeared without eyes. "Let the boy hear!"

Megan covered her son's ears and prayed that Mona had gone for help. She heard a car stop outside, and knew she had to gain as much time as possible. "How did you find out Norma worked for TeleSurv?"

Pollard's eyes darted madly around the garage. Suddenly he yanked the door shut savagely, then with a fierce growl leaped at her, waving the knife. Megan screamed and turned away, weaving in and out of the stacks of mail, a sobbing Thomas pressed against her.

"You can't escape, Megan," Finch called out. "Don't run. You're only frightening the boy."

She heard him a few feet away and let fury fill her mind. He would not hurt her son. She pushed with all her might, toppling a portion of the stack backward. Pollard swore and fell as an avalanche of paper inundated him. She cut to her right, trying to remember in the gloom which door it was. Thomas was crying louder now, and her arms ached with the weight of him.

But she couldn't stop, even for an instant. She climbed up and over a three-foot stack of circulars, dragging Thomas with her. In the distance she heard a siren, and her heart swelled with hope. Stepping up again, she pointed to a box of letters that looked solid. "Thomas, jump over there, then down. Hurry."

His eyes wide with fright, the little boy did as she told him. Bracing herself to follow, Megan felt a hand on her leg.

"No! Let go of me." She kicked violently, but fell to her knees and slid off the mound of slick circulars, slamming into the concrete floor.

Pollard's head appeared from under a mound of paper. He grinned and crawled closer to her, pulling himself on top of her legs. He waved the knife in the air. "You should have waited a couple of hours, Megan. I had a package to bring to you. That's what I do with all my victims. Address a nice, big box to them. When they open the door and see me in my uniform, they never hesitate. Just invite me in with delighted smiles. So happy someone sent them a present. It was all so easy."

Megan held her breath then kicked straight up, knocking the ripping knife out of his hand and through the air. He screeched and grabbed his fingers where her feet had made contact, then lunged for her throat. She hurled a handful of letters at him, screaming at the top of her lungs.

"Run, Thomas. Run back to school," Megan cried as Thomas yanked on the door and scampered out of sight.

Pollard rose and turned toward where he'd last seen the boy, but Megan jumped at him, hitting him square in the jaw with her head. They both fell into the stack of letters next to them, sending the mountains of paper sliding and falling in all directions. A box toppled onto Pollard's back and he cried out.

Megan tried to get her footing, but it rained envelopes. Torrents of them fell from all directions, sucking her down to the floor as if she were a pit of quicksand. Megan covered her head with her arms, but collapsed under the weight. She couldn't see, but she could hear Pollard gasping for breath nearby. He was also making some kind of scratching noise, but she couldn't tell what it was.

"Megan!"

She braced herself at the sound of Jack's voice and tried to stand. Pushing paper out of her way, she still couldn't uncover herself enough to stand. Megan hollered toward the door. "Do you have Thomas?"

"He's here and safe, Megan. Where are you?"

Jack handed the crying boy to Mona. "Run back to your house and stay there." He watched the girl run off, carrying Thomas, then hurled into the garage, shifting a mound of calendars and paper beneath him. "I can't get in, Megan. The entrance is blocked. Where's Pollard?"

"Be careful, Jack. Pollard is here, and he's out of his mind!"

The scratching noise, now accompanied by a metallic hissing, grew louder, then the sound registered in Megan's mind. A lighter. Pollard must have a lighter.

"Get out, Jack! Get out! He's starting a fire!" No sooner had she uttered the words than the acrid smell of burning plastic filled her nostrils. An ominous sound of crackling paper was close by. Furiously she pushed at the debris, but the more she did, the more paper fell on top of her.

Pollard began to laugh, a hideous sound from under the thousands of junk mail envelopes. "I'll destroy all you polluters together," he shouted from beneath his paper shroud. "You can't escape."

Megan began to cough and wheeze. Her eyes stung and her lungs recoiled with the putrid smell of burning ink and glue and paper. The heat was most intense near her right shoulder, so she tried to lean to her left. She felt blood running down her arm, and realized as if in a dream that she'd ripped out some of her stitches. Clawing at the bundles, she moved a few inches, but then a new torrent of mail slid over her. She felt the breath being squeezed from her lungs as the images in her mind dimmed.

Somewhere in the distance she heard what sounded like a fog horn, bleating insistently as a warning. Megan thought of Thomas and her Roxie. Then an image of darling Jack filled her mind. A crash of glass and the splintering rumble of breaking wood reverberated at the edge of her consciousness. By the time Megan blacked out from lack of oxygen she was saying a final prayer for the safety of the three people she loved.

MEGAN AWOKE WITH A SHUDDER and grabbed her chest, nearly jerking out the intravenous needle in her hand.

"Thomas!" she cried out, confused by the dark and strange surroundings. A tall form beside her bed jerked, and Jack's face came into view.

"Megan. It's okay, sweetheart. Thomas is with Mrs. Allen. He's fine. Roxie's fine. You can see them in the morning."

She gulped for air but relaxed, the panic receding at the sound of Jack's calm voice. "I'm in the hospital?"

"Yes. Minor smoke inhalation, a few bruises and contusions, but otherwise, you're fine." Jack kissed her tenderly. "Though, I better warn you, you're also a celebrity."

"Why?"

"You captured the Grim Reaper. Saved Melbourne, one-handed, according to the newspaper. Although they did highlight Mona Hawkins's participation, too. She's thrilled. They're splitting the reward between the two of you."

"Reward?" Megan realized she was sounding like a parrot, but Jack's words overwhelmed her. "I forgot all about that."

"A reward of $25,000 is quite a bit to forget. I'd say your half should let you quit your job at TeleSurv and recuperate a bit before you go to work full-time."

"It sounds heavenly. If I can find a job...."

"You've got an offer already. Lynn Miller from Miller Advertising called yesterday when I was at your house. Wait until you hear this. Darren George called and recommended you for a public relations job there. He said a promise was a promise, and that he'd promised to recommend you to them before this mess occurred. I'm sure your new celebrityhood will make her even more eager to hire you."

"My gosh!" The excitement and unexpected good news was acting like a drug. Megan felt like she was floating above the mattress, but something in Jack's voice made her look closely at him. "Are you okay? You weren't hurt in the fire?" The memory of the smoke and smell and tons of paper flashed vividly into her mind.

"Yes, I am now that I'm sure you're safe." He cleared his throat. "There is so much I want to say to you, Megan. I don't know where to start..."

"Start with 'I love you.' You do, right?" Her voice was easing, but she ached to hear him say those words again.

"Yes, I do love you. And I want to be a family with you and your children. Help you raise them." He took a deep breath. "I've been offered my old job back, and I've also had two calls from the network people in New York."

Megan's hand twitched in his. His words fell on her like blows. "New York? You're going to New York?"

Jack squeezed her hand harder. "No, I'm not. Not now, maybe not ever. I also turned the news director job down. What I've decided to do is free-lance. Your plans were to work, start a career. With the kids so young, I thought it would be better if I were around more."

Tears stung her eyes. She was overwhelmed by the love and yearning in his voice. He leaned over to hug her and she pulled his head onto her chest. "Jack. You darling." Suddenly the memory of Dean's words cut through the euphoria. "We may have a fight on our hands about the kids, though. Dean said—"

Jack looked up and shook his head. "Don't worry about your ex-husband. He told me to tell you he and Reva may be moving to London, and he's happy with the current arrangements. I think the scare over Thomas sobered him up to the requirements of full-time custody."

Megan laughed, then clutched her painful throat. "That little scamp. Is he okay? I'm sure he was frightened out of his wits."

"He seems fine. He was exhausted and went to sleep at six. Mrs. Allen made him cookies. We may have some work to do with him, but I'm sure we're up to it."

Megan blinked away her tears, not wanting to ask the next question. "What about Pollard?"

Jack's face stiffened. He took her hand in his. "He was burned to death, Megan. I rammed the garage with his Plymouth to get you out, but the fire department couldn't get to him in time. All that junk mail, it burned so quickly...."

Shivering, Megan squeezed his hand. "He was insane.... Poor Miss Adams."

"Edna Adams died this morning, Megan. He'd just come back from the hospital when he found you and Thomas. Her death must have sent him right over the edge."

Megan brought his hand to her lips. She felt no pity, only relief. Her kids were safe and so was Jack. "So it's really over?" She kissed the tips of his fingers, reveling in his strength.

"It's over, baby. Now a whole new life starts, starring you and me." He kissed her deeply, then laughed. "Now go to sleep, Megan. Tomorrow I'm taking our family to dinner. And I expect a special dessert later."

Megan grinned. "You've got it, Jack. A double helping."

Harlequin romances are now available in stores at these convenient times each month.

Harlequin Presents **Harlequin American Romance** **Harlequin Historical** **Harlequin Intrigue**	These series will be in stores on the 4th of every month.
Harlequin Romance **Harlequin Temptation** **Harlequin Superromance** **Harlequin Regency Romance**	New titles for these series will be in stores on the 16th of every month.

We hope this new schedule is convenient for you. With only two trips each month to your local bookseller, you will always be sure not to miss any of your favorite authors!

Happy reading!

Please note there may be slight variations in on-sale dates in your area due to differences in shipping and handling.

HDATES

Don't miss one exciting moment of you next vacation with Harlequin's

FREE
FIRST CLASS TRAVEL ALARM CLOCK

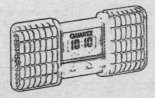

Actual Size
3¼″ × 1¼″h

By reading FIRST CLASS—Harlequin Romance's armchair travel plan for the incurably romantic—you'll not only visit a different dreamy destination every month, but you'll also receive a FREE TRAVEL ALARM CLOCK!

All you have to do is collect 2 proofs-of-purchase from FIRST CLASS Harlequin Romance books. FIRST CLASS is a one title per month series, available from January to December 1991.

For further details, see FIRST CLASS premium ads in FIRST CLASS Harlequin Romance books. Look for these books with the special FIRST CLASS cover flash!

JTLOOK

Take 4 bestselling love stories FREE

Plus get a FREE surprise gift!

REBECCA YORK

Labeled a "true master of intrigue" by *Rave Reviews*, best-selling author Rebecca York makes her Harlequin Intrigue debut with an exciting suspenseful new series.

It looks like a charming old building near the renovated Baltimore waterfront, but inside 43 Light Street lurks danger . . . and romance.

Let Rebecca York introduce you to:

> *Abby Franklin*—a psychologist who risks everything to save a tough adventurer determined to find the truth about his sister's death. . . .
>
> *Jo O'Malley*—a private detective who finds herself matching wits with a serial killer who makes her his next target. . . .
>
> *Laura Roswell*—a lawyer whose inherited share in a development deal lands her in the middle of a murder. And she's the chief suspect. . . .

These are just a few of the occupants of 43 Light Street you'll meet in Harlequin Intrigue's new ongoing series. Don't miss any of the 43 LIGHT STREET books, beginning with #143 LIFE LINE.

And watch for future LIGHT STREET titles, including #155 SHATTERED VOWS (February 1991) and #167 WHISPERS IN THE NIGHT (August 1991).

HI-143-1